No Accounting for Destiny

by Kimberly Emerson

For my mom,
who decided to watch that wedding in
the middle of the night in the first place

3

ACKNOWLEDGMENTS

Left to myself, I would never have published this book. In no particular order, I want to thank as many of the people as I can who helped me to pull this off. Jynae Myklebust has listened to my story ideas for most of our lives and has quietly pushed me to be a better writer and a more confident person. Diana Elizabeth Jordan believed in me so completely that I couldn't help trusting her judgment. She was also invaluable in making the story less ableist than it otherwise would have been. M. Pepper Langlinais, Erika Gardner, Kimberly Grady and Dominic Franchetti read through early versions of the work and helped me bring it into focus. They also pushed me to continue writing when I would have given up. Judy Emerson, Peter Emerson, Holly Foust McKean, and Ann Treleven are some of the best beta readers I could hope for. Without Sharon Eldridge and Gloria Myklebust's invaluable editing, I wouldn't have had the nerve to serve this literary dish up to the public. My wonderful family, Mom, Dad, Peter, Geoff, Karen, Tyler and Ryan all took it for granted that I could do this. Only I was surprised. Well, me and Zoe, my cat, but she has impossible literary standards. If I've forgotten anyone, please know I thank God to have gotten so much help that it's hard to remember all the helpers.

CHAPTER ONE

When I was eight, I realized it was my destiny to be a princess. The fact that I lived in a democratic country and my parents were accountants did not deter me. I couldn't wait to get to London and make it happen.

This October afternoon of 2012, on my thirty-ninth birthday, I had to force myself on to the Boeing 787 that would take me to London for the second time.

Stop feeling sorry for yourself, a voice in my head told me as I shuffled my way on to the plane and down the aisle to seat 32D. Probably my mother, still bitter that she couldn't go. Too bad, Mom. I'd trade you places if I could, knee replacement and all. Surgery paled in comparison to revisiting the land that crushed my dreams.

A half-second before I would have given in and run out of the airport, the line of travelers moved, and I plunked myself down into the particular seventeen and a half inch spot where Virgin Atlantic would hold me hostage for the next eleven hours.

The bald man in the business suit sitting next to me screamed into his Blackberry. "No, damn it! Tell the bastard we need it tomorrow!"

A swift kick accosted my seat. "Watch your language! There are children on this plane!"

I turned around to tell the irate mother that I couldn't control someone else's words when the three-year-old next to her mounted his own screaming rebuttal.

"Would you like earphones?" A flight attendant offered me a set of black earbuds.

I all but ripped them out of her hands. "Oh, for the love of God, yes."

Jamming the cord into the plug in the armrest, I heard the comparatively soothing tones of the Clash. "London Calling." Cute, Virgin Atlantic. I sank back into my seat, my eyes closed, listening to The Clash belt out their tale of post-apocalyptic angst and thought, wow, this song is depressing.

But oh, how I used to love it.

No matter that The Clash described a world falling apart. With the subjective hearing of all adolescents, I heard it as the siren call of a new life, a better life, the one I was supposed to have.

No. I didn't want to think about that. Not ever again if I could help it.

London calling...

It was my mother's fault. (Now I could definitely hear her in my head saying, "Here we go again. Why is it always the mother's fault?") Suddenly I went thirty years back, the television flickering in an otherwise dark living room, my mother curled up under a blanket, drinking a cup of tea.

"Mommy? What are you watching?

"Emmaline, it's two-thirty in the morning. Go back to bed."

"I can't sleep. The TV woke me up. Who's that lady? Is that a wedding dress?"

8

"Yes. That's Lady Diana Spencer. She's marrying Prince Charles, over in England."

"There are princes for real?"

"Yes, and princesses, too."

How could my mother have been so blind? Did she not know her youngest daughter well enough to see that telling me about princes and princesses foretold disaster? Did she really think I'd see Lady Diana Spencer - *Spencer, the same last name as mine* - becoming a princess and not expect to become one myself? Never mind that I was short and my siblings called me Fat Cheeks. This was destiny. The TV didn't wake me up in the middle of the night, God did. I was supposed to be a princess.

Another kick to the back of my seat, here in the cursed land of Coach. "Good evening, everyone. This is your captain speaking." My eyes flipped open at the rasp of the intercom. "Looks like we're going to be on the ground a few minutes longer. Security needs to re-screen a couple of the bags on board. Just a precaution. We should have lift-off in thirty minutes."

The gravel-coated sounds from the speakers and the disgruntled ramblings of my seat mates faded as the music resumed. The music had moved on to Gotye's "Somebody That I Used to Know," but the soundtrack in my head kept playing the Clash.

London calling...

Three girls and one boy, standing in an avocado green kitchen, their mother trying to keep everyone from killing each other before dinner.

"You can't be a princess. There aren't enough princes." My oldest sister, Cordelia. First Child and Executive Assistant to God.

"Don't cry, Emmy." My middle sister, Philippa—Pippa, if you wanted her to answer—who never agreed with Cordie if she could help it. "You could always be a duchess, or a countess, or something. Could you settle for that?"

"I don't want to settle!" Me, crying so hard tears landed on my little brother.

"Of course you'll settle." Mom handed me a tissue. "Everybody settles."

Even though I was too young to understand what that meant, it sent chills down my spine, and not the good kind.

"It's not settling." Pippa put an arm around my shoulders. "They still get pretty dresses and tiaras. Just not as many people want to kill them, is all."

"People want to kill princesses?" Sobbing.

My mother shoved us all toward the dining room table. "No princesses are getting killed in this kitchen. Scoot."

The businessman next to me shook my arm, and the avocado green kitchen faded back into the mist. I removed one of my earbuds. "Yes?"

"You believe this crap? All of us held hostage in this plane because somebody might have nail clippers in their luggage." The scotch in his hand wasn't his first, judging by his breath.

I backed away as far as the armrest would let me. "I'm sure it's just a precaution."

"Just a warning sign that everyone is scared of their own shadow these days. They already checked the bags at the gate. What do they need to pull them off the plane for? Next thing you know, we'll all be flying in one plane and luggage will be flying in another and we'll have to buy it a separate ticket."

I lifted the corners of my mouth in a parody of a smile and closed my eyes again. Two more minutes of this guy's lighter fluid breath and I'd buy a separate plane. Focus on something good, I told myself. You're going to see your favorite aunt. Hanging with Marnie is always a good time.

London calling...

Aunt Marnie in a chic mauve sheath dress, the day I graduated from college. "I've thought and thought about what to give you for a graduation present, and then I realized that I already had just the thing," she said. "I'm giving you my frequent flyer miles."

Marnie, who worked for the Foreign Service and made America look good in embassies all over the world, who had enough frequent flyer miles to go to the moon— business class. More than enough to get me and my best friend, Jane, to London.

Jane, my best friend since the Patron Saint of Dorms put us together freshman year. Jane who graduated in three and a half years, not six like me, and took a job at a bank in Washington D.C., but still stayed in touch. "What should I pack? Where should we visit?" She laughed. "You don't have to worry about it. You've probably had your bag packed and your itinerary planned since you were fourteen."

Actually, I didn't, but I wasn't worried. It was destiny. You can't botch destiny.

"Going to London for business or pleasure?" Mr. Stinky Breath leaned over the armrest, giving me a renewed acquaintance with the redolence of scotch. "Or do you swing both ways?"

Security had a new problem. One more minute with this guy and I was going to plant explosives in the luggage.

11

"Excuse me." Ducking the alcohol fumes, I headed for the restroom.

The one nearest me already had a line, so I headed to the back of the plane.

"...found something in the luggage." A flight attendant with a blond buzz cut stood with his back to me, talking to a curly-haired brunette as he prepared the drinks cart.

"Can I help you?" the woman with all the curls asked me.

"Did they find something dangerous in the bags?" I asked them.

"Oh, no." She smiled and shook her head. "Flights out of California, you sometimes get food in the luggage. Got to be careful of fruit flies."

Blond Buzz Cut's hands moved faster, putting soda cans into the cart's plastic drawers as though competing with someone for time.

I looked back to the brunette. "TSA monitors fruit flies?"

"Any stowaway, they want to know about it." She gave a tight smile and pointed to the folding door on her right. "Bathroom's free."

I walked into a lavatory that, like all airplane facilities, could make one of those dreaded fruit flies claustrophobic, and pushed the door closed behind me.

"Fruit flies?" Buzz Cut's voice sailed through as though the door were made of tissue.

Well, that did it. I didn't want to pee in front of an audience.

"Keep your mouth shut and I won't have to make things up." The flight attendant spoke in a fierce whisper that echoed in my stainless steel salon.

Buzz Cut's tone sank lower. "You know what they found on that last flight to London."

"A bag full of cash, nothing dangerous, and even that was on a flight out of Boston, not San Francisco. We're fine."

"Then why didn't you tell that lady the truth?"

"Shut your piehole, Mark."

The offensive businessman was barking into his phone when I got back to my seat. I settled in, hoping this time he took my earbuds and closed eyes as the "Do Not Disturb" sign that they were. Maybe I'd get lucky and fall asleep quickly. And snore loudly enough to annoy him.

London calling...

Last day in London. No proposals from princes. Did I really expect that? No. (A duke. Maybe a baron.) Something, anything, to tell me that my life would never be the same again.

Maybe I'll hear something in the airport...

Maybe I'll talk to someone on the plane back to San Francisco...

Maybe I'll have a brilliant insight in the cab on the way home...

Maybe I'll walk through the door of my apartment, sit on my dilapidated sofa and realize that I went to England and came home again, and nothing changed.

Three days of tears. Tell me what I did wrong, God. No answer...what's that on the television?..."Confirmation just in from our correspondent in Britain — Princess Diana has in fact been killed in a car accident." The beautiful lady whose wedding had sparked my dreams as a child, gone, never to see her own children get married...it can't end this way...

Crying for three days straight.

13

On the fourth day, my eyes went dry. Message received—princess dreams were over. Now I had work to do.
It was time to settle.

The chirp of the cell phone caught me off guard. Before I could switch it to airplane mode, I saw Jane's name. Couldn't hang up on her. I felt better just picturing her, sitting at her desk at the bank in a neutral-colored suit. I might find fault with her dress sense, but I loved everything else about her. "Happy birthday!" she said as soon as I said hello. "How does thirty-nine feel?"

"Like the cold, clammy hand of forty crept a little closer while I slept. Sorry, hon, I'm on a plane and we're taking off soon. Call you in a couple of days, okay?"

"Birthday vacation? Good for you! Where to?"

"London."

Silence.

I watched the curly-haired flight attendant walk by and ignore a fellow passenger's request for an estimated time of departure before saying, "Jane? Are you there?'

"Just had to go turn up the heat. If you're going to London, hell has frozen over, so I assume earth'll cool down a few degrees, too."

"Hey, Janey, quick question." I lowered my voice so much, I feared she might not hear me. "You work in a bank. If I took a bag of cash with me to England, would I get in trouble?"

"Only if you didn't tell anyone." Her voice slid up, almost making the words a question. "You have to declare it if you leave the country with more than $10,000. If you didn't, TSA could confiscate it, and they'll scour your background looking for criminal ties. Why?"

The loudspeaker crackled. "We're back on track and ready to go," the captain said. "Please resume your seats and fasten your seat belts."

"Trivia question." My voice sped up. "Got to go."

I powered the phone off, put my earbuds back in place, and closed my eyes. Happy thoughts, Emmaline, I told myself. No thoughts of dashed childhood dreams...or random bags of cash.

CHAPTER TWO

"You made it!" My aunt hugged me with a ferocity that temporarily overpowered my jet lag.

Marnie and my mother are a lot alike, from the outside. They're both petite, like me. They have the same heart-shaped faces and perfect cheekbones and originally they both had red hair. Mom let hers go white. Marnie dyed hers platinum blonde and resembles a brassy pixie.

My mother would have worn cords and a sweater to the airport, particularly in the chilly English fall climate. Marnie wore a pearl white Donna Karan suit and matching silk blouse, the requisite London trench coat over her arm.

"Emmaline!" Her voice was as comforting as mashed potatoes with tons of gravy. (She'd hate that analogy. As comforting as a smooth brandy, maybe.) It rang with the cadence of a thousand cocktail parties hosted, a million translations made, countless awkward moments smoothed over. It was similar in tone to Mom's, but with a decidedly non-parental lilt. Mom's voice said *I know what you did*; Marnie's said *don't worry, your secret's safe with me.*

"How are you, lovely girl?" she asked. "All well at home? Job? Parents? Boyfriend?"

Neil. He was the last thing I wanted to talk about. "The job is still boring. Accounting never changes. Mom's in pain with the knee, Dad says he's taking care of her but calls Cordie and Pippa for help every four seconds, and Neil is fine." It was true. I was still mad at him after our last conversation and as far as I knew, he was fine with it. "As always, Harry's job is so boring he never talks about it." When desperate to avoid talking about the boyfriend, bring up the brother.

Marnie doesn't divert on cue. "Neil didn't want to join you on this trip?"

"Too many obligations at work." I grabbed her arm and walked toward Baggage Claim. "Let's get some food before I pass out, okay?"

"Got to hit the ground running, lovely girl. I have an appointment at a dress shop for you, and then we're meeting friends for dinner." She checked a gold filigreed watch. "We're already late. You were days getting out here."

"Stuck in customs. They really grilled everyone about how much cash they brought. Probably a reaction to the Boston bag of money."

For a fraction of a second, my aunt's brow furrowed just like my mother's. "Something wrong?" I asked.

She threaded her arm through mine and smiled, her brow as smooth as if she'd just had a visit from the Botox fairy. "Nothing at all. Step lively, my dear. Dressmakers wait for no one."

***

Two hours later, Marnie signed the bill for her own gown and a little black halter dress just for me, a brilliant blend of sinfully soft silk with just enough spandex so that

17

the dress hugged my waist and absolutely caressed my butt. Good thing Mom couldn't see the price tag. After she fainted, they'd probably need to replace the other knee, too.

Post-couture, we headed to my aunt's favorite Indian restaurant, where we joined two of her friends from the office for a dinner and an obscene amount of wine.

"Officially, Marnie's retirement party isn't for Marnie at all." Bevin, a tall woman in her thirties with beautiful ebony skin and even more perfect teeth, topped off my glass. "It's a gathering for some visiting Saudis, at which Marnie will be unofficially thanked for her service."

I stared at Bevin over the crowded table. "Why did they decide to combine Marnie with the Saudis? What sense does that make?"

"I served at the embassy in Saudi Arabia a few years back," Marnie said. "I came to have an understanding of the language and at least some of the culture. When a big Saudi firm set up in the U.K., the Ambassador asked me to talk to them about investing in the States, too. I think she's trying to set up a job for herself after she leaves this post."

Bevin chimed in immediately after. "Plus, she's a bitch."

"The move backfired." Raj, a man about my aunt's age with the perfect sprinkling of distinguished grey at the temples of his black hair, smiled at the memory. "The Saudi community now thinks Marnie walks on water, and that drives the ambassador even crazier, so she made Marnie share her party with a chance for the U.S. to kiss up to Saudi money."

"She thinks Marnie flirted with her husband." Bevin laughed. "She couldn't stand to give the home wrecker a moment in the sun."

"Oh, please," Marnie sighed, sipping the last of her wine before accepting Raj's silent offer of a refill. "The man grabbed my thigh at a state dinner. It was all I could do to get away from him without elbowing him in the face. Even if he weren't married and the world's biggest jackass to boot, there's a time and a place for these things, and dinner with the Queen doesn't fit either category."

"I wouldn't be too flattered," said Raj. "He grabbed my thigh last week."

"Are you kidding? With the way you work out, I'm surprised he didn't hit on you first."

Raj offered to refill my glass as well. I had barely drunk half my glass, but I held it out anyhow. It wouldn't do for Marnie's niece to appear rude, now would it?

"Word to the wise," Bevin told me. "If the slime tries to kiss your hand, just say no."

***

Marnie took the ambassador's deceptively large home in stride, standing under the Tiffany chandelier where its soft amber light would flatter her best. Peeking around her I saw a long townhouse, the living room giving way to two rooms in the back. Women draped in silk and diamonds mingled with men in tuxedos. I was willing to bet they didn't rent. Discreet servants carried trays aloft with crystal flutes of champagne. The soft strains of Handel brushed past my ears, completing the ambiance of effortless grace.

A step up from Sal's Buck-a-Chianti Night, where Neil had taken me for my birthday three days ago.

A solid-looking brunette with an imperious gaze swirled up to greet us in what I can only describe as a mess of taffeta. Someone in the Better Dresses section of Harrods

19

had done this woman a serious wrong. I could almost see the avenging angels carrying the saleswoman off to the special hell reserved for those who managed to make a woman look less stylish exiting their shop than she did walking in.

She offered a hand. "Marnie. How lovely." A strained smile followed the words.

"Thank you, Madam Ambassador," Marnie said. "It was so generous of you to open your home for the occasion." Damn, my aunt was good. Not only did her words sound sincere, her nose didn't even crinkle at the woman's olfactory onslaught of Chanel No. 19. I'm afraid my own nostrils performed a decidedly undiplomatic flare and retreat.

"Madam Ambassador, may I introduce my niece, Emmaline Spencer? Emmaline, the U.S. Ambassador." She gestured to the formidable pile of fuchsia in front of us.

"Arlene Stevenson." She offered a hand. "Ambassador to the Court of St. James."

"Nice to meet you," I said, trying to shake the Ambassador's palm as it resisted all grasp.

Before I could give in to the temptation to tell Ms. Stevenson that her trim if somewhat boxy figure could be better served by nearly any other piece of apparel than the one in which it was currently clad, a balding man with a hooked nose approached. He kissed Marnie's hand and said, "Marnie Quinn, the woman of the hour."

The Ambassador gripped the hand the man didn't have on Marnie. "My husband, Oliver."

My aunt smiled, and her unassaulted hand gripped mine with a vengeance, making us into a people-chain of discomfort. "My niece, Emmaline."

"Charming to meet you," he said, releasing Marnie's hand to kiss my free one. I gave my aunt a sidelong glance, wondering if she had offered me up as a sacrifice to get her hand back. Was it just me, or did he actually bite at my knuckle while he kissed it? Neil would flip.

Even as it occurred to me though, I could feel the image of my boyfriend losing clarity in my mind's eye. Neil didn't belong in this sparkling world.

Of course, neither did Oliver Stevenson. As I took my hand back, I managed to smack him on the nose. "Sorry about that," I said. Any hope I had of taking my aunt's place in the diplomatic corps had evaporated long ago. Why bother with pretense?

"We should probably go greet our Saudi friends," Marnie said. "I'm anxious to thank them for sharing the occasion with me."

Oliver Stevenson waved us off, discreetly rubbing his nose.

We crossed the room at a snail's pace, because this show starred Marnie, no matter what the Stevensons said. The U.S. Ambassadors to Venezuela and South Africa had come to England just for the occasion. Several Stateside folks found an excuse to cross the pond for the event. Everyone wanted to laugh with her at an inside joke or remember some dangerous spot she'd gotten them out of or get one more picture with her for their personal album. Three-quarters of the well-wishers told her to have her guest room ready because they'd be coming to visit the minute she had a permanent address.

What had my mother said? *You have to be there for poor Marnie, who has no family but us?* Right. "Poor Marnie" could be in this room for a week and not get a chance to say hello to all her fans.

And you wanted to stay home.

Oh, honestly. Five thousand miles away and my mother could still get in the last word.

Raj made his way through the crowd to us, rescuing Marnie from a talkative gentleman who didn't understand the concept of personal space. "Hungry?" he asked. "There are hors d'oeuvres laid out in the dining room."

My aunt smothered a smile. "Emmy and food have been rather out of sorts today."

And she knew why, evil woman. Why had all that liquor seemed like a good idea at dinner last night? Oh, that's right, I was trying to keep up with Marnie, the woman whose life's work had involved chugging down every kind of alcoholic beverage the world had ever fermented. She once drank half a bottle of someone's home-brewed potato vodka in Belarus and then used the rest to start her car. My aunt could drink Marines under the table—and had.

She gave my arm a conciliatory pat. "Try something, lovely girl. You haven't eaten all day. It'll do you good." She gave me a nudge in the direction of the dining room.

Raj glanced toward the hors d'oeuvres. "Not a great selection, but the scones are a treat."

My stomach gave an involuntary rumble, and Marnie laughed. "Well done, Raj. Scones are Emmy's personal opiate."

I made a face at her but scooted off in the direction of the dining room. She wasn't wrong. Scones were the only English thing that still had me hooked.

Raj had summed the offerings up pretty well. Cheese cubes, vegetables sans dip, and trays of small sausages with no chafing dishes to keep them warm tempted me not at all. The saving grace of the table lay at the end—a stack of scones piled with Jenga-like precision, along with lemon curd and—did my eyes deceive me?—real clotted cream! Oh, bliss. If there is one thing the English truly do well, it is clotted cream, a bit of dairy heaven somewhere between whipped cream and butter. My mouth started to water.

I picked up a scone and halved it, putting a spoonful of lemon curd and a large dollop of clotted cream on each side. No sense rejoining Marnie just yet. Not only might I spill something on my expensive frock, Marnie might steal one of my scones. Instead, I eased myself into a nearby chair, next to a group of Saudi women sipping tea and a man preoccupied with his smartphone. I put my plate on an end table and popped a bite of clotted-creamed scone into my mouth.

The moan that escaped my lips was more authentic than anything Neil had heard in the last six months.

Two Saudi women stared at me over their coffee cups. Jet black burqas covered everything except their dark eyes.

"Sorry." To distract myself from their naked judgment, I looked over at the man on his phone. Kind of cute actually. He looked like old money—chestnut brown hair worn a trifle too long, clothes well-made but unremarkable in style, and a sense of perfect ease with the expensive surroundings. "Have you tried these scones?" I asked. "Delicious."

He looked up from the electronic device long enough to acknowledge that I had a corporeal form, made a "Hmm" noise and returned his attention to the phone.

I had a boyfriend. I didn't need to go trawling for strays in the English countryside. It just would have been polite to acknowledge my existence as a human. The English have a reputation as a very well-mannered people. He owed it to his country.

I took a second bite of scone and sighed, to let him make amends. He didn't take the bait.

I decided to ignore him and concentrated on my divine snack.

A seventy-something man with the same dark eyes as the women tsk-tsking my verbal emulations strode into the room. He barked something at one of the women, and my chin jerked up just as I was about to take a bite. Most of my cream-laden scone fell onto my beautiful black dress.

"Oh, hell." I put the scone remnants back on the plate and grabbed my napkin, blotting at the dress fervently enough to expose part of my bra. This caused conversation in rapid Arabic at the other table, and all the inhabitants were now staring at me. Time to escape.

Just then, Mr. iPhone snapped to attention. "Oh, I'm so sorry! Here, let me help you."

I watched with my mouth open as he used his own napkin to wipe cream off my chest. Two seconds ago I was moaning orgasmically over the clotted cream and he noticed nothing. Now suddenly he wanted to play dry cleaner? It strained belief that half an inch of my underwear could inspire that kind of attention. True, it was a La Perla, a $150 piece of lingerie that I bought by mistake (or so I'd told Neil); but I'd hardly expect him to appreciate that.

For whatever reason, he was now completely absorbed by my presence. "I hope this doesn't stain your dress. Such a lovely frock, on such a lovely woman."

"Thank you," I said, brushing him away as he dabbed at my chest, "but I'm okay."

"No, I insist." He moved his hand to my knee. "If it doesn't come out, please send me the bill. I want to take care of you—I mean, it."

As I adjusted my dress, making sure my underthings stayed out of sight, the Arabic-speaking party clucked their

24

tongues a final time and headed to a room further at the back of the house.

"Edward?"

A woman with a mop of auburn curls on her head stopped in the middle of the doorway just after the Saudi folks vacated it. At the same moment, Edward's hands fled my body as though I'd been declared radioactive. "Ashley! I didn't expect to see you here."

She held out a hand as she walked to him. "Kalifa's husband got sick. She asked me to keep her company."

"I'm just waiting for a friend." Edward took a death grip on the arms of the chair. "Haven't seen him yet."

Was it just me, or did he put extra emphasis on the word *him*?

Ashley put a hand on his shoulder as she regarded me. "Who's this?"

"Oh." Edward looked as though he just realized I was there. "No one, she's just…"

"Leaving," I finished for him. "Thanks for the hands-on assistance."

Edward mumbled, "You're welcome," and turned back to Ashley. As I left, I could hear him explain that he barely knew me.

Busted, I thought. That'll teach you to ask before feeling a woman up, even in the name of clotted cream.

After a visit to the bathroom where a nice woman with a beautiful gold hijab came to my rescue with tube of stain remover, my dress looked presentable, so I headed back to the front room, searching for my aunt. I finally caught a flash of a clingy Badgley Mischka silver cocktail gown amidst a dozen tuxedos. She smiled, reaching for my hand. "Lovely girl, where did you get to?"

25

"Mishap with a scone in the dining room. Don't worry, a nice English man was there to grope me under the guise of cleaning it up."

Raj found us and handed a champagne flute to Marnie. She took it absently, still focused on me. "Oliver Stevenson followed you to the dining room?"

I laughed. "No. Someone named Edward. Fortyish, brown hair, old money?"

She put a hand to her mouth. "That sounds like Edward Chamberlain, but it can't be. He's too sweet to grope anyone before dinner. And I rather thought he'd sworn off women since the divorce last year."

Raj looked at my empty hands. "Shall I fetch you a glass, Emmaline? They're supposed to make the toast to your aunt shortly, from what I hear."

I shook my head. "I'll get it."

Navigating the crowded room proved a trick. Just as I was regretting not taking Raj up on his offer, I thought I saw Edward walking toward me and swerved to avoid him, smacking into someone else on the way.

"Sorry!" I backed up a foot.

My victim, a Middle Eastern man who exuded welcome, smiled. "No permanent damage." He topped me by only two inches and spoke with a British prep school accent. "Tony Mehran. Pleasure to meet you." He handed his now empty glass to the man I'd mistaken for Edward, a waiter who probably wondered why I couldn't walk in a straight line.

"Emmaline Spencer." I shook Tony's hand. "Sorry for the full-body introduction. I must be hungrier than I thought —it's affecting my balance."

"You poor dear. Has no one shown you to the hors d'oeuvres?"

"Oh, yes. My aunt directed me."

He followed my gaze to the dining room. "You only saw those meager offerings? No wonder you're hungry. Come with me, my dear. There's a buffet of rather authentic Saudi food set up in the library. Damn good, really. Try the chicken kofta." He looked like the kind of person who knew his food—a little thick around the middle, with a wide, distinguished nose that begged you to ask it the difference between truffles and mushrooms.

"Who is your aunt?" Tony asked, leading the way to the furthest room back.

"Marnie Quinn. The guest of honor."

"Well, between you and me, she's gotten shafted." He took my hand and headed across the crowded room to a buffet that smelled of pepper and ginger. "None of the Saudi community asked the Americans to honor us. I can't imagine why we're such a feature at Marnie's fête."

Boy, the Ambassador really did not like my aunt. Did her husband whisper Marnie's name in bed or something?

A young man, slightly younger than Tony but no taller, walked by, completely wrapped up in a tall redhead. I guess you could say he was kissing her hands, but it looked more like he sucked blood from her fingertips. Three shades grosser than the Ambassador's husband had tried with me. However much she was getting paid—and I felt certain she was—it wasn't enough..

"Good grief," I said before I could stop myself.

Tony laughed. "We're a passionate people." He glanced back at the couple. "Though that could turn anyone celibate, really."

Being a guy, I expected Tony to be at least a little jealous or turned on by the spectacle. I hadn't seen her face,

27

but the skin-tight dress promised that whatever her hourly rate, she made it worth the exchange.

He ignored her, though. "I must confess, Emmaline, I've rather misled you."

"Really?" My surprise had to take a sudden backseat to one more diversion, a Latin Adonis of a waiter. He walked by without noticing me, but I didn't take it personally. It likely took all his faculties to pretend he wasn't gaping at the redhead with the painted-on dress.

"Oh, yes." Amusement bubbled over in Tony's voice. "Don't worry, I won't bother explaining until you're finished devouring the domestics."

The Latino hottie disappeared. This gave me a disturbingly better view of the chubby hirsute man and the woman so clearly out of his league making out. I noticed that, from the side, the redhead looked a lot like Jane. I mean, really a lot. If Jane dyed her hair red, it could be her.

Okay, if Jane dyed her hair red and changed all her views on public soft-core porn.

I turned my attention squarely to Tony. "Sorry about that. You were saying?"

He smiled. "Our meeting wasn't chance. Our mutual friend would like a word."

I stared at him. "The only person here I've known longer than you is Marnie."

"Oh, I understand you and he go back as far as half past seven. One Edward Chamberlain? I believe you two connected over some clotted cream."

My lips twisted. "I should probably get back to my aunt. They're just about to toast her."

Tony's eyes rounded, showing off his long lashes."Only a moment. Please?"

He looked off through a glass door. I followed his gaze and saw the man so drawn to my décolletage standing outside. So it was the Edward my aunt knew, and liked. "Oh, fine." I stood up as high as my heels could make me and walked outside.

Edward looked up as the door opened. He moved forward to close it behind me and wobbled on the uneven terrace floor. I noticed he was leaning on something. There wasn't a lot of light out here, but I took it for a crutch. A cane? Some kind of cross between the two. A permanent fixture, or help with a recent injury? I thought of Mom, trying desperately to do without her cane after the surgery. The way Edward dealt with the item told me that this piece of metal was a friend. He didn't resent it, he used it the way I would use a calculator while doing someone's taxes. It made my life better.

He followed my eyes. For an instant I felt embarrassed, an intruder into a private place.

I cleared my throat and my conscience. Introducing diversity into the *League of Inappropriate Touchers* did not excuse him from joining its ranks. "You asked to see me?"

"Yes. I—perhaps—would you like to sit down?"

A heavy mist hung in the air. Every available surface was damp. "No, thank you. I'd like to go inside, actually. It's freezing out here. Could we talk indoors?"

He looked toward the house and shuddered. "Oh, no —if you'd just sit for a moment…"

This poor dress had already been through enough. "Sorry, no. I'm going inside."

He grabbed my arm, with a strength that surprised me. The instinct to free myself made me swat at him harder than necessary. Edward let go and stepped back with his stronger leg.

29

I'd overdone it, but I didn't feel like apologizing. "That was a warning. I can do worse."

"I don't doubt it. Bony little knuckles you've got there." He rubbed his chest where I'd made impact. "You're a difficult woman to apologize to, you know that?"

I stopped walking. "Apologize? You're here to apologize to me?" I rubbed my knuckles. They were bony, and every single one of those bones hurt right now. The guy had to do a lot of upper-body work. Had he not been so handsy, I might have been more curious about that.

"Yes—well, not so much apologize as explain, but—yes." He looked around. I couldn't tell whether he was checking for eavesdroppers or escape routes. "I can see where you might be a bit...confused by my behavior."

I exhaled. "Fine. You have two minutes before I freeze to death. Go."

"Oh, dear. I wasn't thinking. Here, take my coat." Before I could stop him, he shed his tuxedo jacket and handed it to me.

I wanted to refuse, but my dress didn't do much to fight the cold. "Thank you."

Two men walked out and lit up cigarettes. I coughed. They glared at me.

"Oh, hell." Edward gestured further into the garden, which I could see now occupied perhaps two acres—a gated, mutual back garden for all the townhouses. Lighting subtly worked into the landscape helped me avoid walking into decades-old trees. (Dogwood, maybe, from the scent? Despite Mom's best efforts, trees and I had only a nodding acquaintance.)

"It's rather unpleasant," he began, looking intently at a clump of grass by his foot. "I'm afraid I was using you."

"To do what, exactly?"

30

He took a deep breath and waited so long to exhale I thought he might faint. I didn't blame him. The cigarettes punctuated the air even at this distance, and if we moved further away we'd be at the neighbor's back door.

At the precise moment I considered forcing Edward into the house, a cloth covered my face. Someone said, "There you are, love. Just let go."

The voice had a Scottish lilt to it, and a tattoo stuck out from the edge of the sleeve. Sometimes you catch strange details just before the whole world goes black.

CHAPTER THREE

Light. Somewhere there was light. And voices.

Maybe not voices. Noises, on the other side of this fog that surrounded me. No, surrounded was the wrong word. The fog infiltrated my head. I couldn't see anything, even though my eyes were open.

Were they open?

Maybe not.

Did it matter?

No.

I closed my eyes—or stopped caring whether they were already closed—and went back to the comforting lull of the fog.

Three days ago, I had no intention of visiting London again, ever. Now, swimming in the fog, my mind grasped for sense, playing a fuzzy game of hide and seek with my memories, and landed at my parents' house.

With all the Spencer glamour of drinks, presents, Mom's barbecue sauce on Dad's medium-charred burgers, and someone getting thrown in the pool, we were celebrating my birthday over the weekend, since my birthday fell on a Tuesday.

Mom got stuck in the kitchen, as usual. "Brownies," she said, as I stared at the bowl in her hand. "Isabel wanted to bake, so I told her it was okay. Everyone else is in the back, except Harry. He got called in to work at the last minute."

I ignored my brother's habitual flakiness and looked around for Isabel, my niece. "If she wanted to make brownies, why are you stirring the batter?" I asked.

"Bathroom break. You know how Sneakers is about chocolate."

Sneakers, my parents' five-year-old mutt, a black Labrador-Shepherd-something-unknown mix with the softest, fluffiest ears in the world and light brown fur over each eye that looked like eyebrows, loved to eat chocolate and running shoes. Dad gave up jogging (oh yeah, Dad, like Sneakers had anything to do with that), so the shoes were no longer an issue, but he and Mom both drew the line at giving up chocolate.

I walked with Mom into the kitchen and tossed a kiss onto the top of Isabel's head when she re-entered the room. Intense Isa, my sister Cordie's ten-year-old daughter, gave me the barest acknowledgement, reclaiming the brownie batter from Mom and resuming work on dessert.

Sneakers popped his head and front paws onto the counter to get in on the action. "Down," my mother said, pointing a finger at the ground. Sneakers promptly sank down to the linoleum and lowered his shaggy head onto his front paws, a perfect example of canine obedience.

"You're not fooling anyone," my mother told him. "Out."

"Come on, Sneaks." I headed for the sliding glass door. "Let's go to the pool."

"Oh, sweetheart." My mother put a hand on my arm as I passed. "A word before you go."

For as casual as they sounded, the words stopped me in my tracks.

"I may have told you—Aunt Marnie is retiring. The Embassy is throwing a party."

She hadn't, but I wondered why she needed to tell me that right this minute. "To celebrate her departure?" I asked. "I thought they liked her."

"To honor her years of service," Mom said with a reproving glance. Nobody gives more communicative looks than my mother. When I was younger, she could use an instant of eye contact to tell me to mind my manners, stand up straight, and put the meatloaf in the oven at 5:00 because she'd be home late.

"It's about time," I said. Marnie had been in the diplomatic corps for nearly four decades, serving in American embassies all over the map. Over the years, countless numbers of ambassadors had managed not to stick their feet in their mouths because Marnie Quinn had whispered the correct terminology, name, or greeting in their ears half a second before they spoke.

After a rare second glass of wine one night, my mother had mentioned that Marnie once thought I might follow her into the Foreign Service. She must have been mighty disappointed. I spent my days at my parents' accounting firm, helping small businesses get the best tax refund. Before the London debacle, I'd worked as an administrative assistant at a travel magazine with hopes of working my way up to writing about fascinating English vacations, but that went in the dumpster with everything else that reminded me of my fizzled dream. After Shelley, one of the copywriters, tried to set me up with her English cousin and I threw my iced tea in her lap, I don't think anyone missed me.

34

"She thought so too," Mom said with a hint of a smile. "You could come along with me if you wanted. Your father could handle your accounts for a few days."

In truth, a chimpanzee with a little initiative could handle my accounts for a few days, but I wasn't about to give my mother any reason for hope. "I should probably go over them just to be sure."

My mother gave me a searching glance. "You don't want to go, just because the party's in London?"

"I've been," I said. "It was fun. I don't need to go back." Mom's deep sigh tugged at my conscience. "Won't she come back here to visit? We can throw her a party here."

"Somehow I don't think she'll enjoy drinking margaritas and getting thrown in the pool as much as you all do," Mom observed. "But I suppose we'll think of something. Neither Cordie nor Pippa can really afford to go to Europe, if they want to keep their children in shoes, and Harry's tied up with work."

We both tried to pretend she was serious about ever asking Harry to fulfill a family obligation. I stared at the backyard, where Pippa, Cordie and the rest of my family talked and laughed and ate, not being grilled by Mom. "Marnie'll be happier to have you there than the rest of us."

"Oh, nonsense. She loves all of you. As it is, I'm letting her down by just staying a week. She begged me to stay a couple of weeks and travel around the country with her before she leaves, but you know your father can't survive that long on his own."

This was undeniably true. Left to his own devices my father would stand in front of the oven and wonder why his dinner didn't spontaneously appear.

I fell back on the trite. "She'll find her own traveling entertainment. She's a very capable person."

35

"It's not about the traveling, Emmy. She's leaving the job she's had for thirty-seven years. Even the most capable person appreciates support in time of transition."

"Take Dad, then," I said. "It's October, not April. We can handle things without him." Well, Cordie could, at any rate. I didn't love my job enough to try.

"I think that's exactly what he's afraid of," Mom said, more to herself than me. More firmly she said, "This is not about your father, Emmaline. If you don't want to help your aunt, just say no."

"No." I took a step toward the sliding glass door.

Mom stared at me hard enough to make me turn back around. "You might at least have given it a few minutes of thought first."

"Fine." I put my purse down on the chair. "I'll think about it for a few minutes, and then I'll say no."

My mother sighed. She picked my purse up and moved it to the bookshelf, evidently too quickly for grace, because she banged her knee on the side of it. "Ow." She sank down into the chair she'd just freed up.

"Ooh, was that the bad knee?" I asked.

"Don't change the subject," she said, trying to keep her face calm. Her knee had given her more and more trouble the past couple of months, and while she called it an overre-action, the doctor had brought up the phrase "knee replace-ment" more than once. "It's not like setting foot in London is going to kill you."

I edged another step toward the door. "Probably not, but why test the percentages?"

Thanks to a lifetime of experience with my mother, I got out the door before the next baleful look could land.

When Mom brought the tray of brownies out to the porch an hour later, she sat down to play a hand of poker with us without mentioning the earlier conversation. I thought I'd gotten away clean.

And I probably would have, if it weren't for Sneakers' chocolate cravings.

Placing bets with potato chips, we had played our way through several hands, entertained meanwhile by Aaron, my eleven-going-on-twenty-five year-old nephew who labored under the delusion that the State of California now allowed pre-teens to drink, and kept trying to sample everyone's adult beverages. Neil finally made his way to the party after indulging in an entire day of his favorite pastime, paperwork, and he and I were talking inside when a scream interrupted us.

Through the sliding glass door, I saw the tray of brownies fly through the air and Sneakers scampering away with something clenched between his teeth. Mom, probably calculating the cost of another vet bill, leapt out of her seat to knock the offending item from Sneaker's mouth.

Unfortunately, Mom made this decision at the same time that Aaron tried to have a go at my dad's beer. Falling over the picnic bench instead of stepping over it, she managed to land her right knee squarely on the cement patio.

"Mom!" I screamed at the same moment my father yelled "Megan!"

I flung the screen door open and raced to the picnic table, reaching Mom about the same time everyone else did. She told us she was all right and tried to get up, but her left foot was still trapped on the picnic bench. This time she wrenched her ankle. "Ow!" she yelled.

Sneakers dropped the brownie and ran to Mom's side, eyebrows raised, the picture of doggie devotion.

"Are you okay, Mom?" Cordie asked.

"No, she's not," Dad said, his voice tinged with panic.

"We should get her to the emergency room," Pippa said, fishing for car keys.

"It's not that serious," Mom said, wincing even as she said it.

"Yes, it is," Dad said. "And your London trip is off, Meg."

Oh, crap.

"We'll see," Mom said, her voice getting choppy as she tried to get up. "It's probably just a sprain—ow!"

Mom was back down on the ground again. "I don't want to move her ankle again," Dad said. "Call 911."

Pippa's husband, Danny, was dialing before I could get to my phone. *Please just let it be a sprain, God,* I prayed. *A quick-healing sprain—so she can still go to London.*

We all followed the ambulance to the emergency room, and hours later, the ER doctor dashed my hopes. "X-rays show a broken knee." Dr. Malik, who looked like he was about twelve, pointed out the pictures on the computer monitor. "The ankle is sprained, but the knee is the bigger problem. It looks like you'd need knee replacement surgery sooner or later anyway, though."

She's not a procrastinator, but I have to figure this time Mom would have chosen "later" even to hear this news —after several hours' sleep and some really premium pain killers—much less to have the surgery. The look she gave Dr. Elmo could have frozen lava.

"Anyway," he said, quickly fastening his gaze back on his chart, "your regular doctor can schedule the surgery. Meantime, I wouldn't plan to run any marathons for a few weeks." He made the mistake of chuckling at this and trying to wink at Mom. One look at my mother confirmed that this was a bad move. He tried to stop mid-blink and ended up looking like he'd just been stabbed in the cornea by the Invisible Man.

"But," I said, clinging to the back of a chair, "she's going to be fine soon, right? I mean, knee replacements are nothing nowadays, aren't they?"

"Oh, yes," the doctor said. He tried once more to bond with my mother. "You'll be back on your feet in no time. Most people notice a dramatic improvement right away."

"So, she should be up and walking around really soon, right?"

"Oh, yes. Most patients can resume normal activities within six weeks."

Marnie's party was in three days.

Look out, London—Emmaline's coming back.

The fog began to evaporate. Thoughts of Mom, her bad knee, and Sneaker's chocolate problem receded with the mist.

Could I open my eyes now? Maybe. I took a breath to prepare myself and choked out a cough. Something was trying to suffocate me. Something gritty. Come on, eyes. I steeled myself to open them.

CHAPTER FOUR

If you've never had the opportunity to wake up face down on a dirt-strewn cement floor, I don't recommend it. The experience is every bit as disgusting as you might have imagined.

The third try at prying apart my eyelids brought success, and I immediately wished it hadn't. I lay on my side, my mouth and nose smack up against the dirty floor. The bare concrete said basement to me, but maybe the owners just thought carpets messed with their ch'i. It was hard to tell. I knew for certain, however, that the flooring made an uncomfortable bed.

I raised my head and tried to do the same with the rest of my body. It protested, led in the march by my stomach, which adamantly opposed any state approaching vertical.

Sinking back down, I sneezed and coughed in rapid succession, spraying dirt in all directions. The concrete looked as if someone had smeared it with dust and grease, and I had just rolled my face on it. Good thing there was no one else in the area.

Wait, there was someone. I could hear breathing. Having learned my lesson, I didn't try getting all the way up, but rolled slowly to my other side to see who made the sound.

Edward lay ten feet away from me, curled up in the fetal position.

"What...the hell...happened?" The words came slowly out of my mouth, having to make their way through the fog of my brain and the sediment on my tongue.

The ensuing pause lasted long enough to make me wonder if he was dead, but finally he croaked, "You tell me."

"Where are we?"

"Not a bloody clue."

I scanned the area as best I could without actually moving my head. Not much to see. Dirt. Grey walls—though whether the color stemmed from paint or grime was up for debate. Not a lot of light, but a few windows high up. Boards covered most of those, with gaps around the edges letting in the odd rebel sunbeam. The basement of an old building, I guessed.

"My God." Fuzzy images came back to me. "The party...we were talking and then someone...a rag in my face..."

"Yes." Edward must have woken up earlier than I had, because he managed to move himself to a sitting position. "We've been kidnapped."

"Kidnapped?" I said the word with disbelief, though not because I actually doubted him. We had been away from the main crowd and someone had reached an arm in front of me and covered my face with a cloth. I remembered the smell —chemical-sweet, kind of like the anti-freeze Dad kept in the garage and warned us all not to drink while we wondered why anyone would want to bother. Come to think of it, my mouth tasted kind of like that now, if you threw in some sand for texture.

No, he had the right idea, but following the word "kidnapped" with a question mark happens involuntarily when you are a middle-class woman from Northern California who works as an accountant at her parents' firm, and it defies all logic and reason that anyone should think your loved ones had access to ransom money.

"Don't try to get up," he told me. "You've been out awhile."

"What time is it?" I asked. My voice came out in rasps, as though I'd tried to take the stairway to the top of a skyscraper and run out of water halfway.

He shook his head. "No idea."

I wished I hadn't thought of water. My mouth had gone drier than the Sahara. "Is there anything to drink?"

He pointed to the wall. Oh, hell. An old metal bucket freckled with rust sat near it. If it had water in it, I couldn't imagine it being fresh. How many new strains of bacteria had sprung to life in there? I was certain to find out, because the room held no other liquid, and my lips might crumble to dust and fall off my face if I didn't drink something soon.

I pulled myself to a crouch and waited, but this time my head and stomach seemed okay with the upright stance. I half-crawled, half-dragged myself over to the bucket.

...Whereupon I realized I had no cup, and my hands were filthy from dragging myself across the floor.

In my present state, trying to pour some water out to wash my hands would result in nothing but me sitting in a puddle. I leaned down to try to drink straight from the bucket and discovered that it was too small and the water level too shallow for me to manage it.

"I can't—there's no—it's too—" Words tumbled out with no purpose, as though someone had tipped over a dictionary and all the text had lost its grip on the page.

42

Edward edged himself over next to me. With the cleanest part of his shirttail, he dipped into the bucket and wiped my hands and his with the damp edge. Cupping the palm of his right hand, he scooped up some water and dripped it into my mouth.

I stared at him for three seconds, and then burst into tears.

***

The occasion didn't call for silent, pretty tears, and I didn't provide them. No, I erupted in great, noisy, snot-dripping sobs. Ten minutes of my life disappeared in the first full-blown tantrum I'd had since the age of five. (I gave up on them once I realized they had no effect on my mother.) After a few minutes, I snuffled, wiped my eyes and sat back against the wall, physically and emotionally spent. Edward stared at me in a matter all too reminiscent of Mom. I half expected him to tell me to get moving, my room wasn't going to clean itself. Instead, he said quietly, "Are you all right?"

I nodded, and then gave myself a mental smack on the head. "No, not really. My head hurts, my wrists are bruised, my lip is bleeding, I'm all grimy from laying on whatever is smeared on this floor, and—"

A sneeze interrupted my diatribe. The nasal eruption may have set a record for snot spread per second. "...And I've sneezed all over the dress my aunt paid a fortune for."

Edward glanced at my attire. "I don't think it matters. The dress will probably need some work before you want to wear it again, anyhow."

I looked down at my once to-die-for frock. Dirt coated it, the hem had two rips in it, and something that looked like rusty Crisco lay in a wide swath down the right side. A dry cleaner with a sideline in exorcism wasn't going to save this dress.

Oh, and my beautiful Christian Louboutin shoes had disappeared.

That did it. Whoever did this was going to die.

I looked around for someone handy to throttle and came up empty. The only other person around was Edward, and he was a fellow victim. Or was he? Now that my brain resumed function, I remembered my last moments at the party. Edward had deliberately led me out into an unpopulated, dimly lit section of the grounds. Granted, someone grabbed me from behind to put the rag over my face, but he could have had an accomplice. If so, though, why was he here, looking every bit as close to death as my dress? He sported a gash in his right arm, complete with blood smear on the sleeve of his once-crisp tuxedo shirt. The cuffs on it were wadded up and slightly frayed, as though they'd gotten caught under something. His complexion, already pale, had turned a shade of grey formerly seen only in car upholstery.

Besides, I couldn't convince myself that anyone could drug me and throw me around, finally dumping me (judging from the soreness in my butt and hip) none too gently on a concrete floor, and then solemnly clean my fingers and ladle water to my mouth with his hand.

On the downside, if Edward was innocent, he probably didn't know a secret back entrance out of here.

I took a good look at my surroundings. A basement. A concrete floor. Not much ambient noise. Maybe we were out in the country or maybe the building had good insulation. Stairs up the side of one room, leading to a door. Two small windows on the wall opposite the door, near the ceiling. Both were boarded up, but inexpertly—a couple of inches remained of the windows, letting in enough light for us to see rays of what felt like mid-day sun.

Which day, exactly, I didn't know. Probably Monday, but at this point, finding out that our captors had kept us sedated for three days wouldn't come as much of a surprise.

Of course, if I managed to accept these circumstances as reality, I wasn't sure I could ever be surprised again.

I took a few more swallows of water with my clean-enough hands and eyed the door and windows. True, we couldn't see out, but that meant no one could see in, either. Could they hear us? The room could be bugged. I couldn't see anything, but I've watched my fair share of James Bond movies. Maybe they don't really make listening devices small enough to pass for pocket lint, but maybe they do.

Only one way to find out. I took a deep breath and yelled, "I've found a way out!"

Edward looked at me as though I'd grown a third arm, and hissed, "What way out? Are you insane?"

"Probably. Blame it on the drugs."

"I inhaled the same substance you did, most likely. It didn't give me suicidal tendencies."

I held up my hand, and we both kept silent for a minute. All I could hear was what sounded like an expensive plumbing problem. *Just like mine back home*, I thought. Leaky pipes knew no borders.

I let out the breath I hadn't realized I was holding. "They wouldn't kill us for that. Smack us around, maybe, but it seemed worth the risk to know they aren't listening to us."

Edward opened his mouth, looking ready to argue with me, and then flashed a faint smile. "If they were, they'd probably have come down to check on us. I see."

"I didn't even hear a chair scrape. If they've bugged the place, they're listening from somewhere else and it will take them a while to get here. That buys us a little time."

He shifted off the floor to a sitting position, using some extra care to extend his left leg. "Unfortunately, if no one's listening to us, that means they think they have nothing to worry about."

I sighed. "Only one door, and it's probably locked, maybe even barricaded from the other side. Can you walk, since they took your crutch?"

He nodded. "Might be a trick to boost you up to the window, however."

Scratch a window exit off our list, then. I couldn't help in the boosting department. I routinely needed Neil's assistance opening jars of jam.

What, I wondered fleetingly, would Neil make of this predicament? Probably he'd tell me it was my own fault for straying too far from the party. Or for going to London in the first place.

Check the door.

Ah, yes. The voice in my head had returned. Not Neil —I couldn't see Neil giving me advice without attaching at least a little judgment. No, this was either my ever-practical mother stating the obvious, or Pippa reminding me that she learned everything there was to know about breaking out of a house back in high school, including how to get back in. In retrospect, it's a tribute to her own goodness that she didn't end up a cat burglar.

Focus.

Definitely Mom…or Jane. "What do we know about the door?"

"Solid object, used to separate outside from in."

There are many times when I enjoy the dry British sense of humor. This wasn't one of them. "I mean, do you know how good the lock is?"

He gave a laugh so short it didn't contain a vowel. "I woke up perhaps twenty minutes before you did, and I'm afraid I wasted all of it figuring out how to make the room stop spinning. No time left to concentrate on the finer points of lock-picking."

"Well, no time like the present." I dusted myself off as best I could, remembered the state of my appearance, and set my mental self-assessment to Denial. I would find time to properly mourn the death of my frock later. It would involve tears and a lot of liquor. Right now, I pictured myself looking like James Bond's sexy sidekick and tried to figure out how to get around a locked door.

Behind me, I heard Edward struggling to his feet. I had the fleeting thought that in dumping him on the floor they might have further injured his leg. He could have difficulty walking or at least experience immense pain when he did. Once I heard him moving around, I banished the sympathy. He didn't need my pity. Maybe not ever, and definitely not now. Right this minute, we both needed to stay focused on how to open a door that someone else had determined would stay shut.

I walked up the narrow flight of stairs typical of English houses. Pippa was the only one in my family with a two-story house, and it featured a set of stairs wide enough for her son and daughter to carry skateboards held out lengthwise, without smacking into the walls. (A good thing, because they ran into things on a regular basis. It's not the kids' fault. Pippa is a bad role model for awareness of personal surroundings.) The staircase I walked up now would scarcely allow

47

the width of a person. I feared Edward might have to turn his shoulders sideways.

The syncopated thumps behind me told me that Edward could manage the stairs, if perhaps inelegantly. No problem. Grace didn't count for much right now.

I smacked the door with my palm as a test, and it gave a resounding thud in response. Solid. Good thing I hadn't planned to kick it down. I didn't see a deadbolt, but perhaps it just had a well-hidden one. Or maybe some kind of barricade pushed up against the other side. I tried looking under the door, but no light shone through.

"First things first. Do you have any credit cards on you?" I asked.

Burnt toast wasn't as dry as his tone. "Not just now. I'm sure our kidnappers put them somewhere safe, to return to me later."

"Any weapons, in case there is a guard and he's just deaf?"

"My leg will do."

I stared at him, trying to find out whether this was another piece of misplaced wit. "Your leg is lethal?"

He shrugged. "It's heavy." He rapped his knuckles below his left knee, and I heard a thudding sound.

"It's fake?"

"On the contrary, it's very real. I can reach out and touch it."

"But you can remove it."

He stared at me as though I were a wearisome child. "That's typically the way prosthetics work."

Another time, I might have asked how he lost his leg, or how much he used the cane I'd seen him with earlier. At the moment, my only thought involved Edward whipping off part of his leg and smashing an assailant over the head with it. "That'll work," I said and returned my attention to the more pressing dilemma.

A quick inventory of the room showed no handy lock-picking tools. Me, Edward, and the bucket. My purse had probably ended up in the same Never-Neverland as Edward's credit cards. Other than that, we had only dirt and grease. Whatever vehicle they'd used to transport us here, it couldn't have been pretty, but I would bet good money the doors didn't make any noise. Perhaps they greased the whole interior just for good measure.

"The bucket," I finally said. "Maybe we can get the handle off it and use that to trip the lock in the door." I headed past him down the stairs, but stopped in my tracks when I heard a soft snick.

"I don't think that'll be necessary, actually."

Turning around, I saw Edward standing in front of an open door.

CHAPTER FIVE

I raced back up the stairs. "You said you didn't know how to pick a lock. What did you do?"

"Nothing. I just turned the handle. It was already open."

Open? It was open? That made no sense.

Nothing about this makes sense, Mom reminded me. *Think about that later*. (Maybe it was Jane. Definitely not Pippa or Cordie. Either of them would have said, *What the hell?* Some things do unite us as siblings.) I wanted to argue, but Mom—or Jane—had a point. Later.

The door opened to an alley, and we stepped out into the weak October sun.

Outside we shuffled down the concrete corridor. I tried to run but almost threw up, my head was swimming so much. Damn it. Anesthetics and I had never gotten along well. I didn't even take cough medicine that made me sleepy if I could help it. Aside from that, my feet were clad only in what remained of my silk stockings, and the alley had enough cracks and crevices to rival the surface of the moon.

Edward grabbed me, showing admirable balance, despite his earlier claims. Of course, for some reason they'd left his shoes on. Sexist pig kidnappers. "Can you walk?" he asked.

"Yes. Just not very quickly. Can you, without your cane?"

He nodded. "I don't use it most of the time. I only had it yesterday to—never mind, another time. Just now we need to cover as much ground as possible."

I took a deep breath, trying to steady myself. "Maybe you should go ahead. Try to find help."

He shook his head. "That's not on. We go it together, all right?"

I nodded. He offered his arm and we made our way down the alley as quickly as my head would allow. I looked at him surreptitiously, wondering whether I would have left me behind if I'd been him.

From the high position of the sun I put the time at early afternoon, so there weren't a lot of shadows, but where they existed, we stuck to them. We hit the street without running into anyone, friend or foe, and kept moving as fast as possible.

Suburbia surrounded us on every side. We passed two blocks of semi-detached homes surrounded by tidy yards. No shops that I could see. Realistically, I knew these people couldn't all be in on the kidnapping, but since we'd been stowed in a seemingly innocuous faux-Tudor residence, I didn't feel like knocking on a private door. It occurred to me that I should have made a note where we'd been held. What was the street name? How many doors down from the end was the place? I couldn't remember. When we left, where we ran from hadn't seemed nearly as important as how far away from it we could get.

We looked like something the cat thought about dragging in and decided to leave in the gutter. This didn't bode well for our transportation choices. We had no money for a taxi or the London Underground, and no self-respecting person was going to give us a lift. (Apart from our kidnappers, should we happen to run into them, and we certainly wouldn't like anywhere they might take us.)

We walked several more blocks before I finally asked Edward, "Where do we go?"

He looked around. "The nearest police station, but I haven't the foggiest idea where that might be." He ran a hand through his hair. "Did you notice anything about the people who took us?"

I shook my head. "Not a thing—except a Scottish accent. Oh, and a tattoo. You?"

"Scottish? I remember Irish somewhere in there. I don't think it was in the garden, though. Someone shoved something over my face, but I don't recall them talking. Perhaps in the van—I have some blurred memories of it."

I turned down a tiny walkway through two houses that cut through to the next street over. "Someone put something over my mouth, too. I guess that means there were at least two of them."

"They put some planning into this," Edward said. "They had to figure out some way to get us out of that garden. Being an embassy function, there had to have been a fair amount of security."

"Not an official function," I corrected. "It was Marnie's going-away party. The Ambassador invited a bunch of minor Saudi royals, but it wasn't actually sponsored by the U. S. government, so it probably didn't have as much security." I shook my head. "Enough with the sleuthing. I don't like being out in the open. How do we find the police station?"

"No trouble," he said, staring off into the distance. "They've found us."

I followed his eyes and saw the police car heading toward us.

It shouldn't have surprised me, really. Given the way we looked, if I'd been one of the neighbors, I would've reported us, too.

***

Several breathalyzers later, we managed to evade the public drunkenness charge, but convincing the police that we had a case against someone else proved more difficult. We switched stations as they tried to figure out what to do with us and our story and ended up back in central London. Apparently the London police didn't expect their average tourist to get kidnapped in the burbs anymore than I did.

All the hours spent inside various police stations made me long for the excitement and efficiency of the DMV. Hours one and two had some variety going for them, as they questioned Edward and me separately, then together, even as they asked the same questions again and again. Hour number three brought a sense of dread that perhaps we were caught in a time loop. Hour number four, however, distinguished itself with a particular bouquet of frustration, complete with top notes of despair. I would die here in the ugly metal chair with the inscription *sod off* etched in the arm. I wondered if I'd end up haunting the yellow bug-encrusted light fixture above me.

By hour number five, I had come to numbness of brain and butt.

"Let's go through this once more, shall we?" The detective doing most of the talking, a new one called Detective Chief Inspector ("DCI") Dimmock, tapped his pen on the pressed-wood tabletop.

It was the very last item on my to-do list in life. I'd told the story about a billion times already. (Okay, not a billion, but at least ten.) Everyone involved refused to believe that anyone had actually kidnapped us. From what the police told me, even Marnie didn't worry much when I disappeared that night. They wouldn't actually let me see her, but they related her words: "Diplomatic soirees get old. I figured she'd found someone friendly and thought up something more interesting to do." I wanted to smack her. Did she really think I'd fly all the way to London for her party and then not stick around for the actual event? Evidently yes, because she hadn't grown concerned until I didn't surface the next morning.

"By the afternoon, she had progressed to definite worry, she says." DCI Dimmock related this as though it struck him as fanciful that anyone would worry about me, ever. "When you phoned her from the station, she either believed you or felt guilty about not reporting you sooner, because she made quite the palaver at the embassy about getting the police involved. So, we had to stop looking into actual criminal activity so that we could mollycoddle the two of you." He flashed a smile that would have left Sneakers questioning his sincerity. "One doesn't want to start an international incident, now does one?"

"Marnie's influence doesn't seem to have moved you much." I held my tone at sarcasm, stopping short of outright defiance, but it cost me. "The expressions of everyone we've encountered tell me that no one is taking Edward or me seriously."

"You must concede, a thirty-nine-year-old woman having a one-night stand isn't usually cause to call in the authorities." He sat up a hair straighter in his chair and picked

54

up his pen. "Why don't you go over it again. Why did you leave the party?"

"I didn't 'leave' the party. I went out to the garden, where someone took me away from the party without asking my thoughts on the subject."

"Why did you go out to the garden? Rather cold out for someone from California, wasn't it?"

DCI Dimmock tapped out a steady tattoo with his pen. Psychology 101, I told myself. He's annoying you on purpose, unnerving you so you'll say more than you intended. Of course, that made no particular sense in our case, as I'd been spilling my guts for five hours now to anyone who asked, and no one seemed to care.

Maybe he hoped to irritate me into shutting up? Well, that wasn't going to fly. "I told you before." Taking a deep breath, I prepared myself for the next recital. "I saw Edward at the embassy party and he asked to speak with me privately. I'm from Northern California, where incidentally it isn't always warm and sunny, so I can endure mild drizzle without losing consciousness for at least a few minutes. We walked out into the garden. The next thing we knew…"

"Do you always go off alone with people you've just met?" Dimmock asked.

I sighed. We'd covered this ground before, too. The inspector was baiting us, though for the life of me I couldn't figure out why. "We spoke earlier in the evening. I told my aunt about running into him, and she said she knew him. She spoke well of him. He hadn't done anything dangerous." Weird, but not dangerous. "I had no reason to fear him, and I don't think I gave him any cause to distrust me."

Dimmock peered at me over the edge of reading glasses as he looked at his notes. "You claim that someone took you without your consent. Someone with a Scottish or possibly Irish accent, and a tattoo. Do you remember what the tattoo looked like?"

"A plant." Why had I not listened when my mother tried to teach me plant names? "An ugly plant. Some kind of weed."

His eyebrows went up. "Weed?"

I tightened my lips. "Not that kind of weed. A plant in the garden that you didn't put there on purpose."

Boredom returned to his features. "And this Scottish or Irish person with a tattoo covered your faces with a rag."

"A rag with something on it. Chloroform, maybe."

"Are you an expert in pharmaceuticals, Ms. Spencer?"

"It smelled sweet, in a chemical-ish kind of way." I took a deep breath and tried not to scream. "I'm just saying, there was something on it."

"Something that made you drowsy."

I stopped for a minute, staring at Edward's hand on the table. The veins seemed more prominent than usual. "Not drowsy, exactly. More like being under anesthesia. You know, one minute you're wide awake, wondering if you're going to have to watch them reset your broken leg, and the next thing you know you're in the recovery room and everyone's telling you how brave you were."

Dimmock looked over the tops of his spectacles at me. "You broke your leg at some point? It seems fine now"

My eyes rolled before I could stop them. "I just gave that as an example. I had my only previous experience with anesthesia when I broke my leg at nineteen. We've been over this so many times, I thought maybe you needed me to get more descriptive."

"Ms. Spencer." The detective took his glasses off and looked at me. I felt like a middle schooler summoned to the principal's office. "I'll have to ask you to stick to the facts."

"She's given you the facts." Edward's voice jarred me. He had remained silent through most of the questioning, as much as he was allowed. "She's given you the story several times without variation. I've given you all the information you asked. We've answered all your questions. We were drugged and taken without our consent by people with Scottish and Irish accents. Yet for some reason, I get the feeling that you don't believe a word out of either of us."

The detective narrowed his eyes, but maintained his level tone. If Edward wanted to rile him, he'd have to work harder. "You haven't given us much to go on."

"Perhaps it was a terrorist group." Edward tapped his finger on the table. "I've heard about that group FTP on the news. Several kidnappings have been linked to them recently, yes? Perhaps they took us, too."

"FTP?" I asked. "Isn't that an oil?"

The detective scowled at me. "That's STP."

"Maybe the flower delivery place." That could explain the plant tattoo.

"FTP stands for Free the People." Edward stared at Dimmock. "Extremist Irish separatist group, set on uniting Northern Ireland with the south. They've committed a rash of kidnappings lately."

And the florists, I realized, were FTD. I made a note on a mental to-do list to thank Edward for moving the conversation forward before the inspector could make a crack at my expense. The threshold of my endurance for feeling like an idiot lay some hours behind us.

Dimmock crossed his arms. "Something bad happens to an English aristocrat, you look for the Irishman, is that it?"

"When I get kidnapped, I look for the latest active terrorist group. FTP fits the bill. From what I've read, most of the Irish population doesn't agree with them any more than I do."

I nodded. "Makes sense. They'd probably think an earl was a decently profitable target."

"Someone hadn't done their homework, then." Edward gave half a laugh, stopping short as though he'd suddenly forgotten how.

"Your family wouldn't pay the ransom?" This was more interest in the story than DCI Dimmock had shown all day. I didn't know whether he was leading Edward somewhere with the question, or if he was genuinely curious about this particular aspect of the lifestyles of the English elite.

"My family doesn't have anything with which to pay it."

Was he telling the truth? He reeked of money. Cash poor, maybe, but couldn't someone hock the family tiara for a few pounds?

Edward, however, didn't appear to be joking.

"I'm sure your lot could scrape together a decent amount." DCI Dimmock twisted his mouth so far to one side I thought it might fall off the edge of his jaw.

"I'm sure they couldn't." Edward stared back at him.

"No family estate, no big inheritance?"

"The National Trust took over the family home ten years ago. We lease it back from them at a meager price, in exchange for allowing tours through it. My uncle sold off much of the land years back, and my father died last year of a particularly virulent form of cancer. I'm afraid we spent rather a lot of money on specialists and treatment centers."

The detective didn't look convinced, but said only, "I'm sorry for your loss."

So was I. Lost his dad and got divorced in less than a year's time? How did a person live through that and still get out of bed every morning? I reached over and put my hand over his, giving it a squeeze.

He looked at me the same way Mom looked at Sneakers when he offered her a slobbery tennis ball. I put my hand back on my side of the table, the better to obey the mental *No Trespassing* sign he'd hung in the middle.

"So," he continued, "if it's money they were after, I'm afraid they were in for a rather nasty surprise." He turned to me. "Unless of course they intended to get it from you."

"From me?" I pointed to myself, and then felt like an idiot for doing it and dropped my hand into my lap. "Why on earth would anyone think I had money?"

"You're an American traveling overseas. You were hobnobbing at an Embassy party." He stared at the remains of my dress. "You wore a £1,000 dress and Christian Louboutin shoes. It makes you rather a likely target."

My shoes. The part of me that wondered how Edward knew the label of my footwear took second place to the part that wondered who had my shoes right now. I missed them. I was almost certain they missed me.

Focus, Spencer. The DCI and Edward both stared at me. "The dress came as a once-every-fifteen-years gift from my aunt. The shoes were a very rare splurge." Usually I waited till they were on sale. "My family make their living in accounting. Much as I'd like to think we sprang from elite stock, we're currently firmly entrenched in the middle class. Not even the upper middle. Trust me, if my family pooled all their immediately hock-able assets, including the pinkie ring my brother wants us to forget he owns, the total probably wouldn't make it into the five-digit range. Hardly worth this much trouble."

"Besides, if I'm to believe your story, you heard a Scottish accent." From his expression, I guessed Dimmock's belief was still very much in question. "FTP has only recruited in Ireland, as far as any evidence indicates." He stood up. "You've convinced me. There is no cause for anyone to want to kidnap either of you." He placed his hands on the table. "You want to know a secret? I didn't need to hear your stories. I was already convinced. We obtained the security camera outside the ambassador's house and found some interesting footage."

Dimmock motioned toward the large mirror that I knew full well had people looking through the other side, and after a couple of seconds, the flat screen in the room's upper left corner lit up. A view of the street outside the ambassador's townhouse appeared. I saw a couple of cars go by before a black Mercedes pulled into view. The lighting was good, for a security camera, and gave a clear view of the two people in the front seat. It drove by the house and kept going down the street, not *particularly* quickly.

"The timestamp puts this around the time you two claim to have been kidnapped. You see my problem."

I did.

The people in the Mercedes appeared to be Edward and me, and there wasn't a kidnapper in sight.

CHAPTER SIX

Our protests that the kidnappers had set this up with people who looked a lot like us fell on deaf ears. An inexact kidnapping location and a description of "someone with an accent and a tattoo" didn't qualify as actual clues. DCI Dimmock released us and, in that exceedingly polite British fashion, requested that we never return.

Edward stood by the front desk in a daze. His unflappability seemed finally to have deserted him.

I cleared my throat. "Did you call someone and let them know where you are?"

He stared at the wall. "I called my mother, but since I intended to spend last night at Tony's flat, she hadn't realized anything was wrong. I figured it was as well to save all the gory details of the last twenty-four hours for later, when she could see me in person to know I was all right, so I just said I'd likely not be home till tomorrow. I'll call Tony and have him fetch me."

I intended to offer him the use of Marnie's cell phone, once I found her, but suddenly blurted out, "Would you like to stay with us? My aunt's got room. You can get a decent night's rest and go home in the morning."

A smile floated across his face without actually landing. "Are you asking me to spend the night with you? We've only just met."

Now he wanted to get cute? Hell. "Not likely. I spent last night with you, and you didn't do much for me."

"Not true," he returned. "You were transported to another place."

"True, but it wasn't a place I want to go back to."

The furious tapping of Marnie's heels on aging tile drowned out my rejoinder. "There you are." She practically threw herself at me. "Finally. I thought perhaps you had moved into that interrogation room. Another fifteen minutes and I was going to send for your luggage."

I squeezed her back, hard. "Just a day trip. Or a night trip, I suppose, since it's probably the middle of the night by now."

"It's half-past eight," she said. "Edward, lovely to see you—or it would be, if I saw you anywhere besides a police station."

"Yes." I threaded my arm through hers, for the physical support as much as the emotional. "Can we get out of here, please? I'd like to never see the inside of a police station again."

Edward took a step back. "Good night, ladies. Sleep well."

"Are you going to call Tony?" I put a hand on my aunt's arm. "Do you need Marnie's cell?"

He shook his head. "I'm going home. I need to explain all of this to my mother, before she hears it from someone else."

"You might want to rethink that, Edward." Marnie inclined her head toward the door. "I'll fix you both up with dinner, and then you can get some sleep. You look done in."

"Very kind of you, Marnie." Edward looked as though he wanted to smile but couldn't find the energy. "But I must get home."

"Are you sure?" I asked. "I can always share Marnie's room. You can sleep in her guest room."

"No. I wouldn't impose."

Marnie gave him a quick appraisal. "Looking like you do now, Edward, I don't think I can let your poor mother see you. The two of you have already tested my capacity for heart failure. You need to rest and clean up before you share this escapade with anyone else." He opened his mouth to continue the protest, but she silenced him with a finger. "Really, Edward. Mary's been through enough lately, don't you think?"

My aunt enjoys a fiercely strong will, and that's in the face of people who haven't fallen down Alice's rabbit hole lately. Edward didn't stand a chance. "You're probably right."

"Of course I'm right. Come on, the constable is fetching us a cab."

***

The three of us staggered into Marnie's townhouse. I stared at the stairs to the second floor accusingly, knowing that they represented work, but let them off the hook when I thought of my room. Those stairs led to a shower and bed, perchance to sleep for three days straight. Why not? I had already missed my flight home. While I had basked in the attention of London's finest, Marnie spent the hours on her cell with Virgin Atlantic, explaining that Ms. Spencer hit a snag in her plans. The negotiation of extra fees had concluded with me owing not quite an arm and a leg, but definitely a few fingers and toes.

It could wait, I told myself. The state of my checkbook, the length of the stay, the stories I would concoct to explain my delayed return to Neil and my mother—all of it could wait until my head had some quality bonding time with 1600-thread-count sheets. (My aunt does not skimp on bedding, nor many other areas of life.)

Marnie offered Edward her room and said she'd bunk with me, but Edward turned her down. I guessed it wasn't entirely out of chivalry. Marnie's suite on the third floor (excuse me—second floor, we were in Europe) had the best of everything, but getting there involved two flights of stairs. The couch wasn't as good as a bed, but a ground floor location gave it a definite allure.

While I took advantage of hot water and soap, Marnie ordered up some take-out Italian food. No, in England it was take-*away* Italian. My head felt stuffy, almost like I might be getting a cold. I didn't have the energy to get on a plane and go home right this minute, but part of me wanted to. Enough of this land where everything I said or did felt slightly off. Once upon a time, I'd been sure that England would feel like home. Instead I felt like a glaring outsider. Rather than just speaking with an accent, I managed to exist with one.

By the time dinner arrived, Edward and I both looked marginally more presentable, if no less exhausted. I had changed into yoga pants and a pink long-sleeve t-shirt. Edward didn't have anything to change into, but he'd sponged off his clothes as best he could and washed his face.

Marnie opened all the packages, overwhelming the room with scents of garlic and oregano, and told us to tuck in. After staving off the worst of my hunger, I filled Marnie in on everything that happened at the police station.

"So the police didn't take you seriously at all." Marnie swirled her fork around in the pappardelle pescatore without moving it any closer to her mouth.

"No." Edward hadn't said much since we left the station, and he left this word an orphan.

"It was worse than that." I stared at the spaghetti arrabbiata on my plate. It didn't appeal as much as it had five minutes ago. "They seemed to want to lock *us* up for something instead of our attackers."

"True." Marnie wrapped a strand of pasta around her fork and slid it into her mouth, a thoughtful expression replacing any signs of culinary joy. I felt bad for the food. It deserved more respect than any of us currently gave it. When she had swallowed, she asked, "Why is that, do you think? It's not like either of you exude signs of criminal tendencies."

"They know we weren't making it up. They know who did it."

A dozen words together from Edward's mouth startled Marnie and me both. "Who?" Marnie asked.

"FTP." He looked out Marnie's small dining room window. "They can't let word get out."

"But that's absurd." Marnie put her fork down. "They don't even know for sure that that's who abducted you. Do they really think this one incident is going to frighten people that much?"

"Frighten them, no. Encourage them? Possibly." This time he met our eyes. "The division of classes in our society is as pronounced now as it was in the Dickensian age. Resentment against those with wealth has grown exponentially in my lifetime."

I tilted my head. "But you don't have any wealth. Isn't that what you told the police?"

He lifted the corners of his mouth a millimeter, as though he might have smiled in an alternate timeline. "The estate lacks liquid assets. I struggle to maintain an aristocratic lifestyle, yes, but that's not exactly begging bread." Not even a trace of a smile remained now. "There are those who might see taking from the wealthy—even the cash-poor wealthy—as more public service than crime."

Marnie hesitated a moment, and then nodded as though against her will. "Possible."

I shook my head. Despite the effort it cost me, I had trouble stopping the motion. "No. These are terrorists. They kill people who haven't done anything to them. No one's going to applaud that."

"One less wealthy person?" Edward's eyes sagged, as much from emotional weariness as physical fatigue, I guessed. "Not a great loss. That many more resources to spread throughout the rest of the community. Extra points if it's an aristocrat like me, the kind that outlived their usefulness long ago."

"Enough." Marnie put down her napkin and started to clear away the food. She didn't bother to ask if we had finished eating. No one's fork had moved in the last five minutes. "You two need some sleep. Edward, did you call Mary and tell her where you are?"

I think Edward tried to grin at that. His expression got about halfway there, anyhow. "Yes, ma'am. Now, if you'll be so good as to loan me a blanket, I will go to the sofa and sleep like the dead."

"The couch is already made up for you. Good night, children. I shall see you in the morning, when I am certain we will all find life less maudlin."

Edward said good-night and headed off to the living room. I looked after him, wondering if I should say some-

66

thing, and finally settled on a "Good night" tossed over my shoulder as I followed Marnie up the stairs.

When we hit my room, she took my arm and pulled me inside, shutting the door behind me. "Spill it." She sat on the edge of my bed and folded her arms. "What really happened?"

I dropped down next to her. "Just what we said."

"And that would explain all the surreptitious looks Edward was giving you, would it? I would have accused him of stealing a biscuit, if I had any in the house."

"Biscuit?" The brain cells flowed like refrigerated molasses. "Oh, you mean cookie! You've been in Britain too long, you know that?"

Her lips pursed, a look of impatience flashing in her eyes that made her look disturbingly like Mom.

I gave her the unedited version of the conversation at the ambassador's house. "I told the police all of that," I said when I had finished. "Well, everything except the part about him feeling me up. I don't think he really intended to do that, anyway. Just got carried away with the tidying while he tried to fool the onlookers."

Her mouth twitched, and the Marnie-ness returned to her features. "Understandable omission, to anyone but me. And you're probably right. He's never struck me as the handsy type, even with his wife."

"He's married?" Remarried already, after the divorce? Ah, yes, the woman who showed up right after the clotted cream caper. Ashley. No wonder he wanted to apologize at the party, he was probably rehearsing his speech for the little woman.

"*Was* married." Marnie held up a finger. "Past tense. To a Saudi woman. They split up last year, just after his father died." She sighed. "Poor boy has had a difficult time of it."

So, not Ashley. A huge yawn escaped me. I used the last of my energy to move from the bed to my suitcase. "Sorry for sticking you with an uninvited houseguest. I should have asked first—it was just a spur of the moment thing."

She waved away my apology as she slid off the bed. "I was glad you did. I would have invited him anyhow, and this way he didn't have to worry I was making a pass at him."

I picked out my pajamas and walked to the door of the en suite bath. "Please. He should be so lucky."

"True. His ex was pretty, but more material than a fabric store." She patted my cheek, and then pulled me into a fierce hug. "You'll not run off on me again, yes?"

I nodded, though my sleepy mind couldn't pick through the contrary phrase. Maybe "no, I won't," was the answer she'd been looking for. She seemed content, though, and blew me a kiss as she headed up the stairs to her own room.

I mustered up just enough energy to brush my teeth. After I changed into PJs, the siren call of the bed brooked no resistance. Marnie's blissfully soft sheets wrapped me up and carried me off to Dreamland.

***

Some hours later—not nearly enough hours—a thudding sound jerked me awake.

I froze, straining my ears, but didn't make it all the way to opening my eyes. The covers beckoned and I burrowed into them, intent on returning to sleep's loving embrace.

"Emmaline."

Was I asleep and dreaming already? Probably. Sheets so soft...duvet so warm...sinking into the pillow...

"Emmy, wake up."

My groggy eyes opened in spite of my best attempts to remain unconscious.

"Jane!"

My best friend stood in front of me.

Here in London, when she was supposed to be thousands of miles away in Washington, D.C., working diligently at a bank, wearing something beige.

Instead, she was dressed neck to toes in form-fitting black. "Wake up." She didn't whisper, but spoke in a tone so low it couldn't have made it past my pillow. "Come on, we have to go."

"Go? Jane—what the hell—who's that?"

The gorgeous waiter from Marnie's party stood in the doorway of my room long enough to give Jane a meaningful nod, and then disappeared.

Clearly I was dreaming. Kudos to me, I thought, raising up on my elbow to see if I could catch another glimpse of him. I had never dreamed up someone quite that exquisite before.

"Emmy, we need to get out of here. It's important."

Jane's voice held the pungent tang of reality. Consciousness made this even more bizarre. I blinked. "Okay, I really do want to know who that unbelievably good-looking guy is, but first things first. What are you doing here? Why didn't you tell me you planned to visit London?"

Jane threw my trench coat and my black leather boots on the end of my bed. I managed to move my feet just before they made impact. "We don't have time. If you're not downstairs in twenty seconds, Carlos will come in here and throw you over his shoulder."

I glanced at the hallway. "Would that be a bad thing?"

She didn't even smile. "Get dressed. We have to go."

"Jane, come on. Even if I didn't desperately need sleep, I couldn't just cut out on Marnie."

"Marnie knows we're leaving, don't worry."

"She knows - what did you tell her? Why isn't she—"

Jane closed her eyes and gave her head a micro-shake. "Emmaline, do you trust me?"

I looked at her. She was dead serious. "Of course."

"Then put this stuff on and come with me. I'll explain later, I swear."

I put on the coat and the boots over my pajamas. Jane grabbed my suitcase, already mostly packed in anticipation of leaving after Marnie's party.

I stepped ahead of Jane and headed to Marnie's room, trying to think of the best way to tell her of my imminent de-parture, only to get cut off by the woman herself in the hall-way. She hugged me fiercely, her impeccably manicured nails digging into my back, before sprinting up the stairs and disappearing into her suite.

Jane didn't allow me the luxury of contemplation, guiding me firmly downstairs, out of the house and into a waiting van.

Janey, I thought, whatever this is, it had better be good.

***

Edward was already sitting in the van when we ar-rived. Did Jane talk to him first or had Carlos said something to get him down here? I couldn't imagine Edward putting up much of a struggle. Sure, he looked like he worked out, but Carlos looked like he did little else, and he had a six-inch height advantage over Edward. Waking up in the middle of the night to find Carlos looming over him and suggesting he get moving would have been a daunting experience.

Edward and I found ourselves ushered into the rear seat of a van with few windows. Jane and Carlos rode up front, Carlos behind the wheel, trading comments with Jane in tones so low I couldn't identify any of the words.

"Where are we going, Jane?" I asked.

"You know these people?" Edward stared at me in horror.

"I know her. I have yet to meet this gentleman. Jane, are you going to introduce us to your friend?"

Jane gave me a look that begged me to keep quiet. Her looks were nearly as expressive as my mother's, the only difference being that Jane's usually added a "please."

As soon as she turned around, Edward shot me a look of his own. This one said *Who is she, and if you know her, why are we in the back of a van?*

Great. Apparently, I was the only one in the vehicle who still had to express herself in spoken word.

"We are not being kidnapped again." I tried to make my voice sound reassuring, but judging by the look on Edward's face, I failed.

"Keep quiet." Carlos spoke American English, with the lilt of someone who'd grown up in a family where Spanish and English were equally understood. He was delicious, and in other circumstances the accent would absolutely have enchanted me, but exhaustion changes things. Even if the last twenty-four hours hadn't completely traumatized me, I'd only gotten two hours of sleep. My mind and body had survived too much to play games anymore.

71

"You need to tell us what the hell is going on." My tone came out a lot closer to normal than I expected. "I need several hours, possibly days, of sleep, before I can wrap my brain around what's already happened to me. I don't have any more patience to give you. Now spill it."

Jane and Carlos exchanged a look, and Jane turned back to us. "I can give you the basics. That's all."

I nodded. "That'll do for now."

She gestured toward her ornamental companion. "This is Carlos." She nodded at Edward. "I'm Jane. We're with the U.S. government, and we believe your version of the kidnapping. We think the assailants might still present a threat, so we're taking you to a safe house."

"The government," I repeated. "As in the Foreign Service? You work with Marnie?"

"Not exactly."

I waited for more, but it didn't come.

"Not exactly? How can you be 'sort of' with the Foreign Service? What other branch of government works on foreign soil…" I stopped mid-sentence, as the penny and my jaw dropped at the same time. "Oh, shit—you're CIA!!"

"No, we're not." Carlos replied automatically, as though programmed.

Jane did not. She didn't say a word, and that told me all I needed to know.

My best friend—the beige-loving, makeup-eschewing, quietly witty wallflower—was a spy.

CHAPTER SEVEN

I wish I were one of those dramatic heroines who faints at shocking news. Sadly, my DNA results from generations of peasant farmers who didn't have the luxury of a good swoon when the crops needed harvesting. I remained conscious through the rest of the ride in the van. No one said a word, no matter how much I pestered them. Maybe I could get Carlos to crack, given time, but when Jane chose to keep her mouth shut, the Jaws of Life couldn't pry it open.

We drove onto the tarmac of a small airfield. It had sufficient lighting, but not the intense, tone-it-down-before-I-go-blind array that I was used to in a jetway. Two crewmen in unmarked coveralls escorted us from the car to a small unmarked plane, and we flew to places unknown.

Had I been Jane, I probably could have figured out exactly where we were at any moment, even when we flew through the clouds. Whether it's the maze of one-way streets in downtown San Francisco or the backroads from London to Stonehenge, she never gets lost. My sense of direction, however, tops out at "nothing to write home about," and was no help at all as we flew through the dark. I thought we flew over water at one point, but when you start from London, that doesn't tell you much. As the crow flies, water is never much more than an hour away. (Okay, your average crow would take longer. As the private plane flies—or maybe a crow on some top-shelf steroids.)

The kidnappers had taken my purse and everything in Edward's pockets, so neither of us had cell phones or anything else that might tell time. I tried to guess how much time had passed before the plane came down again. An hour, perhaps? Maybe more. Another van awaited us, with the convenient windowless seating area suitable for transportation of hostages or refugees, whichever status Jane and Carlos had us pegged for at the moment.

Craning to see out the front window did nothing but strain my neck.

Finally, Carlos pulled to a stop. When Jane opened the car door and I could finally look around, I saw only a dimly lit two-car garage, with no other cars besides the van from which I'd just extracted myself. Jane kept up a brisk pace as she walked into the house, hitting a light switch just inside the door. Trying to keep up with her afforded me little time to absorb my new surroundings. White plaster walls and wood floors surrounded us, broken up only by generically charming French country furniture. Decently maintained place, but not lovingly cared for. Utilitarian drapes covered the windows. No throw rugs covered the scuffed wood floor. Walking through, we passed a kitchen, a living room, and a dining room before reaching a flight of stairs. What I didn't see—photographs, knick-knacks or personalization of any kind—told me more than what I did. Nobody lived here.

Jane didn't break stride as she headed up the stairs. I nearly had to jog to keep up, reminding me why I always told her to go running without me when she visited. When she wants to, Jane can really move. On the second floor, a hallway with several doors greeted us. Jane walked over to the

74

second door and opened it to reveal a serviceable bedroom—
a bed with an iron frame, a chair and a desk that could have
come from Ikea. Dickensian orphanage meets college dorm.

"Where are we?" I asked, as Jane put my bag down
on the single bed. I'd posed the question several times over
the course of our nocturnal ramble, only to meet with stony
silence; but if we were staying here for the night, she had to
tell me something.

"The government keeps this as a safe house." She
didn't mention which government, I noticed. "You and Edward will be staying here." She glanced back at Edward, who
had followed us into the room. "Your room is next door."

"Stay here?" I looked at the sparse surroundings. "For
how long?"

"Not sure." Jane opened the tiny closet—cupboard,
providing we were still somewhere in the British Isles—and
handed me a pillow. "For however long it takes to figure out
who wants to get to you, and why."

"I really must get back home," Edward said. "My
mother must be wondering about me by now."

Jane handed him a pillow as well. "You can talk to
her just as soon as things have stabilized, Edward. Right now
it would jeopardize her safety as much as yours." Reaching
one last time into the cupboard, she pulled out two flash-
lights. "In case you need to use the toilet in the middle of the
night. Keep the curtains closed so no one from outside can
see in. Get some sleep." With that, she disappeared down the
stairs. Despite the compassion in her words, her tone told us
not to follow her.

We didn't.

***

Edward and I retired to our separate chambers. After
the events of the last thirty-six hours and a maximum of two

75

hours sleep at Marnie's, I fell asleep as soon as my head hit the pillow, but it couldn't have been more than an hour before I was awake again. A quick peek behind the heavy drapes confirmed that it was still pitch black outside. My mind, hopped up on adrenaline, started running through the events of the last day and a half and kept coming back to one question.

Why was the door open?

Leave the reasons behind the kidnapping itself to Jane and Carlos. The fact remained that we had been purposefully drugged and taken, only to be left in a room where we could get up and walk out.

Who does that?

I spun it around in my brain until my head did the spinning for me, but found no scenario in which this turn of events made sense. Someone put a lot of work into kidnapping us, from sneaking into the party to finding a lookalike of us to drive out of there, to kitting out a basement where they could store us. I doubted it was just to pass the time before the next X-Men movie came out. They wanted something badly enough to take a huge risk.

Had they gotten it or had something in their carefully laid plans gone wrong?

Something else had gone wrong recently. Mom's broken knee...but there was something else before that. What was it?

Chasing a slippery thought made my brain tired. I found myself staring at the one stray beam of light that found its way under my curtains, watching the beam dissolve into the shadows even as my consciousness faded from here into there.

***

Dreams of Italian food swirled through my brain. I was safe, back at Marnie's, sipping chianti and eating mozzarella sticks...Wait, there were no mozzarella sticks at Marnie's.

I was somewhere else. The mozzarella sticks tantalized the taste buds with their contradiction of crispy and gooey textures. The chianti went down smoothly, with notes of sour cherry and basil. Whatever caused my sudden, overwhelming urge to flee, it wasn't the food...

Back in Santa Rosa...at Sal's, the restaurant where Neil and I ate at least every other week. I had expected him to take me someplace else, a place with real silverware, where linen draped the tables instead of red-checked plastic. I liked Sal's, but how was this a special birthday dinner as he kept calling it? Maybe his present would make up for it. I took a sip of chianti and dreamed of diamond earrings. *Sure, they're expensive,* he'd say, *but nothing is too good for you...*

The kitchen door smacked into the back of Neil's chair, forcing him against the table and temporarily robbing him of the ability to speak. As soon as he could breathe again, he moved his chair over, closer to me. "I know you wanted something fancier, but I had to bring you here," he said as the door once again swung open, now colliding with the wall. "This is our place."

I would willingly have made some nicer restaurant our *new* place, but he was right—for now, Sal's was as close to a "place" as Neil and I had. *Take the high road,* a voice in my head told me. Probably Mom. "This is fine. I love the lasagna here."

"I was going to wait until later," he continued, "but it'll probably be a while before they take our order, much less bring our food, and I don't want to wait that long to give you a birthday present."

I smiled. Now we were on the same page.

"Yes," he said, a confident smile on his face. "It took some doing, but here it is."

He picked up his briefcase. I'd wondered why he brought his briefcase into the restaurant, but Neil did a lot of things that made no sense to me. He pulled out a manila envelope. Puzzled, I opened it and saw a stack of paperwork with very tiny writing and multiple signature tabs on it. "What is this?"

He smiled slyly. "It's a bid."

"A bid? For what?" Diamond studs? You didn't need paper copies for that. Maybe Neil didn't grasp the eBay concept.

His smile grew. "The house."

"The house?" My eyes grew as I began to understand what he was talking about. "The house we're renting? I didn't know the house was for sale."

"It wasn't. I called the Espinozas a couple of months ago and asked if they were interested in selling. I wanted to give this to you back on our anniversary, but they needed to think about it. Anyway, they finally agreed."

"They're selling the house?" Of course they were selling. The Espinozas currently resided in Denver. They didn't need the house and they probably wanted the money.

"Well," Neil said, adjusting his tie and doing his best Brooklyn accent, "I made them an offer they couldn't refuse." Neil's best Brooklyn accent sounds kind of like someone stepped on his tongue, and nothing, I'm pretty sure, like anyone who has ever set foot in Brooklyn.

I tried to think of anything to say that would adequately express my feelings on the subject and came up with, "Wow."

"I know," he said, either not hearing or ignoring the lack of enthusiasm in my voice. "All you need to do is sign and initial in the places I've indicated. I'll email the bid back tonight when we get home. We've already pretty much agreed on the price, and they want to do a quick escrow, so in less than a month you and I will be homeowners."

"Are you kidding me?" I asked, my eyes as wide as the platters the servers whisked through the kitchen door.

"No. It's real, Em. Take a look."

I wanted to do many things—scream, cry, laugh hysterically, run from the restaurant, hot-wire the nearest car and drive to Canada. One thing I did not want to do, however, was look through the papers that were going to tie me forever in debt to the man sitting next to me right now.

The bid price, however, leapt out at me before I could stop it. "Neil!" My shriek scared the server in the midst of refilling my Chianti. After wiping the spilled liquid off the plastic, she fled like an escaped convict. "What are you doing? We can't afford this!"

"Yes, we can." He took his laptop out of his briefcase and pulled up a spreadsheet. "We'll have to make a few cuts in our budget—stop impulse spending, eat out less. We might even cut down to one car—"

Stop impulse spending? What kind of madness had overtaken this man? Impulse spending was all that kept me alive.

The muscles surrounding that twitching vein in my neck tightened, particularly on the right side. The strain grew as I turned my head to look at him, and if I didn't do something quick, actual pain would soon follow. I picked up my Chianti and drank it in one gulp. That helped.

He turned the laptop to me. "See, here's a budget with our combined incomes. We each set up a direct deposit to a new account, and we each deposit half the monthly mortgage amount. The way I've figured it here," he pushed a button and the spreadsheet jumped to the last row, "we'll take a thirty-year mortgage, but we'll have it paid off in eighteen years."

Eighteen years. Dear God. I would die in eighteen minutes if I signed this, I was sure. I had to find a loophole.

"Are you sure this is a good idea?" I asked. Trying my best to put a good spin on things, I continued, "I mean, things between us have been so great, the way they are..."

"Exactly," he said, leaning an elbow towards me. "Things have been great. That's how I know we were meant to be."

The neck muscles hurt and the Chianti was threatening to fight back. "Meant to be...but I thought you didn't want to get married," I said. The urge to flee was almost overwhelming.

"Oh, I don't want to get married," he said, leaning back in his chair. "Marriage is an outdated institution. A lot of paperwork and expense to tell us what we already know— that we're a great team."

"We are," I said. Okay, so lots of times I didn't feel like Neil and I were such a great team. More like I was trying to get in a round of poker while he used the cards to play solitaire. "But if you don't want paperwork and expense, why do you want to buy a house? I watched my sisters go through this. We'll be buried in paperwork for the next month, and we'll never be able to eat out again."

The tiniest bit of exasperation cracked through his calm exterior. "This is different," he said. "Weddings are just about sentiment and show. Buying a house is a smart investment. I'd say that's worth eating dinner at home, wouldn't you?"

It didn't matter that he didn't want to get married. I wasn't ready to marry him yet in any case. He just didn't seem to understand that buying a house together, at least in my head, amounted to the same thing…without the presents.

I took a sip of water. "This is crazy, Neil. What do we use for a down payment?"

"We have the down payment," he said, his voice fraying at the edges. "With my savings and the sale of your car—"

"My car?" I repeated. "My car? Since when are we selling my car?"

"Fine, then," he said, struggling to keep calm. "We can use your savings, too."

"I don't want to use my savings!" I said, omitting the fact that I didn't have much savings to use. I drank the rest of my water to make sure I didn't throw it at him.

"Well, you have to put in something." He crossed his arms. "It's hardly fair to expect me to make the initial investment all by myself. What kind of partnership is that?"

"The same kind of partnership where one person decides to buy a house without telling the other person," I snapped.

"It was a surprise!" he said.

"Surprises are supposed to be nice, Neil, not life-changing. Surprises are things like roses or *diamond earrings*," I said, clenching my teeth. "Buying a house is the kind of decision we should have made together." I crossed my arms, too. Defensive posture. "You're always doing this, Neil. You're always making decisions for both of us and I've gone along with you too many times."

"Em, come on," he said with a heavy sigh. "You're overreacting."

"No, overreacting would be pointing out how much I hate being called Em."

He rolled his eyes. "I forgot. Sorry."

Again. Let it go, I told myself. Bigger fish. Deeply in debt fish.

He leaned back in his chair. "What's this really about? It's not the house. You like the house. You always say it's charming."

"It is charming," I said. It was, in the way that only faulty plumbing can be. There was precisely enough hot water for one and a half showers. It didn't matter how fast those showers were. Somehow the house knew, and it would not be fooled. The 1938 Frank Lloyd Wright-inspired bungalow had all of its original features, including hardwood floors, built-in shelves and cloth electrical wiring. If I tried to run the toaster oven and the microwave at the same time, the whole house suffered a brown-out. There was a mysterious corner of the backyard where nothing would grow. I wanted to believe it was a sacred Indian burial ground, but I was pretty certain no self-respecting ghost of any nationality would reside so close to the neighbor's sewage clean-out.

"You have to admit," I said at last, since Neil remained silent, "it has some problems."

Neil's upper lip recoiled. "I've looked around, Em. This house is the only one in the neighborhood that even comes close to being something we can afford. Don't you ever think about our future? Do you still want to be renting when we're sixty?"

I took a sip of Neil's Chianti and suddenly remembered the reason we were here. It was my birthday. I was not going to spend my birthday—even one as un-noteworthy as thirty-nine—having a prolonged discussion about a topic that had my digestion gearing up for rebellion. I broke off a piece of bread and offered it to Neil. "You're probably right about all this, but it's kind of overwhelming, you know?"

The server approached our table just long enough to tell us that I'd have to order something else—they were out of lasagna.

Some days there is no point in getting out of bed.

I switched my order to the baked ziti. Neil shifted in his chair and ended up right in the way of a redheaded staff member emerging from the kitchen with three baskets of bread, managing to shower garlic-laden carb bombs all over Neil's briefcase. While they sorted out the debris, I ordered another Chianti, and told the server to keep 'em coming.

Brushing crumbs off his sleeve, Neil settled himself back in his chair. "Go ahead, just sign it, Em...maline." The exhaustion from the effort of saying my whole name covered his face. "The Espinozas need the paperwork back today."

"Today?" I nearly choked on Neil's wine. "You have to give me a little time to think about this."

He lowered his eyebrows a few millimeters. "I didn't think it would bother you. You're the one who loves doing things on impulse. Besides, we already live in this house. We know exactly what we're getting. There's virtually no risk."

And maybe that's what bothered me so much about it. Buying a house should be a huge leap. There should be the dilemmas of what color to paint the walls and where to put the furniture. A little magic as your beloved insists on carrying you over the threshold. If Neil had his way, we'd just stay in that cold, badly lit house that wasn't good enough to be haunted until we were dead and forced to haunt it ourselves. He probably would carry me over the threshold one day for kicks if I asked, but if you have to ask, what's the point?

That's exactly it, said a voice in my head that sounded like Jane. *That's the point.* (Maybe it was Pippa.) *You're not upset about the house. You're upset about living in the house with Neil.*

No, I am not, I argued back with myself (or whoever else it was). I'm just not ready to buy a house, and it isn't fair of him to pressure me.

So say no, the voice said. (Cordie this time. I could tell by the bossiness.) *What are you afraid of, that he'll leave you?*

Just like Cordie, jumping to the worst possible alternative. Neil wouldn't leave me if I said no to the house.

Would he?

He was sitting in front of me, with those stupid papers and a pen at the ready. As usual, he'd made it so much easier just to go along with him. All I had to do was sign the papers and live in the house I was already living in. He handed me the pen, and I took it. Sign, I told myself. The only change would be who I made the check out to every month. Even the change in the amount was probably manageable, if I avoided the sales at Macy's—like the one Pippa and I planned to hit during lunch on Monday.

"Neil, do I have to do this right now?" I asked. "It's my birthday. The Espinozas can wait one more day, can't they?"

I stared down at the paperwork, wondering if Neil could hear the wild thumping of my heart. Oh, well. Even if he could, he'd probably misinterpret it as enthusiasm.

"Right down there," he said, pointing at the signature line.

I skimmed down the page, checking carefully over all the numbers. It wasn't like I really expected to find anything wrong, because Neil had doubtlessly gone over the information several times in my absence, but I figured if I stalled for time, there was a chance my hand might stop shaking. I glanced down—the down payment amount was high. About $10,000 too high. The total offer for the house was correct, they'd deducted the ten grand from the amount the bank would pay, but I'd have to liquidate my IRA to come up with that much down. That was (a) not smart and (b) time consuming, and thus could not be part of Neil's plan.

"Neil," I asked, trying to keep my voice level, "is this right?"

"I'm sure it is. Let me see," he said, leaning over my shoulder. "It's—wait a minute. No, it isn't. They've put $10,000 in the wrong place. Damn," he said, taking the papers back. "I can't believe I missed that. They'll have to email us a new copy." He kissed my neck. "You're good, Em. No wonder I love you."

Yes, I'd have to face the music later. The proverbial orchestra was just taking five. But at least they weren't playing yet.

***

Neil and unsigned contracts faded into the background of my panorama of crises as I woke up. Figuring out where I was with Neil had to take a back seat to figuring out where I was, period. Whose house were we in and what country surrounded it?

85

CHAPTER EIGHT

One rogue sunbeam had found its way in between the possibly lead-lined drapes, letting in enough light for me to see the diminutive dimensions of my accommodation. I wondered if it had begun life as a closet. Perhaps four feet lay between my single bed and the opposite wall. The interior decorator for this chateau had sandwiched a chair and desk into that space—the desk too narrow for productivity, but excellent for supporting the elbows as one sat pondering grave mistakes in life. The sole window lay just beyond the foot of the bed, hidden behind floor-to-ceiling drapes that might have served as blackout curtains during World War II. If I reached over and yanked them across the single gap, the room would be in total darkness again.

Instead, accepting my wakefulness, I peeked behind the drapes to see a small pond edged with trees, each tree awash in multi-colored leaves. The sunbeam that had disturbed my slumber shone from a break in the clouds, one miraculous patch of blue between encroaching armies of fluffy white. Apparently, the sky changed fast in these parts.

Remembering Jane's instructions to keep the drapes closed, I pulled them back over the window, blotting out the sky. I fished around in my suitcase for clothes that didn't look desperately in need of laundering. Yesterday's boot-cut jeans and a yellow fitted sweater were all that fit the bill.

Now, where was Edward? He couldn't have gotten far. From the looks of things last night, Jane and Carlos wanted to keep a tight perimeter around us. Why? Who did they think was after us, exactly?

I stepped out into the hallway, looking for the other occupants of the house. I needed answers as much as I needed food.

My stomach growled loudly. Okay, almost as much as food.

"She awakes." Edward's voice came from the next room over. He sat on the bed in a room identical to mine. The t-shirt and jeans he wore looked at least two sizes too big for him. Since he didn't have a handy suitcase of clothing to grab, I guessed he found himself at Carlos' mercy, unless he wanted to wear the tuxedo he'd worn for the party/kidnapping.

"Morning."

Edward shook his head. "Afternoon, more like."

You'd never have known it from his room. More heavy-duty drapery covered the room's only window.

I supposed the shrouded windows were standard operating procedure for a safe house, but why exactly did we need to take refuge in a safe house? Why had we flown in the dark of night to a spot approximately six minutes south of nowhere? I mean, yes, Jane probably believed I was kidnapped. She was my best friend, she would want to believe me, even if the police in London didn't. Regardless, she'd only take this kind of action if she had evidence. Where was Jane? For that matter, who was Jane? Questions came over me like waves and I was pretty sure they'd drown me before I found answers to all of them.

One question, however, superseded all others. "Where's the bath—the loo?"

Edward pointed me in the right direction, and I made use of the smallest lavatory ever. I couldn't turn around in there without smacking into something. I could only imagine what hell a taller person might experience in this facility. Maybe the house was built by leprechauns.

Afterwards, I headed down the stairs, only to meet Carlos halfway up. He smiled at me, and I ran a hand through my hair. My hairbrush and my makeup hadn't made it into the suitcase before Jane grabbed it last night. I didn't mind Edward seeing me that way. He'd already seen me regain consciousness after getting drugged and dumped in a basement. Standing with my disheveled hair and naked face before the beautiful Latin James Bond was another matter altogether.

He winked at me. Be still my beating heart. "Just coming to check on you, *bonita*. We'll get you some breakfast."

I heard Edward on the stairs behind me, his gate uneven. I suspected he sustained more bruising from our adventures than he was willing to admit. "And we'll get you some aspirin," Carlos said, nodding in his direction.

We made our way down to the dining room. Jane sat at the table, sipping a cup of what appeared to be tea, and waved to us. As I sat, I found myself scrutinizing the woman sitting in front of me, poised over her morning brew.

Jane Miller and I had been best friends since we shared a dorm room our freshman year at San Francisco State University. A warm and generous heart lay inside her very tall frame, inadequately reflected in her somewhat wan complexion and—let's be honest—mousy brown hair. Jane always was a makeover waiting to happen. I never felt bad about thinking that because if she paid any attention at all, Jane could be *stunning*. She had the height, the almond eyes and the bone structure. A little makeup, a better wardrobe and even now, spitting distance from forty, she'd show up super-models.

In two decades of friendship, it had never occurred to me before that maybe she played her looks down on purpose. I still wasn't convinced of that—her lousy self-esteem seemed too genuine. Given recent events, however, I had to face the fact that she hid quite a bit under that unassuming exterior.

Jane pushed plates of bread and butter toward us, as well as two pots full of steaming liquid. "Tea and coffee," she said, pointing to each in turn. "Help yourself." She cleared her throat. "You probably want to know what you're doing here." With her hair pulled back in a ponytail so tight it could double as a facelift, Jane looked as if she'd rather do anything but answer her own question.

I poured myself a cup of tea, and then took a slice of bread and slathered it in butter. "Yes, please."

"That would be refreshing," Edward said.

Jane exchanged a look with Carlos and continued. "You've stumbled onto something complicated."

"Complicated?" I tried not to spew bread crumbs as I talked. The word seemed like a cop-out. On the other hand, the soda bread distracted me with its deliciousness. "By complicated, do you mean intellectually stimulating, or just bad?"

Jane's look told me that she didn't want my interjections just now. "Complicated," she repeated. "Edward, we've noticed some activity lately with your finances."

"Something weird turned up in Edward's bank accounts?" I stared from Edward to Jane. "In the last twenty-four hours, or did you know him before that?"

Jane shook her head. "Sort of. Well, I didn't know him, exactly." She met his blank stare. "I knew about him. He's been under investigation for a while."

"Investigation?" Edward doubtlessly hated serving as an echo as much as I did, but it was hard to stop. "For what? I haven't done anything."

Carlos pulled his seat closer to the table. "You haven't received some strange deposits in one of your bank accounts lately?"

"Nothing unaccounted for, no." Edward's voice dropped off at the end of the short sentence.

"Repeated deposits in the amount of £50,000, over the last eighteen months?"

My eyes widened so much I feared I might run out of face. "Edward, are you blackmailing someone?"

His gaze ripped from Carlos to me. "What? No! Certainly not!"

Carlos was still focused on Edward. "Then why exactly are you receiving a hefty sum every month for no particular reason?"

"I haven't. I mean, yes, I've received the money, but there's nothing suspicious about it." He drew his lips together and took a breath before continuing. "Insulting, perhaps, but not suspicious. It comes from my father-in-law." He shook his head. "My ex-father-in-law. He gave me some money to help with medical expenses when my father fell ill. Hamid never liked me much, but he understood taking care of family."

Carlos inched closer. "Edward, your father died thirty years ago. What's the real reason?"

90

The blue in Edward's eyes froze over. "My biological father died when I was a child, along with my mother, in the same car accident that took my leg. They left me in the keeping of my uncle. Being a nasty drunk, he was sort of rubbish as a guardian. The housekeeper and the gardener, Mary and John Hobbs, were the closest thing I had to real family. John developed a particularly wretched form of cancer that took his life almost a year ago." Anger pulsed through him so strongly I could feel it pushing the air. "He raised me, so I took to calling him my father. I hope that doesn't confuse you."

Silence can be really loud sometimes.

Carlos cleared his throat. "I understand." The barest second passed before he continued. No more. "But what I don't get is why the payments kept coming after he passed away. Our records show that you liquidated most of your assets to cover the treatments, and you've lived modestly ever since. Looks like your jet-setting days are over, but do you still require an extra £50,000 a month from your father-in-law to maintain solvency? Especially after you and your wife split up?"

"No." Edward stared at his tea. "I've tried to convince my father-in-law to stop sending the money. I thought I succeeded, because for three months, the payments stopped. Then another one came. I called to ask him about it." He set the cup down none too gently. "He said he didn't know what I was talking about and hung up."

"Then your father-in-law must have some interesting connections, because the money came from an account with known terrorist affiliations."

All the air rushed out of my lungs. Edward, on the other hand, looked like he'd just had a triple shot of espresso. "Bollocks. My father-in-law has some antiquated ideas about women and completely misunderstands the West in general, but he's no terrorist."

Jane pulled her chair over toward Edward's. "The deposits came from a bank in Boston, right?"

"He set up an account there to transfer money to Nuriyah—my ex—when she did her graduate studies at Wellesley. He found it useful for business. Easier to have international earnings go to Boston. You lot tend to get dicey about folks making payments to accounts in Saudi Arabia."

"The first few deposits came from the account in your father-in-law's name. The last one originated from an account for a brand new medical charity. Looks a bit suspect."

Edward shook his head. "There's a perfectly logical explanation, I'm sure."

Carlos took a swig of coffee. "We haven't found one."

"Why isn't British intelligence checking this out, if it concerns a British citizen?"

Jane ran her finger along the top of her teacup. "We talked to MI5. They checked you out, and your in-laws, and their investigation came out clean. They decided American bank, American problem. We keep them in the loop, and they allow us in the country. Other than that, it's our problem to solve."

Bouncing back and forth from Carlos and Jane to Edward made my neck hurt. "This is all very interesting, but it isn't getting us anywhere." I rested a hand on my neck, hoping warmth would help. "Why don't we go for a walk or something, look at the local shops, enjoy the country air"— whichever country might claim it— "and we can come back to this later when we've had time to think?"

Good heavens. That sounded so reasonable.

It still didn't work. Carlos could have strained something shaking his head that fast, if he weren't in such great shape. "Sorry, *bonita*, but you and the Lord of the Manor here can't go anywhere. The safe house concept only works as long as no one knows you're in it. You stay in the house with the curtains drawn until we clear up this mess enough to send you home."

I put my hand back in my lap, since it wasn't helping my neck at all. "Here? And we can't even walk around outside? You must be kidding. Tell me he's kidding, Jane."

Jane's mouth puckered into a frown. "Sorry, Emmy. You've already been kidnapped. Someone has tried to pay Edward off. You two landed in the middle of a mess, and the best way to keep you safe is if no one knows you're here."

I looked from one captor to the other. "We're in the middle of God knows where, someone might want us dead, and you're telling us we're grounded."

"I wouldn't put it like that—"

"I would." Carlos put his coffee down and folded his arms. "Read a book. Have a snack. Get comfortable. You're going to be here a while."

Edward looked at his tea and asked for a beer.

That about summed it up.

CHAPTER NINE

The official fiction of the visit cast Jane and Carlos as a couple on their honeymoon. That way, they could get food and supplies in town, but if they spent days on end without leaving the premises, no one in the small neighboring village would question it. In this narrative, Edward and I didn't exist, so we had orders to stay inside and keep away from the windows so as not to mess things up.

Jane couldn't give me online shopping options, but she had stocked up the place with at least a dozen issues of *Cosmopolitan* magazine, a few new Jennifer Crusie novels, and a television that picked up almost four channels. "See?" she said, switching from station to station. "Not so bad, right?"

I disagreed, but she was trying so hard, I didn't have the heart to tell her so. "Oh, who needs extraneous entertainment? I'm trapped in a house with my best friend. This will give us some quality catch-up time." If I couldn't leave this house, I could at least get a few questions answered. Like, maybe, *who the hell are you?*

She put the kettle on for more tea. Not an electric appliance, I noticed. Jane placed an old-fashioned copper one on the gas stove. The simple tea kettle marked perhaps the one touch of personality about the whole house. Jane pulled out loose tea, a ceramic tea pot and a tea strainer and set to make a pot of the good stuff.

"So." I leaned against the tiny tile counter. "When did you develop an alternate personality, and can you switch back and forth at will?"

Jane's shoulders tightened up. When she turned to face me, I caught a trace of a blush on her face. "It's still me, Emmy. I haven't really changed."

"You're kidding me, right?" I crossed my arms and gave her a Grade II glare. "The person that I know works in a bank in Washington, D.C., wears beige suits, and regularly calls her parents." I swept a hand toward her. "The woman standing in front of me right now conducts midnight raids in foreign countries so that she can gather intelligence on international criminals with her trusty hunk of man-flesh by her side. The math here doesn't work." Remembering other people still occupied the house, and Jane probably didn't want them to hear this, I lowered my voice. "I'm an accountant. I notice when things don't add up."

Jane stared at the tea kettle and sighed. "It's a long story."

I boosted myself up onto the counter. "I've got nothing but time, remember? Start talking."

She looked over at the door as though a wild animal might bound through it at any moment. "I can't. It's classified."

"Jane, it's just us. The place isn't bugged, is it?"

"No. We swept the place last night. It's clean."

My Lord, she *could* switch back and forth. In that instant, she'd transformed into a CIA operative right in front of my eyes. All business, cool in the face of danger, able to detect electronic listening devices with her X-ray eyes.

Carlos stuck his head around the door frame. "Need to talk to you."

Jane's eyes moved from me to her partner and back.

Carlos' mouth quirked up on the left side for a quarter of a second. Then he turned and walked back to the dining room.

A moment of déjà vu swept over me, so strong I felt like I'd slipped into a parallel dimension.. Jane looking at Carlos, Carlos walking out of the room. But for some reason Jane's grey t-shirt felt like the wrong costume choice. Why did I feel like she should have been wearing red? Jane never wore—

"It was you!" I shrieked, pointing at her. Possibly the most idiotic gesture ever, since only the two of us occupied the kitchen, but I couldn't help myself. "At Marnie's party, making out with the loser at the Saudi buffet. I wasn't crazy, it was you!"

An earsplitting whistle from the tea pot punctuated my speech. Jane grabbed the rubber-coated portion of the handle and moved it to a burner that wasn't lit. "Me? I don't know what you mean." She licked the edges of her fingers. Evidently the rubber hadn't completely insulated the handle.

"This is insane. What did I do to make the CIA want to follow me, Jane? Tell me!"

"The CIA does not want to follow you, Emmaline. Don't let yourself get paranoid. You were probably just in the wrong place at the wrong time." She looked like a Calvin Klein model, her face completely devoid of expression as she poured water into the ceramic pot and spooned in some tea leaves to steep.

"Okay." I pursed my lips. If my brain kept running in this many different directions, I'd have a stroke. "So what was I in the middle of?"

"I can't say. It's classified."

"Classified from me? I'm your best friend!"

"Classified from everyone. Don't feel bad, okay?" She bit her lower lip. "Even my parents don't know the whole story."

I looked at her for a long moment. No more explanation would follow. I shook my head. "How did your life get so complicated?"

She narrowed her eyes at me. "I could ask you the same question. You're the one getting kidnapped. How did you get wrapped up in this? Was it really just bad timing?"

"As far as I know. Marnie knows Edward, sort of, but I don't think she knew he'd be at her tribute, and she certainly didn't know he had kidnappers on his trail, or she'd have kept me well clear of him. You really think this is something to do with his former in-laws?"

She shrugged. "Most of the family is above board, but we're checking anyway."

"And until something clicks, we're guests of the CIA?"

"I never said I work for the CIA." She reached into a cabinet and grabbed two mugs. Poising the tea strainer over each in turn, she poured the amber liquid from the ceramic pot into them.

"Really?" I leaned forward, watching the tea leaves collect in the strainer as the smell of orange and cloves wafted up to my nose. No. I would not be distracted by the lovely aroma. "Who do you work for?"

"It's classified. I can't say."

Carlos leaned around the door again. "Cali, now?" He gestured upstairs and walked away.

Jane emptied the contents of the tea strainer into a bin under the sink and dumped the utensil into the sink. She picked up her mug and smiled apologetically at me. "I have to go."

I grabbed her arm. "What does 'Cali' mean? Is that Spanish for something sinister?"

"It's his nickname for me." The barest hint of pink crossed her cheeks. "I once had a head wound and mumbled something about wanting to go home to California. That's the only thing about my past he knows for sure." She strode after him with what struck me as unnecessary haste.

I jumped off the counter and leaned out the door. "So officially, we're guests of the Washington National Bank?"

Jane looked back. Her mouth curved into a wry smile. "Enjoy your stay."

Carlos waited at the bottom of the stairs. Jane walked up ahead of him, running her tongue over her lip and pushing a lock of hair behind her right ear.

I didn't bother trying to eavesdrop. Whatever it was, I could get it out of Jane later, because whether she realized it or not she'd just given me a bargaining chip. I might not know anything else about Jane's current life, but one thing had just become clear: she had a big juicy crush on her partner and he didn't know.

It felt good to be sure of something.

***

I was a model hostage the first day.

I survived the second.

On day three my basically short attention span overruled my best intentions. By 3:30pm, I had read half of Jennifer Crusie's latest tale of romantic hijinks and an article on why I should order the eighteen-year-old Jameson whiskey instead of the twenty-one. (The twenty-one was better, but not better enough to justify the price difference.) I switched on the TV and passed by two soccer (excuse me, football) matches, a talk show in Gaelic, and a documentary on Arthur Guinness—the man, the brewer, the legend.

If I didn't get out soon, I would hand myself over to the kidnappers just to end the pain.

Edward looked up at the television, abandoning his other options—Chekhov's short stories and some copies of *The Economist*. His desperation to escape might have exceeded mine.

Carlos sat at the kitchen table, looking at some files on his beloved laptop. I pulled up the chair next to him and sat. "Seriously, Carlos. I need to get out of this house. I know you said we need to stay here, but…"

"You need to stay here." He didn't even look up.

"You don't understand. The boredom. It's moving into my soul and putting up window treatments."

"Deal with it."

"Forget it." I got up and walked to the door. "I'm going to find Jane."

"She went on an errand."

I turned back to him, fists burrowed into my hips. "Where did she go? I thought we weren't allowed to leave."

He pointed at me without looking at me. "You aren't allowed to leave. Jane and I can come and go as we please. Thankfully. Someone has to get food."

"I thought you said the house was wired. I didn't hear any alarms go off."

"They go off when someone without permission gets in. They don't go off when anyone goes out. Especially not someone who has permission to go out."

The bastard didn't even have the good manners to look apologetic. "Fine." I gritted my teeth. "I'll just find something to do, like unravel the afghan and teach myself to knit."

"I could use a new sweater."

Funny. Carlos' beaming smile became quite resistible when flashed at my expense.

Edward headed up the stairs. After a few minutes, given the options, I decided to follow him.

I found him in his room, with his leg off.

Now with the limited number of times I've encountered that scenario—this would make a grand total of one—it should have drawn my focus. Oddly enough, however, neither the lower part of his left pant leg hanging flat beneath his knee nor the prosthetic itself, lying on the bed, grabbed my attention. The strange game he played with his right leg was something else again. It involved rolling his foot over what looked like a tangerine, and then picking it up with his toes.

"Don't tell me." I turned around and headed back out the doorway. "I don't want to know, I really don't." I turned back. "Just tell me you're not going to eat that. Please?"

"No." Disgust stretched the word out a few syllables. "I have to do exercises with this foot, and I didn't get time to pack the proper equipment. I saw the fruit in the kitchen and thought it might work."

"Does it?" I couldn't take my eyes off his foot. Toes were not supposed to do that.

"Well…almost. Bit squishy, though."

I might never eat a tangerine again. "What does this do?"

"Exercises the muscles in my foot. It's supposed to help the injury heal more quickly."

I stared in disbelief. "How does nimbleness with your toes on that leg make the other leg heal?"

Edward looked at me for a full second, and then burst out laughing.

I tapped my foot. "What?"

He wiped a tear from his left eye. "Not that injury. I assure you, abusing a tangerine isn't going to make my leg grow back."

My cheeks burned. "That's not what I thought."

"You'd need at least a grapefruit for that. Possibly a small melon."

I straightened my spine, reaching possibly five-foot-three and a half. "You are enjoying this way too much. You know that, right?"

He smirked and put the tangerine on the low dresser next to his bed. "It's an exercise to help my other leg. You know, the one that's still attached. I tore the plantar fascia while running, and it's only finally beginning to heal."

"You run?"

"Yes." His mouth twitched to one side. "Why do you look so surprised?"

I shook my head. "At Marnie's party, you were walking around with a crutch. I guess I just assumed you used it all the time."

"No. Well, yes and no."

I drew my lips together. "Not helping."

"I've been using it since I tore the plantar fascia. With the injury, my balance has been off. When my right foot isn't stabbing me with pain, I don't need it. But even when my foot functions normally, I use the stick at night if I have to get to the loo or shut off a light. It's easier to use a crutch than to put the prosthesis back on."

I thought about all of that for a minute. It made sense, and most importantly, it meant I was right about his relationship with the crutch. It was a friend. I like it when I'm right. In trying times, you have to cling to the little things.

"Does it still hurt? The plantar whats-it." No sense letting him get all silly at my expense again.

His smile slipped. "Sometimes. Better than it was, though. Right after I injured it, I had to use two crutches to get about."

"Good upper body workout. That explains the buff arm muscles."

His eyes caught mine and held just a fraction of a second too long. Then he turned away and scratched at something on the duvet that I couldn't see. "Spend a lot of time looking at arm muscles, do you?"

I couldn't very well help it, could I? A girl has to be dead not to notice some things. "Part of working in accounting. You notice details."

He exhaled sharply and looked in my direction, if not at me. "If you must know, I find it useful to keep my upper body in good condition. I began doing so at school, not long after the accident. I was still learning how to deal with the leg. It helped to know that if I couldn't run as fast as the other lads, I could damn well beat them at climbing a rope."

He picked up the prosthesis and gave all his attention to cleaning it with the edge of a nearby blanket. "Nuri always wondered why I was so obsessive about my exercise regimen. 'Manic,' I believe she called it. Made her insane."

"At least you concede your neurosis. My boyfriend Neil insists that all the compulsive things he does make sense."

"Boyfriend, eh?" He looked carefully at the attachment, as though inspecting it for flaws. "Been together long?"

"About a year."

102

"Ah. Sounds serious."

"I don't know. I'm not really sure it's going any-where." The words fell out of my mouth before I realized it.

Oh, honestly, Emmaline, I thought. A man takes off his leg in front of you and you want to throw yourself at him.

He didn't show any signs of wanting to catch me, so I changed the subject. "If you're finished with your daily exer-cises, let's discuss ditching this place. I think I know a way."

Edward listened patiently enough to my theory, but looked at me quizzically, one of his eyes half closed. He was either squinting in concentration, or he'd suffered a minor stroke. "So, if you threaten to tell Carlos about this crush, you think Jane will offer us a weekend furlough?"

I sighed. "Of course she will. Otherwise, I can threat-en to tell him that she likes him. She'll do anything to make sure that doesn't happen."

"Why?" Edward's eye relaxed. I ruled out the stroke. "Perhaps she already has, and they're having a torrid affair."

"You don't know Jane," I assured him. "She does not have good luck with men. He's probably dating someone at work and she has to watch them together. Even assuming he's not dating someone else, he'll reject her as soon as he finds out. I've known her for twenty years, I've seen it be-fore. It just happens to her for some reason."

"Why? There's nothing wrong with her." He stared at the wall as though he could see through it and down the stairs. "Maybe he's had his eye on her, too. She's actually quite a lovely girl. Smashing legs."

It was my turn to squint. "She's worn pants the entire time you've known her. How would you know what her legs look like?"

"She's tall and athletic." His cheeks turned a shade too rosy, even for an Englishman. "Extrapolation."

I stared at him. "You recognized her, didn't you? From the party."

He tried to hide a smile, and his cheeks went positively crimson. "It took me a bit to put them together, but she was hard to miss at that reception."

I sighed. "True enough. Anyway, I'll bet you a drink. If I'm right, you owe me a pint."

"Safe bet, seeing as how we may both die of old age before we see the inside of a pub again. We'd probably best just stay put. People want us dead."

"The police don't think so," I reminded him. "Besides, how slick can these kidnappers be? They abducted us and then left the door open."

"I keep going back to that, too." He shook his head. "Why would someone go to so much trouble to kidnap us, just to let us go? It took a lot of planning to get us out of that party. They couldn't have gotten us back through the ambassador's house, I don't think. That means they most likely arranged access to one of the other houses. Had an in at the security company, perhaps? They must have had a reason to get to us. They may still."

I rubbed the bridge of my nose, trying to get rid of the headache I felt looming. "But what reason? Neither of us can claim fantastic wealth. Do you have political or social influence that you neglected to mention?"

"Not particularly. You? Does your aunt have the ear of your country's president? Could you be used as bait?"

"My aunt met the president twice, and both times he got her name wrong. She knows people, yes. You want to eat at a restaurant in D.C. that has a six-month waiting list, she could get you a spot tomorrow. But as far as actual political policy? I don't think so. She's never wanted that much influence, probably precisely so she didn't get mixed up in stuff like this."

Edward slunk down onto his elbows. "Square one, we meet again." He looked at me, a touch of desperation in those azure blue eyes. "You really think you can sway Jane?"

"I'm sure of it."

"At least it's some possibility of escape. I could kiss you."

So lightly made, the comment could have floated on the breeze for half a day. Our eyes met.

He cleared his throat. "I've got to get something to drink."

I learned one more thing: Edward could put a prosthesis on in a very short amount of time when he wanted to get away.

CHAPTER TEN

I tried to get Jane alone for a friendly bit of extortion, but for the rest of the day Carlos needed her constant attention. Was I wrong? Maybe he did like her. Or maybe he suspected I was plotting something. I had the uncomfortable thought that Carlos could read people better than I'd given him credit for.

On day four, I started in on my fourth copy of *Cosmo*. Six different sexual positions to try while standing up. I looked at my surroundings and wondered if that would ever be relevant to my life again.

Out of sheer boredom, I took a nap that afternoon and woke to the sound of heavy breathing. Oh, my. Evidently erogenous zones figured in someone's reality here. Had Jane talked Carlos into a naughty game of Spy vs. Spy? One could only hope.

The sound was indeed coming from Jane's room, down the hall from mine. No wonder I could hear—the door wasn't completely shut. Dear Jane was shedding inhibitions right and left.

I tried to avert my eyes, but couldn't help a glance when I heard a male voice. Not Carlos—Edward. He was doing a yoga pose, downward-facing dog. Just like I'd seen

Sneakers do a million times. Front paws on the ground, rear end sticking up in the air. He had on black sweats that looked like they'd fit Carlos better, and no shirt.

Damn.

Jane had one hand on his stomach and one on his lower back. Teaching him a yoga pose? I hadn't heard the offer of afternoon yoga classes. I might have joined in, just to do something different. But then again, maybe they didn't want company.

"Just keep breathing." Jane pressed both her hands more firmly on him. "Now relax through here." She ran her hands across his lower back. "Oh!" Her hands flew to her mouth. "Sorry!"

"Don't be." Edward bent his knees to the floor and raised up to a kneeling position. "Having my arse patted by a pretty girl is the only bit of good fortune I've had this week." He winked at her. They both erupted in laughter.

I slipped away from the door and went downstairs before either of them spotted me.

Edward and Jane? No. That couldn't be right. I was so sure she wanted Carlos. She'd certainly done a good imitation of flirting with Edward, though, and meaning it. Jane didn't have it in her to blush on command.

So what? You have a boyfriend. You have no reason to care what they get up to.

I ignored the voice in my head - probably Cordie, the booking agent for guilt trips - and went downstairs. Carlos sat at the kitchen table in front of the laptop to which I had begun to suspect he was surgically attached.

Presently, Jane came downstairs again and went into the kitchen. Edward didn't come down. Probably worn out from the foreplay, poor boy.

Well, finally a chance to catch her alone. I followed her into the kitchen. "Hi."

She stood at the refrigerator and flashed me a smile before reaching inside for a bottle of mineral water. "Hello. Need something?"

"Just wanted to find out if I could get in on the next yoga class. Every day my confinement extends, so does my waistline."

Jane jumped. The refrigerator door handle slipped out of her hand, and the door shut with a soft click. She turned to face me. "Yoga class?"

"Yeah. You know, the one you and Edward had upstairs?"

She backed up to the refrigerator. "We didn't have a class."

"Oh, really?" I leaned on the counter and played with a loose thread on my lilac sweater. The house's antiquated washing machine made my clothes smell better, but it attacked my sweaters like a terrier with badly cut nails. "Look, Edward is cute. If you think there might be something there for you…"

"There's nothing between us, Emmaline. Nothing. He's nice looking, but I'm too tall for him. It would be a problem."

For Jane, anyway. Edward hadn't shown any signs of discomfort with her height when she had her hands on his butt.

She cast a wary eye at me. "Do you and Edward have something going?"

"No. I mean, once you get kidnapped with someone, you do develop a connection to them, but that's the extent of it."

"I'm sure Neil would be relieved to hear that." Her fingers drummed the countertop. "He must be so worried." Her eyes relaxed, but the veins in her forehead picked up the slack. "I'm sorry you have to go through this, Emmy."

Her concern wrapped around me like an old wool blanket, familiar and soft. I reached over and put an arm around her. "Thanks. I don't know how you do this all the time."

"I don't. Ninety-five percent of my life is spent going through paperwork. I just have to stay in shape for the occasional flare-ups."

"And a little groping at Embassy parties?"

She took a step back and closed her eyes, breathing out through her nose. "That was one of the most regrettable job requirements."

"I'd ask what ranks as the favorite," I looked back at the dining room and lowered my voice, "but I think I know."

Her eyes darted back and forth like a crazed animal, alternating between darting looks toward the dining room to see if Carlos had overheard and glaring at me. Her eyes told me to shut up, without her vocal cords having to do a thing. She headed out to the living room, where we could see Carlos but were technically further away, and when she did speak, her voice came out a raw whisper. "Don't get excited. He's a co-worker. That's all."

"Uh-huh. Are you sure about that?" I threw a glance over at Carlos.

Her mouth tightened to a straight line. "I am, and I'm pretty sure his girlfriend is, too."

"Girlfriend? Bummer." I watched her try to avoid my gaze. "Have you told him how you feel?"

Jane's eyes moved to Carlos as if against their will before coming back to rest on me. "I don't feel anything. He's a colleague."

"A colleague, huh? So you're telling me you haven't noticed the bedroom eyes or the Adonis-like cheekbones?"

Her own cheekbones flashed scarlet. "Of course I noticed." Her voice came out so faint I had to lean closer to hear her. "But even if there were the remotest chance of anything happening, which there is not, our jobs demand a certain level of professionalism. We have a good working relationship." Her lips tightened. "And there's the girl friend."

"Is it serious?"

"Seems that way. Some chippy in Boston. They met a couple of months ago. She helped us check out the bank where the transfers to Edward's account originated. Now, he texts her all the time. They're planning a romantic weekend as soon as this wraps up."

"A couple of months, they can't be that serious, right?"

Jane narrowed her eyes at me. "And if I'd asked you that about Neil, when you'd dated for a couple of months?"

I rolled my eyes. "That's hardly the same. Neil and I saw each other more. We moved in together after three months."

"Exactly my point. For all I know, they could move in together if the weekend goes well. Leave it, Emmy. Do not interfere."

"I'm not going to *interfere*." The innocence I forced on my face probably fit as well as a plastic clown mask. "Maybe just—plant a seed. See what grows."

"Emmy!"

The word came out louder than she'd intended, I was sure. Carlos looked over at us, his eyebrows lifted in question.

"We're fine," Jane said, plastering a smile on her face until he looked away.

I gave a long exhale. "I'm bored. Seeing how Carlos feels about dating you could be just the distraction I need, to keep me from thinking about all the stores and restaurants I'm missing here in—wherever we are."

Her eyes narrowed. "Read a magazine. Watch a movie."

Underneath the suspicion, she looked a little scared.

"Fine, I won't rat on you...probably." I threw my head back on the sofa cushion. "But you know how I am with confined spaces. Staying inside is making me nuts. You're sure we couldn't manage a field trip or two?"

After the tiniest peek at the pretty man, Jane concentrated all her energy on rolling her eyes at me. "I'll see what I can do about more entertainment. Let's teach you some Virabhadrasana. The Warrior Pose—it tones your thighs and sharpens your focus."

Like toned thigh muscles or sharpened focus mattered here at Camp CIA.

***

I'm not rebellious by nature. Pippa filled that role in our family. Me, I fell somewhere in the "relatively agreeable as long as there are no brussels sprouts involved" category. So when Jane told me and Edward to stay away from the curtains, I intended to follow instructions. I don't normally spend a lot of time staring through windows, unless there's a display of shoes on the other side.

Four days in lockdown, however, and nature held an attraction I'd never known before. Every afternoon, I told everyone I was going upstairs for a nap. Instead, I went upstairs and peeked around the edge of the curtains.

The house sat on a small lane, a low stone wall running alongside a row of tall skinny trees. Several hundred yards down the street I could see the next nearest house, separated from us by the pond and a field, far enough away that I couldn't tell whether anyone was inside staring back at me.

Each time I did this, I heard Jane's voice in my head, telling me how important it was that no one see me in the house so that I didn't screw up her honeymooning cover story. But then, the image of her and Edward and the yoga episode would pop into my head.

I had no claim on Edward. There was no reason in the world he and Jane shouldn't have some fun. Yet somehow, the idea of the two of them engaging in hands-on flirtation made me want to throw up a little.

You have Neil waiting for you back home, and Jane only wants you to stay away from the windows to keep you safe. Cordie's voice this time. *Can't you just do what you're told?*

Well, hell. If disobeying Jane held some allure, irritating Cordie was downright magnetic.

I told myself I'd only look outside for a minute, but each day, I stared a little longer.

The fifth day, a boy of seven or eight exited the nearby house with a fishing pole. He walked down the abbreviated dock, climbed into a small rowboat and made his way to the center of the pond.

My parents put the pool in our backyard when I was ten, and I remember a lot of lectures about water safety that year. Rule Number One was "Never go in the pool by yourself." This kid's parents didn't seem to worry about it. Maybe they had trained that large bird walking around the edge of the lake to report anything out of the ordinary? The bird had a comb on the top of its head, like something exotic, but feathers of a very unglamorous brown and grey. My knowledge of birds made my grasp of flora look extensive. It looked to me like a peacock and a turkey had spent too much time with each other and a bottle of tequila. I couldn't see this creature filling in for Lassie and telling the local humans that Timmy had fallen in the lake. If it noticed the kid going overboard, it might comb its hair before making a sound.

I monitored him from my room and breathed a sigh of relief when he finally rowed back to the dock and returned to his house.

I really wanted to say something to Jane, maybe ask if she'd seen the kid's parents, but of course, that would mean confessing all the time I'd spent staring out the window. I hadn't seen anyone out there but the kid, and he showed no signs of having spotted me, so I didn't see the harm in it, but Jane would.

At least the Jane I knew would. This new Jane, who made out with repulsive men in the name of justice and practiced wanton yoga? I wasn't sure what she thought about anything.

CHAPTER ELEVEN

Sleep eluded me that night. Too much napping, I told myself. After the last week of my life though, sleeping issues were only to be expected. I could nod off during the day after digesting yet another Cosmo article, but at night, when darkness reigned, I couldn't help imagining all the things that might pop up on my personal horizon. Another kidnapper? An additional friend-turned-CIA-agent? Maybe my mother snuck off at night to disable nuclear devices. If Jane could live a double life, anyone could.

I peeked out the window. I couldn't see any risk to it now, with the moon making it lighter outside than it was in the house. Trees stood silhouetted in the moonlight, the night breeze bringing them alive, stirring their branches into a ritual dance to summon evil spirits from the pond. If you wanted to set the scene for a tale with fairies—not the Disney knockoffs, but the old-fashioned kind that stole babies—you couldn't ask for a better setting. I dropped the curtain and fell back onto the bed. The view did nothing to convince me into unconsciousness was a good option.

Soothing thoughts, I told myself. Scones. Warm, fresh, just out of the oven, with a huge dollop of clotted cream and someone's homemade raspberry jam. Okay, the jam could be from the store. I probably couldn't tell the difference. Wash it down with a cup of tea made by my mom, with the cup properly scalded...

"Eeeeeaaah..."

I sat straight up and looked out the window. The noise came from outside. High-pitched, almost keening—a child crying for help.

On the other side of the glass, everything remained as obscure as before. Shadows all over the place. I didn't see anything out of the ordinary. It still looked spooky, and seeing winged creatures with suspicious bundles wouldn't have surprised me, but I could only make out long, wavering shadows of trees. The wind picked up. See, I told myself, it wasn't a kid. Just the wind.

The sound came again.

I didn't imagine it. Something was out there. I grabbed my flashlight and ran out of my room. Someone else had to have heard it, didn't they? Edward had closed his door, and no light came from under it. Jane's door lay open a few inches, but everything inside seemed still. Forget it. Carlos and Jane slept in shifts. I ran downstairs. No one around. A beam of light off to the right suggested Carlos had need of the facilities. Should I wait till he was done?

A great splash came from outside.

Forget Carlos. That little kid from next door. Crap, maybe he'd decided to go fishing at night and fallen in the pond? I opened the hall closet. A trench coat over pajamas didn't count as the height of fashion, but I didn't have time for anything else. Unlocking the back door, I ran outside in the direction of the pond. The door swung closed behind me with a soft snick.

I knew we were out in the countryside, but as an indoor hostage, I hadn't appreciated the lack of exterior lighting. No streetlights, no neon signs, not even any light from the house I'd just exited, since Jane and Carlos had so carefully covered all the windows with heavy curtains. The wind ushered in clouds to obscure the moonlight. The thin beam from my flashlight constituted the only illumination around.

Something splashed in the water. It rocked back and forth, then dipped under the surface.

"Hold on!" I yelled. "I'm coming to help you!" I ran forward and shined the flashlight at it, but saw only a black mass. *Don't dive into the water,* Mom's voice told me. *Drowning people like to pull you under with them. Find something to lower to them.*

A gust of wind blew my trench coat around my legs. A branch from the tree slapped me in the face. It snapped back out over the water. I ran out onto the dock and grabbed at it, trying my best to break it off with one hand while holding the flashlight with the other. It fought back, springing back out over the water, and I felt my feet slipping off the end of the dock.

"Emmaline!"

Hands grabbed my waist, pulling me back on to the walkway. Regaining my balance, I turned and saw an agitated Carlos pulling me back toward the house.

"Let me go! A kid just fell in the pond. We have to find him!"

Jane ran out of the house. Carlos looked in the pond. "Where?"

I flashed the beam of light in the water, but didn't see anything. The poor thing could be unconscious already.

"EEEEAAAAH!" The sound came again, from somewhere off to my left, the opposite direction from the lake.

Two kids around these parts couldn't find themselves in peril on the same night, could they?

I moved the light over to the left. A flash of something green and blue, about a foot off the ground, moved behind the nearest tree.

I stared after it. "Oh, you have got to be kidding me."

Jane tossed her head toward the house. "Inside. Now," she hissed.

"A peacock? What the heck is a peacock doing out here?" The funny-looking bird I'd seen earlier. Female peacock. Peahen, that's what it was called.

Carlos chased me inside. Jane followed swift on his heels and locked the door after us.

"You know you're not supposed to leave the house!" Carlos' voice came out in a strangled roar, trying to settle between yelling at me and keeping quiet so the whole world couldn't hear. "What the hell were you doing?"

"What else could I do? A kid was crying…"

"A *peacock* was crying!"

Jane put a hand on my shoulder. "It's not her fault, really. The bird does sound an awful lot like a child crying for help."

Carlos shot me one more glare and then looked at Jane with his jaw set. "We should move."

"We have cameras set up outside, Emmy." Jane held up a finger to stave off Carlos while aiming her words to me. "We knew one of the neighbors kept peacocks. We'll get on it if any kids fall in the pond, I promise."

"What's going on?" Edward leaned over the stair rail.

Carlos threw up his hands. "Gang's all here. Great."

Jane took a sharp breath. "Emmaline thought she heard something outside."

117

Edward came down into the room. "There's someone outside? Should we leave?"

"There was no one outside."

Carlos twisted his mouth. "Unless you count the peacock."

Edward stared at me. "You ran outside for a peacock?"

"It sounded like a kid!" My hands flew to my hips. "What are you all, deaf?"

Jane took a stand in the middle of the room and pointed to me and Edward in turn. "You and you, go back to bed." She crossed her arms and leaned a shoulder back toward Carlos. "I'll call the boss and explain what happened. Assuming she doesn't die laughing, she can tell us what to do next."

CHAPTER TWELVE

"Boss said to sit tight." Jane's words greeted me the next morning. "Aren't you glad? You don't have to pack. Oh, and she enjoyed the story immensely, if that helps. Actually laughed over the phone. I didn't know she was capable of that. The few times I've seen her smile, she doesn't even show teeth."

I sank into the chair at the table next to her and accepted the cup of tea she pushed toward me. "Glad someone benefited." Stupid peacock. If I ever ran into one again, I'd carve it up for dinner. "Where's Carlos?"

"Upstairs sleeping."

My eyes flew to the ceiling. "Good. After a decent night's sleep, he might be less mad about last night."

"Don't count on it. Headquarters wants to do more analysis on Edward's money. Our next assignment after this is going through a mountain of records, detailing the entirety of his family's financial history."

I winced. "Unhappy camper, huh?"

"Hostile camper. Forced to camp against his will."

"I know the feeling."

If anything, Jane sugarcoated Carlos' feelings. Later that day, when I asked if we could go out to lunch, Carlos pushed out of his chair and asked me if I'd like to have his laptop force-fed to me. Jane held out a hand to him as if to pin him in place with her mind. She ushered me out of the room, yelling back to him, "Killing your protectee will look bad on your record."

Aside from that faux pas, I did pretty well for the rest of that day, and the day after. By day seven, however, paranoia set in. Not, oddly enough, about potential kidnappers. I couldn't worry about external things when my immediate surroundings threatened to suffocate my brain. I had nothing to fear but this house itself. I had entered a world in which life no longer existed beyond its walls, where I spent all my days leafing through Cosmo finding out about new erogenous zones I would never get to use. Not even death could save me. This hellhole existed beyond life and death, an eternity in the Purgatory of Light Amusements.

One small ray of light broke through this haze of self-pity. When Jane got back in touch with her superior that day to report in, the boss told her and Carlos to chat with the locals and see if they'd heard about my encounter with the peacock. To accomplish that while keeping up the newlywed fiction, they were going out to lunch. Together.

"Just a quick bite," Jane swore to me. "You'll be perfectly safe as long as you stay inside. We'll be monitoring the outdoor cameras over the phone. Just stay inside and keep away from the windows, and all will be well. We'll be back by 3:00."

Edward looked from Jane to Carlos. "A romantic lunch? Shouldn't you go for dinner?"

Jane put some money in a small clutch. "Lunch will have to do. I don't think anyone knows you're here, but if they do, they're less likely to go after you in broad daylight."

Carlos got a coat out of the closet and handed another to Jane. "We're on our honeymoon. They'll just assume we want to get home early to have sex."

Jane the Super Agent blushed so furiously I was tempted to check her for fever.

I wanted Jane to go out with Carlos for her own happiness, but not nearly as much as I wanted them gone so I could escape.

For preference, I would have escaped alone and skipped the possibility of hearing the details about more yoga positions Jane might have taught him, but taking Edward with me ranked ahead of coming up with a reason to elude him.

As soon as they left, I darted over to where he sat, watching a movie. "Come on. This is our chance. Let's get out of here."

"What?" Edward sat up. "Have you lost your senses?"

"Not yet, but I will if I have to spend one more minute in this house." I pointed at the TV. "You were watching that same movie two days ago. Tell me you don't want out of here as badly as I do."

He looked at the screen and then put his head in his hands. "All right, yes. I'll slit my wrists by the end of the week. Happy?"

"Ecstatic. Let's go."

"How will we get out without them knowing? They've got alarms and cameras here."

"The alarms don't go off when we go out of the house, just when someone tries to get in without the code. I'm figuring they won't check the exterior cameras until they get to the restaurant."

"So we just leave and hope they don't notice?"

"Exactly." I raced upstairs for shoes and a coat and came back down trying to throw everything on at once. "This is definitely one of those 'better to ask forgiveness than permission' moments."

"Assuming we live to ask it?"

"We're going to live," I told him. "The whole kidnapping thing freaked me out, but now that I've had time—so, so much time—to think about it, I think the London police have a point. Nobody's said boo to us since I went outside and chased after our avian neighbor. Our kidnappers let us get away after they took us. What kind of threat do they really pose?"

"So you think the CIA is worried over nothing?"

"I think the CIA saw the money from your Saudi relatives and went directly to 'global terrorist threat.' It's what they do."

"And you're willing to gamble on the guess that they're wrong?" Edward arched one eyebrow. I'd always wished I could do that.

"You know your ex and her family. Do you think they're terrorists?"

"Of course not."

"I trust your instincts. Besides, I heard a Scottish voice and you heard an Irish one. Neither of us heard Arabic. Come on!"

It took me another twenty minutes to convince him, but finally he caved. Once he changed into the least ill-fitting clothes he could pilfer from Carlos, we walked out the front door.

...Into Ireland.

***

I didn't know where we were at first. The greenery that surrounded us could have been many places in the Sceptered or Emerald Isles. Or maybe these plants existed only in Ireland, but I didn't know either place or plants well enough to determine that. It wasn't until we passed the first sign printed in both English and Gaelic that the truth occurred to me.

"We're in Ireland." I have great talent at stating the obvious.

Edward looked at the sign. "This was a bad idea. We should go back."

The thought had run through my head, too. "I guess in comparison to getting kidnapped again, my third nap of the day doesn't sound bad." I sighed. "Well, not as bad."

"Boring, but safe." He turned around.

I reached back for his arm. "The alarms. They're set to go off unless you have the right code to get in. I don't suppose you memorized it?"

"I've never seen either of them use it. We're always on the other side of the door."

"What do you think happens if it goes off? Immediate occupation by agents currently hiding in the bushes?"

Edward studied the door. "Probably just Carlos and Jane come home, none too happy with us."

Thoughts bounced around in my head. "Millions of people live in this country. They can't all want to kidnap us. What are the odds that we run into that one guy?"

He looked skeptical, and I couldn't blame him. This week, the odds hadn't favored us. After a second, however, he shrugged. "We can't re-enter the house unnoticed, whether we try now or later. I suppose since we're in trouble either way, we may as well go ahead. We don't have a reason to feel in any particular danger this far from London."

He held a hand out toward a walkway around the pond. Trees surrounded the water and were too thick along the far side for me to see what came next.

We walked in silence for a few minutes. I seldom walked at home just to walk. If I want a workout, I go to the gym and use the stair master, closing my eyes and cranking up Pink on the iPod until I feel like I've burned enough fat to keep me in a size four. (Okay, my workouts only keep me in a size six, but they *feel* like they should get me into a four.)

I looked at the surroundings, keeping an eye on how to get back. The lushness of the landscape almost overwhelmed the eye. Delicate trees surrounded us, dropping water from the morning's rain on our heads in erratic sequence. We walked a mile, maybe more, along a road that probably wouldn't have merited a street sign back home but seemed to act as a main thoroughfare here. We passed five or six people, most of whom nodded or smiled at us.

Edward walked quickly. I nearly had to jog to keep up. "Foot not bothering you today?"

He shook his head. "It's much better lately, actually. Feels good to walk, after so much sitting about."

I had to agree. "Couldn't ask for better scenery, either."

His lips curled up. "We visited Ireland once when I was small. It was years back, but I remember it enchanting me. I loved the tales of creatures living in the woods."

I nodded. "I heard some of those from my grandfather. He moved to the U.S. from Ireland when he was four. His parents told the stories to him, and he told them to my mom and my aunt, and then to my sisters and brother and me.

Usually about some evil troll ready to rip your legs off if you didn't eat your veggies."

Half a second later I realized what I'd said.

"Sorry!" My hand flew to my mouth, as though that would do any good.

He laughed. "Trolls! And here I was blaming the car accident."

We walked in silence for a minute, the only sound coming from the soggy leaves squishing under our feet.

In the midst of this tranquility, I heard myself ask, "How old were you?"

He didn't answer right away. I probably should have kept my mouth shut, and I would have, except that I wanted to know. My good judgment rarely keeps pace with my curiosity.

Finally, he said, "Ten. The brakes on my father's car gave out just as we went round a sharp turn."

"Hell. I'm sorry."

He smiled, but no pleasure lay behind the expression. "I was the lucky one. My mum and dad both died in the crash."

He kicked aside a tree branch with unnecessary force.

"You didn't mention any brothers or sisters when you told Carlos and Jane about your life. No one else in your family?"

He shook his head. "At a guess, I'd say my parents didn't sleep in the same room often enough to make it feasible. Not the happiest of relationships."

We walked on, strolling in silence. I couldn't guess his thoughts, but mine focused on how to stop bringing up awkward subjects. Eventually, we turned onto a picturesque road with medieval-looking shops and pubs. The local mall, six hundred years ago. With the exception of electrical wire and a few signs declaring acceptance of Visa, nothing had changed. A few people wandered in or out of a shop, and a couple with two kids walked ahead of us. Clearly, hustle had never come through these parts, let alone bustle. If they ever arrived here at the same time, the earth would stop spinning.

We walked along the cobblestone street. I stared in the shop windows, just for a second the ordinary tourist I thought I would be on this trip. The green sweater with the wooden toggles in the window to my right would make the perfect Christmas present for my mother. Cordie would drool over that lace tablecloth. The storefront across the street boasted a beautiful green and blue Aran knit throw that I would tell myself I'd give to Pippa, but would really keep for myself because let's face it, Pippa would spill juice on it and this blanket deserved better than that.

By the time we passed a pub called the Cook & Castle, I couldn't resist anymore. I grabbed Edward's arm and pulled him toward the dark green door. "Come on. Let's go have a pint."

"We can't."

I slid my hand down to his and threaded our fingers together. "We're supposed to stay under the radar, right? Well, what could blend in more in the Irish countryside than a couple having a pint?"

That artificial leg clearly worked just fine, because he held his ground like he was growing roots there. "We can't pass for a couple having a pint."

Maybe I should have felt up his butt. He hadn't had any trouble canoodling with Jane, but he couldn't sit with me long enough for one stupid beer? "You're a man. I'm a woman. Presumably the pub can supply the ale. What are we missing?"

"Money."

Damn.

Jane and Carlos made sure we had clothing, shelter and food. They'd even taken a stab at entertainment. Since we weren't supposed to leave the house, though, they didn't bother supplying us with cash.

I looked longingly at the pub, a place so traditionally Irish a set designer might have created it for a period film set in the 1500s. "Come on," I said, heading for the door. "I'll flirt with the bartender."

"What if the bartender is gay?"

"Then you flirt with him."

My fingers closed around the door handle as he said, "Flirting's not my strong suit."

Before I could argue, the door opened of its own accord. A dark-haired man, even shorter than I, leaned out and smiled at us. "Are you coming in, then?"

"Yes," I said, at the same moment that Edward said, "No."

"Ah, having a bit of a spat, are you? We can't have that. Sweet couple like you arguing on the street. I don't recognize you folks. You here on holiday?"

"Yes," I said. What was it Jane had said? Newlyweds on honeymoon in that house? The safe house sat in the country, in between two towns. Jane had said they were heading east. Edward and I had gone west. Not much chance of running into them then. I grabbed Edward's hand.

"Do I detect a bit of an accent, then? Where do you come to us from?"

Had Jane said they were American newlyweds? I couldn't remember. I affected my best English accent. "Manchester," I replied, picking a city completely out of the air. It was a big place, right? So the owner was unlikely to have cousins living there who knew everyone in town? "We'd love a pint, but I left my purse at the house and Albert," I squeezed Edward's fingers, "just realized he left his wallet behind, too. Silly boy." I gave him my best adoring smile.

"We're so sorry to trouble you." Edward squeezed my hand back and gazed at me, semi-convincingly smitten. "Victoria and I are on honeymoon. I suppose our minds have been on other things."

"On honeymoon!" The proprietor beamed at us. "Well, that settles it. You'll come in and have a pint on the house. I've a romantic streak in me a mile wide. In with you and we'll toast to love." He winked at Edward. "Got to have something to keep your strength up, don't you?"

Edward quirked the right side of his mouth up and glanced at me, then quickly looked away. He released my hand and put his on the small of my back, ushering me through the door the proprietor held open wide.

The man could improvise. Who knew?

We followed our host to the bar and sat on high leather stools. He gestured to the woman working the taps. "The missus." His wife, a good five inches taller than he, inclined her purple buzzcut head toward us and smiled, then blew a kiss to her significant other. He grinned, looking not unlike a leprechaun discovering that he could have his gold and pint to drink, too.

Patrick and Fionnula ("Call us Paddy and Fi, or we're not like to answer") supplied us with pints of ale and baskets of fish and chips, then drew up stools of their own and drank with us. They toasted our health, happiness and fertility (dear Lord, no, not even in my fictional marriage) and we drank to them in turn. When we reached fertility, Fi laughed and said we'd waited too late, she was already drinking for two. I almost asked if she shouldn't switch to something less—well, alcoholic, when I remembered I wasn't supposed to be American and that Europeans had a very different relationship to liquor than we did.

Reluctantly, I stopped Paddy from pouring me a third Guinness. I hadn't finished my second and couldn't if I wanted to remember the cover story I'd invented. (Jane had invented. Whatever.) Part of me wanted to let him keep pouring. For an hour there, I'd felt as though I were actually on vacation.

Edward nodded at the clock over the bar, advertising Jameson Whiskey. "We should probably get back, Vicky."

I followed his gaze. The hands registered four o'clock. "Oh, hell. Jane and Carlos are going to kill us."

Fi looked at me, shaking her nose ring. "Jane and Carlos?"

Paddy squinted. "You brought another couple on your honeymoon? Have you gone right round the bend?"

"Our corgis." I smiled beatifically. "We take them everywhere. If they don't eat at 4:00 on the button, they get ever so cranky."

"Thank you for everything," Edward said, bracing himself as I leaned on his arm. The room had begun to spin a wee bit. Somewhere, the Irish ancestors in my family shook their collective heads in disbelief at my lack of drinking capacity. "I'll send you the money for those drinks."

Paddy shook his head. "Wouldn't hear of it. You two have a lovely honeymoon trip. I can only hope you're as happy as my Fi and me."

Fi forced a smile, and I got the feeling Paddy would hear a "babies are expensive, you know" speech as soon as we cleared the premises, but she wished us well anyhow.

Edward and I waved and walked back out to the street. When we were safely out of the village, I wobbled toward the woods. Not a bad idea actually. "We'll take a short cut. We can get back to the house faster." I shot him a sideways glance. "Victoria and Albert? You didn't think that was overdoing it?"

"This from the woman who named the corgis Jane and Carlos? I don't think you're in any position to judge."

"You're just upset that I brought them on the honeymoon."

"I think it is grounds for annulment." Edward put out a hand to steady me. "Lucky for you, I like a woman who can't hold her liquor."

"I'm fine. Just needed to walk a minute to clear my head." I shook his arm off. "Just try to keep up, okay?"

Crack.

The sharp retort came just before a large tree branch fell inches from my head and crashed to the ground.

Edward pulled me behind a tree trunk. "What the hell was that?"

When two more deafening blasts followed, we both knew the answer. Gunshots. Someone was shooting at us.

At least it definitely wasn't a peacock. This time I was sure.

CHAPTER THIRTEEN

We crouched behind the tree, trying to become one with the bark. First someone kidnapped us, and then a week later in another country, they try to kill us? For what possible reason? I could almost buy someone kidnapping me to steal my fabulous designer shoes, but homicide for the Keds I wore at the moment didn't wash.

I heard an engine in the distance. Thank God. The trees spanned perhaps two miles from the small village to the street where the safe house sat, but we'd only walked two hundred yards, and the growth never got thick enough to block the view from the road completely. They couldn't keep shooting us with witnesses, could they?

Yes, they could, as the next volley of shots proved. "They're insane," I declared to Edward's shoulder. He threw an arm out, shielding me between him and the nearest tree. He provided decent body cover, but that made his lack of bullet-proofness a problem for us both.

Edward ventured a glance around the tree. "Maybe they're just bird hunters and don't realize we're here."

Another shot. "Bloody hell!" Edward yelled so loud they probably heard him back in England. He grabbed at his ear, which the bullet had just grazed, and then pulled both of us even lower to the ground.

No one called out, "Sorry, mate! My fault!" or anything of the like.

Probably not bird hunters.

"We have to move." I peeked around him "They'll get the right angle to kill us eventually."

He nodded, his chin hitting my head. "Probably soon."

Another cracked tree limb went down, further away. "That wasn't even close. Are they just messing with us?"

"I don't know, but that makes this a good time to run. Let's go."

Before we could move, the small van that had delivered Edward and me to the safe house a week ago pulled up onto the sidewalk at the edge of the woods. The side door slid open. Carlos jumped out took cover behind an adjacent tree. One more shot rang out, followed quickly by something falling hard onto the leaves. Carlos' face appeared around the edge of the tree. He signaled back toward the road. Two more shots flew, away from us. He shoved Edward toward the van on the sidewalk. Me, he picked up and threw onto the backseat.

Righting myself, I saw Carlos jump in the driver's seat. Jane came running from the woods, slowing only once to fire back behind her. "You go," she shouted to Carlos. "I'll track the shooters."

"Not a chance," Carlos said, opening the passenger door. "I'm not leaving until you get in the car."

Jane looked back once and then got inside. "Go!"

Carlos put the world's mini-est van into gear and went. Jane leaned out the window and took one more shot as we sped off.

I didn't know what messed with my head more—the idea that people wanted to kill me, or the fact that my even-tempered best friend, the one who calmed my nerves with her very presence, spent her days shooting people out the windows of moving cars.

"They were trying to kill us." Edward's face reached a new shade of white, even for an Englishman. "They were actually trying to kill us."

"After they went to the trouble of arranging your kidnapping, you expected a fiesta?" Carlos asked. He stared back at me in the rearview mirror. Mirrored sunglasses hid his chocolate brown eyes, but I could feel his glare just the same. "We told you not to leave the house. One damn piece of instruction, and that was too much for you?"

His Spanish lilt did not make the words any more pleasant. I appreciated that I couldn't see his eyes, half suspecting they had lasers of death shooting from them. I sighed. "We got bored. You can't ask a person not to leave the house for a week and expect them to stay sane. What were we supposed to do?"

"You were supposed to stay in the fucking house." Carlos could really enunciate, especially on K sounds. His mother must be so proud.

"The boredom was going to kill us anyway. How do you know someone wanted *us* dead, specifically? Maybe we just stumbled on some unfortunate local violence." That sounded lame, even to me.

"Here's a little-known fact: when people are shooting at you, they usually have a reason." He turned to Jane. "Did you call this in?"

Jane shook her head. "I can't get any reception."

Carlos fished in his pants pocket. Without looking at him, Jane put an arresting hand on his leg. "Don't bother."

133

Carlos stopped fishing, and I guessed it wasn't because of her words. I couldn't blame him—Jane had inadvertently put her hand close to something vital there. She removed it, unfazed. "I think it's better we stay off the grid anyhow. That was too easy for them."

Damn. When this girl was in the zone, she could out-cool an iceberg. No wonder she did the window work and made Carlos the wheel man.

"Of course it was easy. These two decided to play tourist. We might as well have sent up a flare." Carlos smacked a hand on the armrest. "Where to now, then?"

"I don't know. Anywhere but here. Just get on the highway and give me a chance to think."

***

The silence in the van put me to sleep, so I don't know exactly how many hours passed before we pulled into an industrial section of a large city. I guessed Dublin. Did Ireland have any other big cities? I didn't know. We certainly hadn't seen any others since Jane and Carlos put us on the plane. Marnie once told me that Dublin had beautiful parts to it. This wasn't one of them.

Presumably my current overlords had come to a decision about our destination while I slept because Carlos pulled up to a garage in some sort of storage facility. Jane jumped out and punched a code into a keypad, which opened a garage area. Once we drove inside, Jane closed the bay door and opened the car, shooing us through yet another door into a warehouse.

It was small for a warehouse and stuffed with boxes. Narrow windows high up on the front wall let in some natural light, but most of the illumination came from fluorescent

134

lighting fixtures suspended from the ceiling. Cabinets lined the walls, a folding table with two plastic chairs sat in one corner, and a flight of stairs led up to a loft office over the back half of the space. The sort of place where a predominantly online business might store its inventory, with the owner using the office space to keep track of the bookkeeping.

"What's this?" I asked. "Are we picking something up?"

"Nope." Carlos walked to the back wall and started opening cabinets. "These are your new accommodations. Get comfy."

Edward looked around at the concrete floor, bare plaster walls and stacks of dusty boxes. "But there's nowhere to sleep."

Carlos opened the second cabinet on the side wall and flashed a smile. "Either Jane or I will get blankets and food."

I rubbed my arms. "Assuming we don't freeze."

"The place has heating. You'll live—unless you do something stupid." He slammed the cabinet closed. "Something *else* stupid."

I climbed up the stairs and looked inside. Clearly the manager's office—more boxes and an old metal desk. Industrial carpet in every color of grey coated the floor, giving the space all the warmth of a dentist's waiting room. Nothing around here would make for a cozy mattress.

"Make yourself at home." Jane stood on the stair landing outside the office. "You and Edward will be sleeping up here. One point of access. Carlos and I will sleep in shifts."

"In here?" I took another look. The desk took up most of the room. "Where?"

"You'll figure it out." Carlos flashed me a smile. He reached in his pocket for his phone.

His smile faded when Jane held out her hand for it. "I'm sorry. No contact, just for now."

"That's taking things too far, don't you think? It's a secure line."

Jane walked down the stairs, gesturing for Carlos to follow her, which he did. They spoke in low tones. I caught Edward's eye, and we both made our way quietly down the stairs behind them. I managed to catch "...right after you called your girlfriend. It doesn't look good."

Naughty boy, Carlos, I thought. Sounds like teenagers weren't the only ones forbidden from calling their crushes while babysitting.

He clenched his jaw, but handed Jane the phone. She gave him a tight smile. "I'll be back. Sorry, you get to watch the kids."

She disappeared into the garage. A second later, I heard the engine start and the van drive off. "Where is she going?"

"That information is given on a need-to-know basis only. You don't need to know."

I scowled. "Does this place have nothing to drink? I'm thirsty."

"Faucet in the bathroom probably works." He pulled out one of the plastic chairs around the table. "Sit, *bonita*. The bad guys are out there. Stay in, stay safe."

Edward looked up at the narrow windows, where presumably he saw the same nothing that I did.

My fingers curled into my t-shirt. The air vents in this room wheezed like they had asthma. Loud hum, a fan working too hard, the noise breaking off and then coming on again at uneven intervals. I could swear the ventilation system pumped poison gas into the air. Get out. *Get out.*

"I can't stay here."

"You don't have a choice." Carlos' even tone didn't match the danger in his eyes. "In fact, why don't you figure out your sleeping arrangements now? Go get a really good look at that office upstairs. You two have caused enough trouble for one day."

My eyes flew from the cell-like office upstairs to the door leading to the garage. How long would it take me to run out? Was there a chance in hell I'd get past Carlos? No, but that wasn't what stopped me from trying it. As I looked frantically about my new prison, I got a glimpse at Edward.

His face had gone a shade of grey that managed to clash with his blue eyes. The cool he'd kept through the past days of kidnapping, flight to another country and mindless detainment had disappeared. He looked as though he might keel over in a second.

I took a cautious breath, decided the air might not have that much poison in it, and walked up the stairs.

Edward followed me, and Carlos walked up behind him. Once Edward and I were inside the smaller-by-the-minute room, Carlos grabbed the door handle and shot one dark look at us. "I'm locking the door for your own safety, and I'll shoot the first one of you to come through it. Good night." The door banged shut behind him.

I looked at Edward. "He's exaggerating. He's trained to protect people."

Edward stared at the door. "He's trained to shoot and not miss."

Fair point.

CHAPTER FOURTEEN

I told myself to relax. At ten feet square, the room made a spacious cell. Never mind that it didn't even have a bathroom. Damn, now I desperately needed to go. I could bang on the door and yell to Carlos, but he probably wouldn't believe me. Heck, I wouldn't believe me either.

I sank down to the floor. "Edward, would you do me a favor?"

"What?"

"Talk to me."

"Talk to you." His voice was somewhere between a question and a statement. "About what?"

"Anything. I know this sudden claustrophobia is all in my head, really, but—just distract me, okay?"

He sat down next to me. "I suppose I still owe you an explanation for what happened at your aunt's party."

"You know something about the kidnapping that you didn't tell Jane and Carlos?"

"About what happened before the kidnapping." He shifted a few inches away from me to rest his back against the metal desk. "When you came into the dining room, some of my ex-wife's family were already seated nearby. You might remember them. Rather severe-looking Saudi group."

I did. I could still feel the stares of judgment. "They seemed like loads of fun."

Edward gave half a laugh. "Just so. In defense of Nuri's family, I must say those particular people constitute the dourest of the group."

"Every family's got someone who can't remember how to enjoy themselves." I would bet money Cordie hadn't had a genuinely good time since the mid-1990s.

"I don't know exactly why they dropped in. Not the party-going sort, really. I think perhaps they wanted to see if Nuriyah was there with me."

I tried to remember the Saudi women near him that night. "Was she?"

"Good Lord, no. Nuri moved out a year ago, when the money ran out."

"Ouch. That's harsh."

"Is it?" He stared at the door. "It just seemed logical at the time. She was accustomed to a certain standard of living, and I couldn't provide it anymore."

"What happened? You've got the house and the title. I'm guessing your family had money at some point."

He exhaled. "We did. Back when my father was the Earl, he had businesses all over England, Scotland and Ireland. My mother and I scarcely ever saw him, but we had plenty of money. After he and my mother died in the accident, my uncle came to take care of me. He did see to it that I had the best medical care to rehabilitate from the loss of my leg. After that, though, he resumed his twin careers of gambling and alcoholism."

"Let me guess. He bankrupted you by drinking Château Lafite by the gallon."

"No. He preferred an aged whiskey, but if that wasn't to hand, anything alcoholic would do." He tapped a finger

139

against the floor. "We actually owned a whiskey factory for a time. He should have managed it magnificently, knowing the product so well. Unfortunately, he didn't have the first clue how to manage any business at all. Before long, he sold off all the investments for less than they were worth and gambled away much of the profit. Thankfully part of the money went into trust for me. After he passed away, I used a fair bit of the trust clearing up his debts. John, Mary and I would have lived the rest of our lives in low-level affluence if my adopted father hadn't chosen to contract a rare form of cancer."

"The national health care didn't cut it?"

He shook his head. "Once you stray toward experimental treatments, the funds go rather quickly."

"Didn't your ex get the memo about marrying for richer or for poorer?"

Edward's mouth quirked into a wry smile. "It's a nice idea."

He didn't throw off angry vibes. His eyes showed no bitterness. The emptiness in them worried me more than anger would have. With anger, you still have energy. Edward seemed to have entered a void and gave every indication of having made camp there.

"You miss her."

He flinched, but if I touched any inner wounds, they had scar tissue already. "I miss what she was to me."

"What she was to you?" I shook my head and batted the sky, dismissing his statement in syncopation. "No. She's a person, not an idea. You miss her. Don't deny it."

"She's gone and she won't return. There's no point in missing her." His face clouded over.

I didn't like the tension, but it beat the emptiness. "So if you want her back, why were you flirting with me in front of her relatives? Trying to make her jealous by proxy?"

His cheeks burned as scarlet as though he'd developed a taste for burning charcoal briquettes. "I owe you an apology for that."

"For feeling me up without knowing my name? Yes, you do."

"I didn't mean to do that. I just meant to help you clean off the clotted cream..." He sank his head back against the desk, heaving a sigh so long I thought he might pass out afterwards from oxygen debt. "It's a long story."

"Go on, tell me. We've got nothing but time."

He drummed his fingers on the floor, which must have been frustrating. Grey berber stretched from wall to wall and absorbed any sound he might otherwise have made. "Believe it or not, flirting with you had nothing to do with Nuriyah." He sat so close to the desk I thought maybe he hoped to morph with it to get out of the rest of the conversation. "It just didn't have anything to do with you, either."

"So, who did it have to do with? You wanted to coax the burqa off one of her cousins?"

Those clear blue eyes frosted over. "No. I did it to influence my former father-in-law."

I glanced sideways at him. "Really? Not that I'm judging, but that could explain a lot about why your ex left."

He glanced at me through narrowed slits. "You know, if you'd truly like to hear this story, you could try keeping your pretty little mouth shut for perhaps two minutes at a go."

"Fine." I leaned back against the wall. "Proceed." I made a motion of locking my lips, wondering if he did indeed find them pretty. Jane would've said it was a meaning-

141

less remark, but I've found when people say things off the cuff, they speak more honestly than they realize.

"When my father fell ill, Nuriyah and I lived in a flat in Kensington. We moved back to the estate to help my mother out. At that point we still owned the estate, and maintenance ate away at the money I had. Mary had a small baking business, supplying scones and a few other baked goods to restaurants in the area." He looked toward me without making eye contact. "That's why there was a great cracking pile of them at Marnie's party. Your aunt had sampled Mary's wares before and liked them, so when they put together the occasion, her coworkers asked if my mother would provide some."

"Ooh, I bet she sells tons of them. They're unbelievable." Yes, I had promised to keep quiet, but even the memory of Mary's scones made my mouth water.

"They are at that." A faint smile of pride escaped him, hard as he tried to keep the tale stuck in neutral. "She was on her way to building up a respectable local business, but she couldn't keep it going after John got sick. He needed twenty-four-hour care. We hired a full-time nurse, but of course he wanted Mary with him. We tried everything we could—spas in Switzerland, experimental surgeries, several varieties of powder flown in from a noted Chinese herbalist—but nothing worked. Nuriyah let her father know money was running short, and he made several substantial deposits in our joint account."

"To make up for the fact that his worthless son-in-law couldn't support his baby?"

He shook his head. "He and I didn't agree on much, but he believed in taking care of family. I think moving home to take care of John was the only thing I ever did that he re-

142

spected." He traced a pattern on the carpet. "The difficulty came in convincing him to stop."

"Ah, yes. The mysterious deposits."

"Those, yes. Nuriyah said she'd speak with him, and I thought that ended it, but then another check turned up. When her cousins turned up at the party, the thought overwhelmed me that with the money I couldn't stop and her family around, I'd never be able to get on with my own life. Her aunt and uncle receive invitations to lots of Saudi ex-pat events, so they had every right to be there, but I'm sure they really wanted to check and see when I planned to go to Riyadh to win Nuriyah back. They didn't like her with me, but even less do they like divorce and spineless Englishmen who permit their wives to leave."

"They sound like a lovely bunch." I tried to imagine Cordie leaving her husband and Marnie paying him a visit to tell him to force her to come home. Nope, couldn't do it. Showing up to poison his drink, yes. But to tell him to pull a caveman? No.

Of course, I could see Cordie giving those instructions to Danny if Pippa ever left him. I guess every family has its traditionalists—and maybe its ideas about which members will disgrace the clan with no one around to monitor them.

"Anyhow," Edward continued, "I thought perhaps if they saw me with you, with anyone who wasn't Nuriyah they'd tell her father I was no longer worth his generosity."

"She left—what, almost a year ago? Haven't you seen anyone since then?"

"Well...no, not really." He stared at the window as though he could see through the blinds that covered it. "I went out to a few dinners with Ashley, one of the tellers at my bank." He went crimson again. "You likely remember her dropping into the dining room as well."

When you suddenly remembered to keep your hands to yourself, I wanted to say, but didn't. If his blood came any closer to the surface of his cheeks, I feared it might burst through the skin.

"Anyhow, after the third date I had to beg off." He glanced at me, then looked away. "I kept finding myself tracking her similarities to Nuriyah. She had the same mouth Nuri did. She once ordered the same drink Nuri used to. Ashley is nice. I couldn't use her to move on when I had no hope of seeing her as her own person."

You have a boyfriend, Cordie yelled in my brain. Only Cordie can bring down a room when she's not even there. *It should not make you happy that he's single.*

Shouldn't, no. But it did.

"That caused me a problem at the party. You were convenient to flirt with, to shock Nuri's family."

It shouldn't have made me upset that he kept using his ex's nickname, either.

"When I saw Ashley, though, it changed things. I didn't want her thinking I'd thrown her over for someone else. She deserves better than that."

"Very noble of you."

"Very disingenuous of me." He licked his lips. "I didn't think I wanted to get close to anyone after Nuri, but then you walked into my life, and I had no trouble getting closer than I had any right to." He gazed at me, and this time the blue in his eyes didn't have a trace of ice.

All of a sudden the temperature in the room rose. I stared at him. A couple of his shirt buttons were undone, and I kept thinking of what he'd look like with his shirt off, with all those toned pec muscles exposed...

144

A voice in the very back of my brain—probably Cordie again—told me that we'd had a stressful couple of days, and that this moment wasn't real. Just the result of hormones with too much proximity.

Sage advice, of course. Even if he didn't have complications, I did. Neil sat back at our house in Santa Rosa, waiting for me, worrying about why I hadn't come home. I hadn't thought rationally enough to phone him after leaving the police station, and Jane and Carlos had forbidden us all lines of communication since. Marnie knew we were leaving, and Jane had offered her some kind of explanation, but given that my best buddy now made her living as one of Uncle Sam's invisible elves, she'd probably whispered something like "The cockatiel stands on one leg" just before she and Captain *Americano* whisked us off into the night. Neil wouldn't find that reassuring — assuming, of course, that he noticed I was gone.

Edward was looking at me like he'd just noticed his favorite dish, back on the menu.

Damn. I couldn't remember the last time someone looked at me that way. "The clotted cream." My voice seemed stuck in the back of my throat. "You wanted to help me get the cream off my dress."

"I could have asked one of the staff to help you. They probably would have fetched you stain remover or something truly helpful, and you could have gone back to your aunt unscathed."

"And you'd have had no need to apologize, and we'd never see each other again."

"Never."

He didn't close his mouth after he finished saying the word. Instead he leaned over to kiss me. I wasn't surprised, and the fact that I met him halfway probably let him know it.

Yes. Oh, dear God, yes. He licked into my mouth, catching my lower lip between his tongue and teeth. I shivered, in a way I hadn't for Neil in ages.

Who was I kidding? I hadn't shivered for Neil, ever. I had completely forgotten this kind of want existed.

My mouth firmly in possession, he moved his hands down to my waist. I caught his right hand in mine and moved it under my sweater. He moved both our hands up under my bra. I leaned my body in to him, my right leg sliding over till I straddled him, balancing on his lap.

"Emmy? Are you all right?"

I blinked in confusion, wondering how Edward's voice had gotten so high, and then realized that Jane had entered the room.

Sure. Wait until Edward and I start to enjoy confinement, and then open the door.

CHAPTER FIFTEEN

My companion in lust and I both scrambled to re-claim body parts. I pulled my bra back down to serve its in-tended purpose, and Edward bent his knees in front of him-self.

"Oh," Jane said, leaving the room as abruptly as she'd entered. The door closed behind her with a thud.

I got up and followed her out of the now unlocked door. "Jane!" I called after her, trying to get her attention without shouting. "I didn't realize you were back."

She started down the stairs ahead of me. "Didn't mean to interrupt. Go back to who—I mean, what—you were doing."

"It wasn't like that."

She glanced at me over one shoulder. "It was exactly like that." She gave her head a shake. "Whatever. Not my business. I wouldn't have bothered you, but I was worried when Carlos told me he confined you to the office. I know you don't like being closed in."

"Thanks. I couldn't believe he did that."

She took the stairs carefully. "I couldn't believe he had to."

"He didn't have to. He could have just—"

"Just what? He said you were working up a good head of steam, complaining about the new arrangements, and he thought you might try something stupid. I couldn't exactly blame him for that."

Carlos stood by the counter, ripping open a case of Guinness. He handed one to Jane, who removed the cap by smacking it against a cabinet with her hand. The Jane I'd known could barely get a bottle cap off with an opener. This one looked like she'd grown up in a brewery.

I expected her to offer me one, but she didn't.

"How long have you been back?" I folded my arms. "Did you really stand around listening to his excuses before you unlocked the door?"

"He just took a few minutes to get me up to speed. Besides," she said, taking some groceries out of a paper bag, "from what I could see you weren't suffering."

Carlos looked from one of us to the other and muttered something about needing to check the van. He made it out the door to the garage in under a second.

I watched Jane place each item on the table with precision. "What is with you? You're mad at me for making out with Edward? What could it matter to you? You said you didn't have anything with him."

Her cheeks tightened. "Of course not. He's in my custody. That would be unprofessional." She took a deep breath and exhaled. "We're in close quarters. It makes things more difficult when hormones get involved."

"Oh, hello. Where was your no-touching policy the other day when you were grabbing Edward's ass?" I tossed my head toward the garage. "You can't have him and the Latin lover out there, you know."

Her eyes flew open. "That's not what happened! I was showing him a yoga pose to help with the plantar fascia heal-

148

ing. He couldn't go out for walks, so I showed him some stretches. I accidentally touched his butt in the process. That was it." She pointed up the stairs. "What I just walked in on didn't look like an accident, unless you accidentally held out your sweater and fell on his hand."

"It was a spontaneous thing. I don't know, maybe the tension of being locked up together for days got to us. I didn't know any yoga moves to show him. Let me guess, you're a certified instructor."

She breathed in deeply through her nose and looked away.

Oh, for pity's sake. She was. Of course, she was. Secret agent, crack shot, naturally she could also bend herself into a pretzel and achieve a state of existential transcendence. She could probably move objects with her mind while finding the best deal on car insurance, too.

"Forget it." She sat down at the table in front of the laptops that never seemed too far from her and Carlos. "It sucks for Neil that you're cheating on him, but whatever."

"I didn't cheat on him."

"From the looks of it, only because you didn't have time." She took a long pull on her Guinness, spilling two drops on the keyboard in the process. "Doesn't matter. Neil's problem, not mine. What is my problem, however, is your safety. Your denial about your situation has reached epic proportions. People are trying to kill you. Do you get that?" She stabbed at the wall. "People out there want to end your life, and you keep giving them the chance to do it. I can't believe I actually worried about coming up with more entertainment for you. I should have known nothing I came up with would be good enough to stop you from running out to get yourself killed. Oh, and you put Edward's life up for grabs along with your own. Do you understand that? The guy you're so hot for

149

is in more danger because you convince him to follow you around. Does it matter to you? Or will you just go on your way, forgetting about him as fast as you forgot about Neil, and find someone new to take care of you?"

"What is your problem?" I stared at her, giving a fleeting thought to dumping her beer over her head just to crack her statue-like exterior. "Yes, I know the danger. I was there, remember? They shot at me! I know if it were you, it would be different. You'd shut it down and compartmentalize the whole thing into a little safe deposit box in the back of your head, and freeze out any sexual tension, so you could be all about strategy. Or you could sit and play Scrabble all day until the danger passed. I can't do that. I have all these emotions running around in my head and I have to deal with them the best I can. And that's what I'm doing—the best I can. I'm sorry you don't like the way I process things, but being a kidnapping victim isn't something I ever trained for!"

"Go to bed, Emmaline." She waved at me like the Queen acknowledging a particularly unwashed subject. "Stay in the room with Edward. Carlos and I will take care of everything for you, and if it comes to that, Edward will probably stand between you and the bullets. You don't need to worry about a thing. Fortunately, I'm a sexless loser with dry ice where my libido should be, so I can concentrate on my job. I brought blankets and pillows in the car. Hope you brought your own condoms. I didn't think to pick any up."

"Don't worry about it." My fingernails dug into my palms as I got up from the table. "Conniving slut that I am, I never leave home without them."

She didn't look up from the computer. "I'll send Carlos up with the blankets."

I stalked back up the stairs. "Don't bother."

I slammed the office door hard enough to make the window shake. The impact reverberated in my arm, mimicking the way Jane's sermon still rattled around in my head.

"What happened?" Edward rose from his seat on the edge of the desk, facing me as though prepping for battle.

"Jane decided to turn into the morality police. Evidently you and I are a disgrace to kidnapping victims everywhere. Well, maybe not you. I cause problems. You just fell victim to my seductive machinations."

Edward's right eyebrow rose a quarter inch. "That doesn't sound like Jane."

"You don't know her that well." I walked over to the window and peered through the crack in the blinds. Fog obscured all but the highest watt street lamps. My fingers threaded through the cord to raise the plastic slats for a better view.

Edward put a hand on my fingers. "Let's not give her anything else to complain about, shall we?"

I looked at him without moving my hand. "Now you're going to get on my case too?"

He moved his hand away and sat against the far wall. "Wouldn't dream of it."

I let go of the cord and kneeled next to him. "I didn't mean that. You're not mad, are you? I can't handle having two people mad at me right now."

He patted my hand. "The past few days have driven us both mad, I think, but I'm not angry. I expect we'll both regain our sanity once this adventure comes to an end."

"If it ever does." I unfolded from the floor and sat on the desk chair. Tucking my knees under my chin made my tailbone dig against the wood. This room had all the comfort of a prison cell, and it wouldn't get any better tonight. "Sorry in advance," I told him, trying not to get sucked into those blue eyes. "We won't be getting pillows or blankets."

"No? Your punishment for snogging your fellow prisoner?"

My laugh came out as a cross between a sneeze and a snort. "No, my grand gesture. She offered them and in my huff I refused. I find great satisfaction in working against my own best interests."

Edward sat on a file box next to the desk. "I'm glad I could inadvertently support you in that. Any other side effects of your tête-à-tête that I should know of?"

I gave him a basic rundown of the conversation. After sharing the gory details, I added, "I think she might have a crush on you."

He laughed. "No, she doesn't. I'd be flattered, she's a beautiful woman, but you had the right of it before. She only has eyes for Casanova out there."

I shook my head. "Then I don't get it. If she doesn't want you, why was she so mad about seeing us kissing?"

"She's not wrong, I suppose." He stared at the window, as though he could see through the cheap blinds to a deeper truth outside. "You're involved with someone. Our current situation is enough of a cock-up without adding something else for you to tidy up once the gunplay ends."

Visions of Neil popped up in my head. For someone as bad as I'd told Jane I was at compartmentalization, I'd certainly managed to forget about him during all of this. A cold sweat ran down the back of my neck.

I was attracted to Edward, yes, absolutely, but he also made a convenient distraction, now didn't he? Fact was, I really, really didn't want to buy a house with Neil. Edward, poor Edward, was a handy way for me to prove Neil didn't control me.

A cough drew my attention back to the present. Edward turned away from the window, back to me. "She may have a point about the other matter as well. We haven't excelled at protecting ourselves."

I sighed and wrapped my arms around my knees, trying to work my tailbone into a less painful position. Beating myself up for my disloyalty to Neil and getting angry at him for his high-handedness would both have to wait until we resolved the current situation. "You threw yourself in front of me to protect me from gunfire. That has to count for something."

He leaned over to scrape at something on the box next to him. "If I'd done my job as a protector, I'd never have let you leave the house."

"You didn't let me leave." My protesting tailbone finally won out. I got up and walked to the door and then walked back to the desk. Stupid tiny office. "I talked you into leaving."

"Not terribly sensible of either of us, then."

"No." I kicked at the carpet which, given its industrial berber weave, was like trying to hurt the feelings of a statue. "I just couldn't believe anyone really wanted to kill us. Think about it, Edward—even when someone kidnapped us and went to a hell of a lot of trouble to do it, they left the door of our prison open. What does that mean? Who does that?"

Edward sank down to the ground and leaned his head back against some boxes stacked against the wall. "That bothers me the most, but how they made it look like we drove ourselves out of the building is a close second. I bloody well didn't drive us."

"As you were unconscious at the time, I'd have avoided getting in the car with..." I trailed off as a vision of me thinking I was avoiding him popped into my head. "The waiter."

"I'm sorry? Did one of the waiters offer you a lift?"

I shook my head. "One of the waiters looked like you. I'm suddenly thinking that wasn't a coincidence. The footage we watched wasn't high definition. They didn't need a perfect match. As long as they had someone who could pass for you at a distance, they just needed to toss me in and jury-rig a way to keep my head up."

He moved his head in what would have been a nod, had his head moved straight down instead of over toward his right shoulder. "That would explain it."

"But the door, the escape—that I don't get."

"Let's consider." Edward moved his hands back behind his head. "One person couldn't have pulled this off. I don't remember seeing anyone grab you or put something over your face, or I'd have tried to stop them. As well, you heard a different accent than I did."

"So that's at least two, to grab us simultaneously." I put two fingers on the desk, and then tucked one back toward my palm. "One of them changed their mind."

Edward started to nod, forward this time, and then stopped midway. "But judging by the gunshots, the other person is still committed to the mission." His forehead wrinkled in concentration. "And there we return to the question of the hour. Who despises either of us that much?"

"I don't know who'd hate me." I propped my feet up on the desk. "At least, not enough to track me to London to get even. But Marnie—she works for the Embassy. Someone might have a problem with her and used me to get to her. Maybe the ambassador. Ever since her husband made a pass at Marnie, she's hated my aunt. Or her husband, who hates Marnie for turning him down."

154

"You think either one would have you killed for that?" Edward's disbelief covered his face as plainly as his five o'clock shadow.

"Stop thinking rationally. We can judge merit later. Just give me your best shot at why someone would hold a grudge against you. Don't you have any good scandals in your family? What about the money your ex's father gave you? Maybe he wanted it back."

"He knew I didn't want the money. I tried to return it to him. He wouldn't take it."

"Maybe they were laundering the money. Maybe they have terrorists in the family."

Edward sat up and stared at me, his blue eyes scanning me like a new breed of insect. "Because anyone from Saudi Arabia must harbor a radical jihadist agenda? Is that it?"

I tucked my knees into my chest again, curling into a fetal position. I couldn't seem to keep from offending people today. "I'm sorry. I'm just grasping at straws."

He shook his head. "I watched Nuri deal with a lot of prejudice while we were together. I suppose it still rankles." He shook his head. "That aside, though, the angle doesn't work. You forget, I was married to the woman for five years. I know that family. Her father could make the most ardent pacifist want to stab him, but as far as I know he's never wanted to kill anyone for religious reasons or any other."

"You're right. Forget I said it."

He kept silent for several minutes. At last, just as another apology formed on my lips, he said, "The only true scandal in my life happened when my parents died, and they caught the man who did it."

My eyebrows twitched up. "I thought your biological parents died in a car accident."

155

"They did. The car crashed because the brakes had been cut."

My jaw fell to the point where I thought I might need surgery to put it back in place. "Who did it? Why?" I clamped a hand over my mouth. "Sorry. It's not—you don't have to talk about it if you don't want to."

"It's all right. The local mechanic went to prison for it. My father refused to pay him for some work on the Jaguar, said the man had taken it out for a drive and dented it. They argued and my father said he'd see to it the man lost his job and would never find another. The next day, we had the accident. The police later found evidence that someone had tampered with the car."

I walked around the desk and sat on the floor next to him. "They caught that guy?"

Edward nodded.

"What a sick person he must be. To kill two people and risk killing a third, and for what? It wouldn't benefit him."

"I spoke to John about it once, years later." Edward put his hand on his knee and traced a circle with his thumb. "He didn't like to speak of it even then, but after a few pints, he told me about the trial. It went on for months. It was the one time he, Mary and my uncle were united. After he hired the best law firm in London as counsel, my uncle took me to a doctor in Switzerland for therapy. Either John or Mary attended every day of the trial. John said they couldn't bring my parents back, but at least they could make sure I grew up knowing that justice had been done." He cleared his throat. "He did say, though, that the garageman never gave up maintaining his innocence."

"Everyone accused of a crime does, don't they?"

"Mary took me to see the sentencing. John didn't want her to, but she said I needed to know that the man who took my parents away would pay. The man had bright red hair. His wife held a baby with a big pink bow. I remember the bow getting wet when the wife started to cry." He dusted off his hands as though action might brush away the painful memories. "Enough. Let's solve the mystery tomorrow. I'm tired."

I wasn't, but Edward's face had a "Closed for Business" sign on it. I moved two boxes to clear out sleeping space.

Edward looked around the room and then back at the box. "Well, they may as well serve some purpose." He dug out some of the account books stacked inside. "Better than no pillow, I suppose."

I laughed. "Debatable."

"Fine, then. You can rest your head on the floor."

"Oh, hell. Why not?" I took three books out of one of the nearby boxes and tried to arrange them into a comfortable shape. Closed, they had awkward angles that poked into my face. Open, the old and possibly moldy book smell might choke me.

I stashed the books back in the box, closed it as best I could and opened another couple of them, hoping for better. The newer files clearly resided downstairs. Nothing here dated past 1980. The latest box had thicker volumes that had somehow evaded the scent, however, so I picked up two of them and tossed them on to the floor. The cover of the second one fell open. I glanced at the title page, and then looked for real.

"Edward, what was your father's first name? The Earl, I mean."

"Arthur. Why?"

I handed the open book to him. "These accounts belonged to him."

Silence reigned as Edward and I flipped through the books. I didn't have a watch, but I guessed ten minutes passed before the sound of books hitting boxes made me look his way. He looked through the other boxes sitting around us. "These are all the account books from the businesses he owned in Ireland," he said at last. "Why do Jane and Carlos have these?"

I thought back a few days. "Jane made some comment a while back about them having to go through your family's financial history, as part of their investigation. I guess when they needed to take us somewhere in a hurry, they decided to move on to their next place of work."

We spent hours — okay, maybe an hour, time does funny things when you can't escape the smell of mold — going through accounts of his father's financial past. Long enough, at any rate, for my hands to cramp. I gripped the books more tightly as I went through each one, registering certain patterns. "Edward, have you noticed something about these records?"

"Yes. I've noticed it was a miracle my family stayed afloat as long as we did. My father's businesses scarcely broke even." He ran a hand through his hair, looking as though he might pull it out. "I don't understand this at all. I always thought my father did well with his investments. He certainly never spared any expense in our lifestyle."

"Your father did much better than he told anyone, I imagine. Especially Her Majesty's Internal Revenue Service."

"You mean Revenue and Customs?"

"Whatever." I cleared my throat. "Edward, I think your father was a crook."

158

CHAPTER SIXTEEN

Edward's eyes widened until the whites around the irises were visible on every side. He put down the book he held. "What on earth makes you think that?"

I wished I'd thought of a way to break it to him more gently, but there was no going back now. "Did you notice some of these books are for the same months?"

"Duplicates, yes? These were from the days before computer files. I assumed they wanted an extra copy for some reason."

"Not quite duplicates. They have the same deductions, but one set lists an extra set of deposits, always coming in two days after a particular sale. It's not ironclad, but I think maybe your father got kickbacks from somewhere." Feeling his stare, I winced. "Don't panic. I could be wrong. Maybe there's another explanation."

Edward blew out an extended sigh. "Actually, this one explains a great deal." He got up and walked to the other side of the room, leaning back against the wall. "My parents were barely speaking to each other before they died. The day of the crash, we went to see *The Nutcracker* at Royal Albert Hall. It was the first time we'd done anything as a family in months. He traveled constantly, always bringing home presents and leaving again. I wasn't supposed to know, but Mum had our bags packed. That night signified an attempt by my father to get back in her good graces. I think this might be why he fell out of them in the first place."

I stared at him. "It might also be a reason why someone wanted to kill him."

He nodded. A short, careful nod as though all his energy needed to go elsewhere, so he had little left for the motion. "In the morning, we should tell Jane and Carlos about all of this." He tapped his fingers against the wall rhythmically. "Right after we apologize for being such ungrateful protectees."

I choked. "Yeah, that's going to happen." A spot on the carpet suddenly absorbed all my attention.

"She's your best friend, yes? Don't you want to patch things up?"

My head jerked up. He had moved closer to me while I stared at the stains in the berber. I looked back at the carpet fibers. "She said some fairly awful things. I love her and all, but I still want to punch her."

"Fair enough. I've wanted to punch Tony a few times, too. But I don't know how I would have made it through this past year without him."

"Tony?" I almost asked who he was talking about, but the mental search engine kicked in just in time. "Oh, our mutual friend from Marnie's party." Assuming someone I talked to for ten minutes counted as a friend, exactly.

He nodded. "We met at Oxford. He's Nuriyah's cousin. He introduced me to her eight years ago when she came to visit from Boston. He stood by me through the divorce, even though she's his blood family. He's been there for all the biggest moments of my adult life, and I've tried to be there for his. He told me he was gay before he told his

160

family. When he finally did tell them, I went with him for moral support."

"Ah. That explains his lack of reaction to Jane's spectacle at the party."

Edward smiled. "I don't think Jane's partner in spectacle impressed him."

I grimaced at the memory. "Tony has good taste."

"I like to think so. The first person he fell in love with was me."

My eyes widened. "He told you that?"

Edward nodded. "Right before he left for parts unknown. Since he knew I was straight and would never feel the same about him, he said he had to get away and clear his head."

"Wow. That must have been awkward."

"He left just after he said it, and he didn't talk to me again for a year. I tried to get hold of him, but he didn't answer. By the time he finally phoned, I was so glad to have my friend back, I didn't care what awkwardness we had to overcome. Of course, by that time he'd fallen for someone else who adored him just as much, so the point was moot."

I leaned my chin on my hand. "So, you're telling me that if you and he could get through that, Jane and I can get through this?"

"Something like that."

I sighed. "Jane's been there for everything major in my life since college. She knows me better than my mother."

"So you think she said precisely what she knew would hurt you the most." Edward leaned against the wall. A pair of spectacles to peer over would complete his psychiatrist image.

"I know she did." I tried to keep my tone even, but the note of asperity sidled in anyway. I stretched out on the

161

floor between boxes of books, turning on to my side as if it might be comforting to curl around one of them. "She said I always expect everyone to take care of me. That's not true. My sisters, the ones who got married right out of college? They've always had caretakers. I've gotten by just fine on my own. She forgot about that."

"You've never married?"

I shook my head. "Never even thought about it."

"But you're involved with someone."

"Well, yes, but I wouldn't say he takes care of me."

Edward nodded. "And you were probably on your own before that."

"Well, no. I lived with a guy for almost a year. Things were going badly by the end, and I met Neil at the pharmacy while we were both waiting for prescriptions. After things fell apart with Daniel, I called Neil. We moved in together about two months later."

"I'm sure you've been on your own for quite some time over the years, though."

"Of course." I ran one foot against the other. "Well, kind of. I mean, there were times when I wasn't really *with* anyone, if you know what I mean. Just because you date someone for a few months doesn't mean you're truly together."

Edward's upper lip moved, but he stilled it before any actual words came out.

"Okay, so I've probably been in a relationship with someone or other since I was in college. That doesn't mean I haven't taken care of myself."

He nodded. "Likely not all of them fulfilled the care-taking role."

I pulled my legs up and wrapped my arms around them. "I wouldn't call them care-taking, no. Controlling. A lot of them thought just like Jane does, that I couldn't take care of myself." I stared at the wall and found my mind's eye skipping through the last twenty years. "And I let them. I always let them make decisions for me, even when I wanted to do something else. I thought I was being accommodating, making compromises, like you have to do in relationships." After so many years dreaming of London, when I got home and had to figure out what I'd do with the rest of my life, reality threatened to mow me over like a truck. "Maybe Jane has it right, sort of. Maybe deep down I didn't think I could take care of myself."

Edward stared at me appraisingly. "You've survived getting kidnapped and shot at. You can do anything you like."

I chewed on my lip. "Jane's always told me that, too."

"It sounds like she's a good friend to have, generally."

"She's the best." I almost smiled. "Generally."

Rain crashed into the window, a storm erupting so quickly it made my heart pound. California rain sauntered in, taking its time before it decided to commit. Precipitation in the British Isles seemed to prefer a climatic blitzkrieg.

Edward got up and walked to the side of the window, trying to look out without moving the blinds. "I missed it. Usually my leg gives me a warning when a storm moves in."

"There's been a lot of tension around here. It might have masked the weather."

He laughed. Moving a box out of the way, he sat down next to me and closed his eyes. "Let's get some sleep. Maybe telling Jane and Carlos in the morning what we found here will let them know we're taking our peril seriously."

I nodded, and we both stretched out on the floor. Within minutes, the sound of rhythmic soft breathing let me know he'd fallen asleep.

Fatigue pulled at me, but my eyes didn't close as readily as Edward's. I found myself wondering what emotional weather pushed Jane to her sudden storm. Throwing her for a loop took some doing.

At last, as I rolled over on to my side, my eyelids grew too heavy to keep open anymore.

***

Once I finally gave in, sleep took me over like a drug, freeing my mind to take another merry acid trip down Memory Lane.

Waves lapping against the shore...huge waves...so massive they lapped over the concrete edge of my parents' pool, because Pippa's boys, Aaron and Carter, were practicing their cannonball technique. I was back at the birthday pool party again.

Emerging from the guilt sauna of my mother's kitchen, I saw my nephews laughing at the impact of their aquatic attack. Their sister, Jodie, a brand-new teenager, yelled a few words I couldn't understand, but from Pippa's sharp, "I heard that!" profanity featured prominently in them. Jodie shouted a hasty and thoroughly unbelievable apology and went back to practicing her butterfly stroke. A redheaded girl I'd seen her pal around with before treaded water next to her, staring longingly at Cordie's seventeen-year-old son, Colin. Colin, saddled with the burden of being the oldest cousin, lounged on an Adirondack chair, reading a book and trying to pretend he didn't know anyone.

When people talk about the joys of parenting, I assume they drink.

The parental types at this party certainly did. Various beers and margarita glasses lay close at hand as Pippa, Dan-

164

ny, Cordie and my dad sat at the wooden picnic table on the left side of the yard, playing poker for potato chips. "Hey, Emmy," Dad yelled. "Want us to deal you in?"

I shook my head and sat down. Sneakers, who had followed me out of the house, took off to join the boys in the pool, perhaps because he saw that as a wet shaggy mess, his destructive powers would increase ten-fold. "I'll just sit here and watch you all cheat," I said. "Maybe I can pick up some pointers."

"It's all in the wrist," Pippa said, palming a disposed card.

"What is?" Danny asked. His chocolate brown skin glinted in the sun, contrasting nicely with Pippa's freckled fair complexion. "Everyone saw you."

"Then there's distraction," she said, giving him a kiss.

He smiled and kissed her back. "Okay, that works."

"Not for the rest of us," Cordie noted.

"Sure it will," Pippa said. "Danny, kiss Cordie."

Danny obediently leaned over and kissed Cordie on the cheek.

"Cut it out," Cordie told him, shoving him away. She tried not to laugh and failed.

I was struck for a minute by the sound, realizing that I couldn't honestly remember the last time I heard Cordie laugh for real. Her ex-husband Joe, a worm in human clothing, had taken off with a twenty-six-year-old the previous year. My sister had worked full-time before, but now she spent every spare moment trying to expand our family business, so she could bring in extra money. For balance, she spent her nights helping her children through homework, soccer practice and bouts of depression when they realized their father had left them as thoroughly as their mother. For a guy who hadn't helped much when he was there, Joe still

165

managed to leave a gargantuan hole for her to fill. Cordie was always uptight, but she used to be a happy uptight. Now she looked like someone perpetually trying to put a queen-size sheet on a king-size bed.

I need to be more grateful, I scolded myself. By comparison to Joe, Neil won the merit badge for significant others.

As if sensing my thoughts, Pippa asked, "Where's Neil?"

"He had some stuff to finish up at the office." And, I didn't add, he hates pool parties. "He'll be here in a bit." I sat down on the bench next to my father. "What the heck. Deal me in."

Dad fetched me a margarita and some potato chips for betting, and Cordie dealt a new round to all of us.

I won the first round handily. Pippa was too busy kissing Danny to pay much attention, and Danny was enjoying the distraction. Dad pretty well sucks at poker. He's good at reading business opportunities. He stinks at reading people.

My only true opponent at the table would normally have been Cordie, who has a poker face like a computer with all its memory deleted, but today she got sidetracked monitoring the little redhead lusting after her son. Cordie had no worries—Colin showed no trace of recognizing the prepubescent friend of his cousin's even existed. Once she grew into that bikini, I guessed the story would change. She had a determination about her that reminded me of Neil. She'd get what she wanted.

My attention to a possible straight was diverted by Aaron, trying to sample my margarita. I was explaining to him that California had not yet lowered the drinking age to

166

eleven when I heard a loud "Emmaline!" come from the other side of the yard.

Neil stood at my parent's back gate, a little out of breath, holding his briefcase. An odd accessory for a pool party, for anyone but Neil. "Hi there," I said, getting up to close the gate after him as he came into the yard. "Where've you been?" Neil hated family barbecues, but they were a social obligation, and no one does obligation like Neil.

"I've been—oh, hell," he said, seeing my dad and Sneakers coming over to say hello. "We'll talk in a minute." To my dad, he said, "Hello, Sam. Good to see you."

He and my father shook hands, and I could see Neil straining to keep his voice in check.

When Dad got distracted by Aaron trying to take his beer, Neil took my arm and guided me over to a relatively quiet area at the end of the table. "I need to talk to you."

Those words never foretold anything good between me and Neil. I looked around for escape. I could tell him Jodie needed me to coach her on her butterfly kick. She was probably a little old for the "pretend you're a mermaid" speech my sisters had given me, but...

"Emmaline! Are you listening to me? We need to talk."

"What about?" I asked. I sat down on the picnic bench. Where was that drink? Oh, yes—in my hand.

"The Espinozas just called me. They sent the paperwork back for the house with the adjusted numbers. They need us to sign it today."

I hit myself in the chin with the margarita glass.

"Are you all right?" He put a finger to my chin.

I barely registered the touch. "We have to decide about buying the house today?"

My increased volume made my dad turn around. "You two are buying a house? Good investment," Dad said. "A little effort and you can have it paid off by the time you retire, if you buy the house now."

"Buying a house?" Aaron the budding alcoholic asked, eyeing my drink. "Why would you guys buy a house? Are you getting married?"

"No!" I drank the last of my margarita to spite him. It was a lot to drink at one time, but it was worth it. Call it my bid for eleven-year-old sobriety.

"Who's getting married?" Mom asked, carrying Isabel's brownies out of the kitchen.

"No one," I said.

"Can I talk to you in private?" Neil asked, glaring at me.

"They're not getting married, they're buying a house," Dad told her.

"It's not definite yet," I said, getting up to grab one of the brownies. My head started to throb. The explosion in my forehead was equaled only by the revolt my stomach suddenly mounted.

I wasn't a good church-goer. Religion had lost me after the London episode. I went at Easter and Christmas because Mom insisted, and once in a while in between because somebody was getting baptized or died. But I still found prayers running through my head just now. Please, God, I prayed. Please don't make me buy this house with Neil. Mom hasn't finished glaring at me for not wanting to go see Marnie in London. I can't deal with this right now, too.

"Neil, this is my birthday party. Do we really have to talk about this now?"

Neil stared at me. "It'll only take you a few minutes to sign, Emmaline, and it's for our future. Isn't that worth missing a few minutes of a party?"

I led him into the house and sat on the couch in the family room. No, it wasn't worth missing a few minutes of anything, but I didn't want to argue in front of my entire family. They'd all take his side. As Dad said, the house made a good investment.

Neil put the paperwork on the coffee table. "Just sign it, and you can get back to the party. I can go home and take care of all the details."

One signature and I'd never have my financial life to myself again. "Neil..." I grasped at words in my head, but settling my stomach required so much energy I didn't have a lot left for my brain. "I need time to think."

"What's to think about, Em? This is our future. We don't want to get married. This is all there is."

I didn't want to get married now, but I didn't necessarily want to rule out marriage forever. How could I tell him that, though? The right words wouldn't come.

"You know this is the right thing to do." He dug into his briefcase and pulled out a pen. "Just be logical about it. If we don't buy this house, what are we really doing here? Just wasting each other's time?"

You don't want him to leave you.

Definitely Cordie this time. Not fair, I thought. Neil isn't Joe. He was just saying that to bait me into signing the deal. He wouldn't leave me.

Then again, as rotten as he was, none of us had ever thought Joe would leave Cordie, either. She earned most of the money. She paid the bills and kept the refrigerator stocked and made dinner every night. She made it possible for Joe to be the waste of good oxygen that he was. We

couldn't imagine anyone else signing up for that, but someone did. What if someone else lay in wait for Neil, too? And
almost a year later, no one had come for Cordie. Mom said
that it was just a matter of time, and Jane said Cordie probably needed some time on her own, but Mom hadn't known
singlehood for almost half a century and Jane seemed content
with little else. I wasn't like them. What if no one was waiting for me?

Neil held out the pen to me. With shaking fingers, I
took it and began to sign.

CHAPTER SEVENTEEN

I woke up the next morning sweating. Relax, I told myself. You didn't sign the papers. You aren't really tied to Neil. It had taken Sneakers' brownie theft and my mom's subsequent medical emergency to derail the conversation, but even Neil couldn't bring himself to talk about home ownership in the E.R. After that, my imminent departure for London had taken center stage.

For now. He'd still expect me to sign the minute I got back.

Coming to full consciousness, I realized there might be another reason for me to sweat. I was curled up in the fetal position next to Edward, his arm resting on my shoulder. Oh, hell, Jane was right. I really did gravitate to the nearest protector in any situation.

All the memories of yesterday came flooding back before I could stop them. Jumping Edward, fighting with Jane, discovering that Edward's father could have had criminal tendencies—was there a hornet's nest in the Emerald Isle that I hadn't stirred up in the past twelve hours?

I extracted myself from Edward's grasp without waking him, a move I'd perfected with a number of former beaux. In my experience, unless you plan to have sex with them immediately, it's best to let men wake up in their own time. I headed downstairs to use the facilities. As soon as the office door closed behind me, I spotted Jane waiting at the bottom of the stairs. She started when she saw me.

"Jane." I took the stairs slowly.

"Hi." She looked at me, then quickly at the ground, then back at me again.

I looked around the ground floor. "Where's Carlos?"

"Napping in the car."

"I guess it's more comfortable than the floor in here," I said, looking at the cement that made the berber upstairs look spongy. Which reminded me of the boxes. "Hey, last night Edward and I—"

"Oh, God. Please don't. I want to forget last night ever happened."

I caught a glimpse of her bloodshot eyes before she looked at the floor and decided that maybe the news could keep. Pippa looked better than that when her kids had colic. "Get some sleep, Jane. Edward and I will stay in the room. We'll even keep our hands off each other if it makes you happy."

"I'm so sorry, Emmy." The words came out in a rush, like a verbal cork had come loose and she couldn't stop them. "I wish I could take back everything I said."

I turned around and took a step closer to the stairs, where I could get a view of the office door. Still shut tight. I lowered my voice till Jane probably had to use her CIA-issued bionic ear to hear me. "Janey, do you want Edward? Because if you do, I'll get out of the way. He's not...I mean, last night we both needed comfort and distraction..."

Jane's head snapped up. "Oh, God, no." She brushed a tear off her face. "I mean, yes, I thought about it. Especially during the yoga pose, because it was nice to have a guy around who'd actually flirt with me." She sniffed, tilting her head to one side and sounding almost objective. "And let's face it, he does have a really nice butt."

I sighed. "No argument here."

She flashed a weak smile, veins and earnestness on equal display in her eyes. "But no. Really."

I scrutinized her face, but it gave no evidence of a lie. Granted, she did work for the CIA, so maybe she had just gotten that good at deception, but I had to believe I still knew Jane's heart underneath the cool agent façade. "Then why did you get so mad last night?" My lips pinched together and I found it difficult to exhale. "Not that you were completely, absolutely wrong about some of the things you said." My gaze sank lower with each adjective. "Especially the 'looking for a protector' thing."

"Oh, Emmy. Forget everything I said. Please. What you and Edward do is none of my business."

"You're right about that." I couldn't keep a tinge of bite out of my tone. "But that doesn't make everything you said untrue."

She glanced up at the office and spoke in a tone softer than mine. "Is he awake?"

I shook my head. "He was out when I left. We were up pretty late last night."

Jane bit her lower lip and looked away.

"Looking through files." I put my hands on my hips. "You don't want him, remember?"

She closed her eyes and sighed. "I just envied you. A lot. Not for the guy you were with." Her words tumbled over one another. "But damn it, Emmy, you've known this man for a week, and he's all over you. I've known Carlos for three years, and if you asked him what gender I am, he'd have to think about it."

173

"I knew it!"

Jane's eyes opened their widest, darting toward the door that opened into the garage. It hadn't moved.

I lowered my voice. "Sorry. I couldn't help it. I'm all for it, Janey. He's gorgeous. The two of you make a movie-star-beautiful pair. You should have a combo name. Jane and Carlos—Jaylos."

She rolled her eyes, looking two seconds from smacking me.

"It has to be Jaylos. Carlane sounds like the location of an accident."

"Stop it." Her eyes teared up. "He doesn't look at me that way. He never has, he never will. I tried to flirt with him a couple of times. He didn't even notice. Just kept treating me like one of the boys, like he always has. Men always see you as sexy and approachable. I want to be like that."

"Maybe it's him. Maybe you're entirely too sexy for him. Have you seen him with his girlfriend? Maybe she's cold and emotionally unavailable."

She didn't look convinced.

"And you overestimate my prowess with men." I said it to calm her down, but as I did, a cloud appeared on the edge of my mood. "Things haven't been so great with me and Neil lately."

Jane pressed her lips together as if trapping words that begged to escape.

"I know, I know." I flashed on that moment of having Edward's tongue down my throat. "Understatement of the year."

"I wasn't going to say anything."

"You were thinking it, and you're right. I did some thinking about what you said last night. Neil makes so many decisions for me, and I let him." I slunk back against the wall

174

next to the bathroom and didn't stop till I sat on the floor. "Neil wants me to buy a house with him."

She sank down next to me. "And how do you feel about that?"

"Like crap." My head sank into my hands. "Like everything I've eaten for the past year wants to make a sudden, violent exit."

Jane sighed. "That's not a good sign."

"I thought I loved Neil. But I can't stop thinking there has to be more to life and, if I buy a house with him, I'm giving up on all of it. He was really nice, he did all the work for me, getting the paperwork together for the house. By the time he told me about it, all I had to do was sign. But—"

"He picked out a house by himself?" Jane's eyebrows flew up.

"He didn't go shopping around. It's the house we live in."

"So, you never looked at any other houses?"

I shook my head. "We hadn't even talked about buying something. He showed up on my birthday with the paperwork. Done deal, or so he thought."

Jane narrowed her eyes. "This is the guy who doesn't want to get married, but he fully expects you to tie up your entire financial life with his by buying a house with him? Without even talking to you or giving you options? I wouldn't call that nice, Emmy. I'd call it controlling." She twisted her mouth like she'd just bitten into the briniest pickle ever made. "No wonder you were tempted to cheat on him."

"It doesn't matter. I don't want to be the person who cheats. Not even with provocation." I rubbed my temples. My head throbbed, whether from personal growth or lack of sleep, I couldn't quite determine. "It's over with Neil. It has

175

been for a while. I was just holding on to him because I didn't see anyone else on the horizon, and I don't want to be that person, either."

She squeezed my left hand with her right. "I'm sorry, Emmy. I really am."

I squeezed her hand back. "I know. And I know the odds of Edward and me building a relationship together for real are pretty slim. He was there. I'm mad at Neil, I needed distracting from the death threats, and I didn't have any liquor." I twisted my mouth. "You're right. I am shallow."

She shook her head. "You are not shallow. You sincerely try to find happiness with each guy that comes into your life."

"That's why I love you, Janey. You see better things in me than I do in myself."

A smile floated over her lips, as much as she tried to suppress it. "I excel at analyzing other people's lives. It's only with my own that I am an utter failure."

"You are no failure."

"Not sure my boss would agree with you." She reclaimed her hand and twined her fingers behind her head, pulling her head forward and stretching her neck in a way that didn't look like her neck enjoyed the sensation. "People shot at you yesterday, Emmy. I was supposed to be protecting you, and I almost got you killed."

"That was my fault. I left the house when you told me not to."

"Oh, please." Her head snapped back up." We've been friends for over twenty years. I should have known better than to leave you alone. I suggested gathering intel under the newlywed cover as a joke, but my boss thought people might open up more if we approached them as a couple. I should've said no, but we'd had no trouble for days, and I

176

couldn't resist a pretend date with Carlos, so I convinced my-self it was okay." Her forehead furrowed so deep I thought I might see her brain in a few seconds. Intensely disturbing. "If anything happens to you, it'll be my fault."

"Because you should have known better than to trust me with my own safety?"

Her mouth smiled, but her eyes didn't. "You're a civilian. You get to hope for the best. I'm supposed to plan for the worst."

I nudged her with my shoulder. "It wasn't a total fail-ure, right? None of us died. You got to go on a date with Car-los."

"Yeah, it was great. We ordered food, he disappeared to make an against-the-rules call to his girlfriend for ten min-utes, and then we talked to the waiter about whether he knew of any terrorist cells in the neighborhood. Totally romantic." She stood up. "Damn it. I can handle failure with men, most-ly, but I'm good at my job." She stabbed at the air as she said the last phrase, and I'm pretty sure the air took a step back. "My gut tells me we can stay off the grid, as long as we're holed up here." She looked from one edge of the ceiling to the other and finally turned back to me. "But if we somehow manage to tip someone off to our whereabouts this time, Emmy, I don't know what to do next."

I stood up next to her. "I trust you. We'll be safe. I'll stop trying to bolt, honest." I looked her in the eyes. "Do you trust me?"

She turned her head part way toward me, her eyes still down. "Put it this way. I might not trust you with your life." Her head swiveled toward me, and at last a genuine Jane smile snuck across her face. "But I'd trust you with mine."

"Okay. Then trust me when I say, you are not a failure." I squeezed her hand hard, as though I could shove confidence into her skin with sheer force. "And what you said yesterday, when you called yourself a sexless loser? Trust me when I say, that is not true. Even if Carlos can't see it, you are gorgeous."

"I—I didn't really mean it. I was just being a pain."

If only she hadn't blinked before she started the denial, I might have believed her. My jaw tightened. "You listen to me, Jane Miller. You don't ever get to talk about yourself that way again. Not even in jest. You are my best friend, and I don't let anyone talk about my best friend that way." I wiped a tear off her face. "Not even you."

"Thanks." She hugged me like she'd never let go. "And you're not a slut, either. Just a really passionate person who deserves to be happy." I could feel her tears roll onto my neck, and they must have been contagious because a few tears fell from my eyes, too.

Which reminded me...

"I'll be right back. I love you, honest, but I really have to pee."

CHAPTER EIGHTEEN

By the time I took care of business and washed my hands, Edward had sat at the table with Jane and an electric tea kettle percolated on the counter. Carlos came back in shortly with bread and tea bags. Edward made a face, but refrained from requesting the fresh-brewed article. Carlos dug out a knife and some paper cups and spoons and began doling out breakfast. If either of the guys noticed Jane's blotchy face, they kept the knowledge to themselves.

Edward cleared his throat, even though he hadn't eaten a bite yet. "We need to tell you about last night."

Jane turned a shade of red reminiscent of Santa suits. (Did they call him Santa in Ireland? Or Father Christmas? Or something in Gaelic?) I guessed the flush didn't stem entirely from the tea she was preparing. "We don't need to talk about last night. At all."

"Not that." I accepted a piece of what smelled like Irish soda bread from Carlos. "We found something interesting last night, going through the files."

Jane started, spilling a drop of the tea on her foot as she handed it to Edward. "What? How come you didn't tell me earlier?"

I pursed my lips. "I tried, but you had other things to discuss, remember?"

Carlos sat down and put his feet up on a box. "Please, enlighten us. The suspense is killing me." Sarcasm did not become him.

Okay, it did. Everything became him. But I still resented it.

Edward made a face, but I think it had more to do with the second-rate beverage than Carlos' comment. "My father did business in Ireland. Years ago."

Jane nodded, handing cups of tea to Carlos and me before grabbing one for herself. "We knew that. We have his business files upstairs."

"We know," I cut in. "We opened them last night."

"Emmaline noticed something odd when we started to go through them." Edward took another sip and abandoned his cup. "Tea bags. Terrible invention." He shook his head. "Anyhow. It appears my father may have been involved in some underhanded practices. Possibly extortion. Maybe a spot of blackmail." He stared at the tea as though it might bear responsibility for his father's misdeeds.

Jane leaned toward Carlos. "I don't know how, but do you suppose this has anything to do with what we found?"

"What exactly did you find?" I asked.

Carlos shot her a *not-in-front-of-the-kids* look.

"Forget it, Carlos. We're out of ideas. Maybe they can help." Jane sat on a folding chair, pulling her legs up in front of her.

I thought maybe Carlos sacrificed a second of his apathy as he watched Jane fold up her legs, their toned outline clearly visible through the tight denim. Before I could reach a verdict however, I got distracted by a stab of jealousy when I saw Edward glance over at Jane's legs, too. I couldn't blame him. Legs like Jane's were the reason someone thought up skinny jeans. You don't have a reason to feel jealous anyway, I reminded myself. You don't really want him. He's just convenient.

Jane didn't notice the boys watching her or me watching them. "I talked to my boss just before we left the safe house. Edward, that last fishy deposit in your account did have some suspicious origins. Just not Saudi ones."

"No." Carlos focused his intense brown eyes on Edward in a way I didn't trust. "Irish ones."

"What?" Edward and I asked simultaneously.

"You might have heard of a group called Free the People? FTP, for short?"

I pointed to Edward. "You mentioned them at the police station. Latest group of freedom fighters, right?"

"An expensive hobby, freedom fighting." Carlos tapped his finger on the table. "If they're giving you money, it makes sense that they expect something in return, right?"

Edward stood up, placing his hands flat on the table. "Now I'm the terrorist?"

"No," Jane assured him.

"Probably not." Carlos' tone carried a lot less certainty. "But giving us a reason why an organization with known violent tendencies sent you money couldn't hurt."

"I've no idea!" Edward paced the five steps he could in our limited temporary abode. "This is the first time I've set foot on Irish soil in thirty-five years. I have no ties to any Irish organizations, terrorist or not. My father had business connections here, but that was decades ago. My last girlfriend was the woman who handles my accounts at the local bank. If the deposit came from anywhere unusual, she would've mentioned it to me."

181

Girlfriend? They only went out a couple of times. That didn't merit girlfriend status. Unless they'd gotten more involved than he admitted to me.

"Stop it!" I told myself.

"Stop what?" Edward asked.

Crap. Apparently, I'd said that out loud. "Stop protecting Ashley. Maybe she was stealing from you." Damn, I am good at covering my tracks. "Did you check to make sure the money went back to the right place? Maybe it left your account and went to hers."

Edward opened his mouth to say something, but Jane beat him to it. "If he didn't check, we did. One of the last two deposits, about four months ago, went back to his father-in-law's account, just like he said."

Ex-father-in-law, I thought before I could stop myself. Stop *caring*, Spencer!

"The last one didn't go anywhere," Jane continued. "The money was deposited a month ago and is still sitting in Edward's account."

Edward folded his arms. "But that doesn't necessarily tie in to this. When the kidnappers took us, Emmaline heard a Scottish accent. The detective told us FTP only recruits in Ireland."

Looks flew back and forth between Jane and Carlos with such intensity I thought they might be communicating in some kind of eyebrow code. "You don't suppose they're branching out?" Jane asked.

Carlos moved his feet from the box to the floor. "Could be someone faked an accent, to throw people off."

Edward watched them, his blue eyes flitting from one to the other as though watching a tennis game. His summer-day, not-a-cloud-in-the-sky-blue eyes, which I did not permit myself to stare at for more than the briefest of instants. "But

182

all of that happened thirty years ago. It can't possibly be related to anything happening now, can it?"

Carlos and Jane diverted my attention with more eyebrow choreography. At last, Carlos said, "Stranger things have happened."

After living through the last week, nobody in the room could dispute that.

***

After we devoured the soda bread (okay, I devoured it and everyone else ate a socially acceptable amount), Carlos kept watch downstairs while Jane, Edward and I went upstairs to see what else the account books might reveal. The more I looked at the late Earl of Alderwood's records, the more inconsistencies I found. Questionable records for businesses in Ireland, Wales, and Scotland. Loans made to the Earl by business partners, which were regularly forgiven. Notes about other people's debts to the Earl, which were never forgiven and seemed to carry an ungodly interest rate. Buried in one of the boxes was a newspaper article from a hotel fire on the Isle of Man, with "Avoid paying reparations?" written on one side and underlined twice. If FTP wanted to convert from the Northern Ireland issue to a general "The English Are Assholes" platform, these records held a world of possibilities. No wonder Edward's biological father and mother grew apart. He probably never told her anything at all, just to keep from telling her anything incredibly awful.

I dropped the account book on the floor without the care I should have given to something with forty-year-old binding. "It's all suspicious, but what does it have to do with the kidnapping? Someone took us from that party and then let us go. Why?"

183

Edward put his ledger down more gently and stretched. "Perhaps someone found out we had no funds to offer, and they couldn't make use of us. Or possibly they only had so many people at their disposal. If our kidnapping was part of a larger enterprise, maybe they decided we weren't a priority."

"We haven't heard of any other kidnappings at the same time."

"We haven't heard of anything, you and I. Where would we have heard the news?"

He had a point, at least about the isolation. I looked over to my best friend, her attention buried in an account book. "Anything?" I asked.

She shook her head. I believed her, even though I had no idea how she might know. If she or Carlos tuned in to *Good Morning, Ireland* each day, they didn't tell us how they managed it.

I switched my gaze to Edward. "At the very least, though, they should have taken your prosthetic leg. I would have, if I were them. Wouldn't you? What easier way to incapacitate you?"

"Yes, I would." Edward stared at the windowsill. "But then, I'm used to taking it off."

I tilted my head and stared at him. "What would that have to do with it? I've seen you remove it, the procedure isn't that complicated."

"More so than people think, but some people find the idea of a damaged limb itself to be inherently untouchable. Nuri took a while to get used it. Fundamentally, though, I think it means they didn't find us a tremendous threat."

Funny, when I was crawling on that limb, my only thought was how quickly I could get clothing off the body attached to it. Do not think about that, I told myself. Aloud, I said, "They seem to think differently now."

"The police didn't believe us, but the CIA did. Maybe FTP found out about that and decided we must be good for something."

It made sense, now that I thought about it. "We talked about the idea of partners in the kidnapping before. They plan the operation together, but once they have us, one member of the team changes his mind. Then one or both of them hears we've disappeared and panics?"

He leaned against the wall, three feet to the right of the window. "Who knew where we'd be?"

"Jane, Carlos, and someone at the CIA, presumably. They kept checking in until we left the house, didn't you, Jane?"

Jane knelt in front of a box, wedging her finger in between two spines as she placed the book she'd been looking at in the space she'd created. "Yes."

"Who did you tell when we left England?"

"The only one who knew was Marnie. She's actually the one who called me to come get you."

Carlos walked in. "Time to switch posts."

I ignored him. "Marnie knows you're with the CIA?"

"I never said—"

"She knows you don't work in a bank. She knew you were in London."

"Yes."

I got up, intending to pace, and realized the lack of necessary real estate. Instead, I sank into the desk chair. "How did she know? How long has she known?" And more importantly, why didn't she tell me?

"How does your aunt know anything? She knows people, and they trust her."

"She knows people at the CIA?" At this point, I wasn't even sure that surprised me.

"Maybe. I think it was the FBI."

"You work for the FBI?'

Jane's head shake made her ponytail whip her at her cheek. "Of course not. The Feebs have no jurisdiction over here."

"HA! You do work for the CIA!" Maybe Marnie did, too. I rubbed my temples. My head was going to explode any second now.

"Bigger question." Carlos took a sip from the cup of water next to Jane. "Did Marnie tell anyone?"

"No!" My mouth constricted into lemon-bite formation as soon as the word left my lips. I crossed my arms over my chest.

"Not willingly, no." Edward's voice took me by surprise. I hadn't noticed him moving closer to me. His eyes went wide when he caught sight of my face. "Not that anyone would try to coerce your aunt into saying anything. Oh, hell."

Visions of Marnie and the nasty end of a cigarette floated through my brain and my stomach started doing gymnastics. Even Edward's proximity couldn't steal my attention—at least, not all of it. My throat felt like someone had coated it in broken glass. "How much did you tell her?" I asked.

"I told her we were going to Ireland. I don't know why. I shouldn't even have told her I was taking you with me, but I like Marnie and I knew you wouldn't want her to worry." Jane raised her gaze up from the floor. "But still. She wouldn't breathe a word about where you were even if I had told her the exact coordinates, which I didn't."

I held my head in my hands. "But if someone wants to kill us, what are they willing to do to get her to talk?"

Edward patted my shoulder. "She'll be all right."

Jane pulled up a box and sat next to me. "Your aunt's tougher than she looks."

Did they have more faith than I did, or did they just want to make me feel better? I looked at Carlos. "You think she's in trouble, don't you?"

He thought for a moment, weighing the idea. Just as I started to break into a cold sweat, he shook his head. "Unlikely. As a truth serum, torture doesn't actually work as well as TV would have you believe."

I stared at him. "You're saying people don't talk when you smack them around? It's hard to believe we've all evolved that much since junior high."

"People talk. They say anything they think you want to hear in order to make the pain stop. If you want facts, you can't put a whole lot of trust in anything told to you by someone under duress. Stress messes with people's memories."

"But these people who are after us—do they know that?" My nails dug into my palms. "Or will they try torturing her, just in case?"

Jane put an arm around me. "No need to think the worst. We don't know that anyone gave FTP details about our movements."

"We don't?" It took all my decorum—and I have a very limited supply at the best of times—not to spit. "Someone sold us down the river. How else did they find us and start shooting at us?"

"Someone might have tracked the cell phones. I thought Carlos' and mine were clean, but maybe not. We've certainly had a quieter time with them gone."

Typical Jane, reasonable at all times. Or just more paranoid? I gave my head a non-committal toss. "It's possi-

187

ble. But my money's still on a source from within our allies. Who did you tell about the plans?"

"I talked to my boss at the CIA, a person I've worked with for five years. She kept the ambassador in the loop, to an extent. That was the end of it." Jane stared off for a moment, evidently lost in her own thoughts, and then said, "As far as I know, the only other person Carlos talked to was his girlfriend. Can't see where a receptionist at Boston Federal is going to care much." The fact that Jane cared about Carlos talking to the Boston bank babe lay naked on her face.

"Who did you tell when we moved to Dublin?" I asked.

"Just one person—Kevin, my contact in the accounting department. Normally, we don't look through the financial statements to this depth. We leave the hardcore bean-counting to the pros. They're better at it. As it happened, Kevin had just called to say that they'd collected all of the files connected with the Alderwood estate. They started storing them here since the largest amount of the businesses were in Ireland, so they figured they might as well pile everything together. When we had to vacate the safe house, I texted him that I needed the code to the warehouse. I promised I'd have a drink with him if he didn't tell a soul." She shook her head, as if trying to shake off the memory. "Lucky me."

Carlos stared at her, his face a mask of confusion. "You promised to go out with Jennings?"

Jane glanced at him and turned away. Carlos probably couldn't see the faint pink on her cheeks, but I could. I smiled. Jane didn't. "It's nothing."

"He's what—seventy-something?"

Jane rolled her eyes. "He's fifty."

"And talks non-stop about his tropical fish?"

"Only sometimes." Her head tilted forward like her neck had trouble holding it up.

"That's right. The rest of the time he talks about the ferret." Carlos' face split into a grin. "Are you up for that kind of reckless abandon?"

"It's not like I had a choice!"

If someone shot Carlos, we wouldn't have to look far for a suspect. I stood up. "Unless you want to ask her out yourself, Carlos, I think we can leave Jane's love life out it for now." The look on her face said we could add me to the list of people Jane might kill. "Jane, you said your boss at the CIA kept the ambassador in the loop. How many people did the ambassador tell, do you think?"

"Officially, no one." Jane's face regained some of its composure as she tracked back to business.

"Officially?" Edward's eyebrows quirked up. "And who might she have told, unofficially?"

"I don't know if she talks in her sleep." Jane's mouth twisted into something that might have become a smile some other time. "Her husband, or whoever else might be in her bed to listen, might know something. Hell, for all I know, she might have told everyone in her yoga class."

Edward caught her eye. "Strange things happen under the influence of yoga."

This time, she did smile.

Carlos didn't and neither did I.

If my mind kept yo-yoing back and forth between fear and lust like this, high blood pressure would kill me before FTP got the chance. "I would so love to go for a drink right now."

Jane gave a short laugh that almost sounded like a cough. "In Dublin? Might as well hang a bull's eye on your back."

189

I stared into space for a moment as a thought rico-cheted around my brain and then looked at her. "What if we did?"

Jane stared back. "What?"

"What if I gave these mysterious foes somewhere def-inite to look?"

"You want to make yourself a target?" Edward's voice went low, as though someone might overhear us. "Are you mental?"

"Maybe. Perhaps too much downtime and paranoia has pushed me over the edge, but I'm tired of sitting here waiting, trying to figure out what game this lunatic is play-ing." I looked at them, balling up my hands and fixing them at my waist. "Aren't you?"

Jane stared at me and then Edward in turn.

Edward looked at the fluorescent lights screwed into the ceiling and then fixed his gaze on me. "Yes. I am."

Carlos stared at us both, open-mouthed. "You want to play decoy? Is that what I'm hearing?"

Edward and I both nodded.

"Where are you hiding the crack? This level of deci-sion making doesn't come from anyone who's clean." He looked at Jane. "Back me up here."

Jane took a deep breath. "Actually, maybe it's not a bad idea."

Carlos gave her the full power of the dark chocolate eyes. "Do you want to be the one to explain to the higher-ups how we came back with two corpses instead of protectees? Because I don't think my career can take it. I don't have Jen-nings in accounting to vouch for my character."

New life sparked in Jane's eyes. "You're assuming we'll make it back."

Carlos shifted his weight, looking very much like he wanted to hit someone. The cautious role didn't come naturally to him. "Be honest, Cali. You were the one to make the off-the-grid call. Do you want to take this kind of risk?"

Dirty pool, Carlos, I thought. Using your pet name for her, a nickname that reminds her that she told you where she comes from?

My jaw fell so far it nearly came unhinged when she turned to him with a cat-like grin and said, "Come on, Carlos. Where's your sense of adventure?" She crossed her arms and leaned back against the wall. "We're safe here, but only for a short time. No matter what I promise Jennings, he can't keep the rest of the accounting department out of here forever. We need to figure out the bigger picture."

"Do you really think it has something to do with these old accounts?" Edward sat against the wall, rubbing his knee. I wondered what things he might need to take care of his leg, that he didn't have access to. "I know grudges don't always die over time. Sometimes they get stronger. I could understand someone wanting to kill my father, were he still alive, but why punish me for something my father did? Wasn't losing my parents and part of my own body punishment enough?"

"Your father died in a car accident, with his reputation intact." Carlos leaned agains the edge of the table. "Perhaps someone felt he got off too easily and wants to punish you by extension."

Edward gave a noncommittal tilt of his head.

I didn't buy the theory, either. "Why now? Edward must have had more vulnerable moments than that party. Aside from all the security, it had to make things more complicated to take me, too."

"Maybe you were a bonus." Carlos steepled his fingers together and rested his chin on top of them. Damn, he was pretty. No wonder Jane didn't want to go out with Kevin Jennings. He probably wasn't as bad as they'd made him sound, but anybody would have a hard time measuring up to the face currently in front of me.

"I want to do some real research." Now Jane looked like the one who wanted to pace. "I want to run all the names we've come across. I can run the ambassador's, too, as soon as I can get on the net."

Carlos raised his head. "Time to get back on the grid?"

"Do you think it's safe?"

I would have expected Carlos to be all for it, in order to talk to the bit of stuff in Boston. Instead, he stared across the room for a second and then shrugged. "I don't know. We've had a lot less company being out of touch with the digital world. No denying that."

Jane looked at Edward, and then me. "We have to end this deranged vacation sooner or later. Let's do it."

"Where do we start?" Edward asked.

I could see the gears turning in Jane's head. "I want to talk to Marnie, see if she recognizes any of the Earl's former business associates." She smiled and socked Carlos in the shoulder. "Congratulations. First thing tomorrow, you get your phone back."

As soon as Jane looked away, Carlos rubbed his shoulder.

CHAPTER NINETEEN

The phones themselves, it turned out, had gone with a passing garbage truck down to wherever trash went to die in Ireland. Fortunately, getting the connected phone numbers assigned to new phones didn't take long. Jane picked up new mobiles at a nearby electronics store and asked her boss at the CIA to have them connected to her and Carlos' old numbers. Once you don't care if anyone finds out where you are, logistics get much simpler.

I suggested that both of them contact the same people they'd called in the twenty-four hours prior to the shooting near the safe house.

Jane looked at her phone as though she didn't trust it, and at Carlos' as though it might explode. "There is always the chance that it was someone in the town that you and Edward visited who sent the message."

I conceded that with a reluctant nod. "That would have to be a huge coincidence, though. Somehow they had people on the lookout in the very sleepy town we snuck off to?"

"It's possible." From the look on Jane's face, though, it wasn't likely.

Jane walked outside to call Jennings while Carlos chatted with the girlfriend back in Boston. I heard him drop a word about his location in case anyone managed to tap the line. Sounded like she wanted a souvenir from Dublin. Nice life Carlos had, really. The girlfriend far enough away to remain mysterious and Jane here to worship him even as she talked to the Ferret Whisperer.

Unfortunately, none of us had time to straighten out love triangles today. "There's a van parked down the street," Jane said as soon as she came back inside. "It was there when I went to get the phones and it's still there now. Could be nothing."

Carlos met her gaze. "Could be something."

That sounded thin to me. FTP had found our hideout within a day? That was quick work, for people who'd had no contact since we got here. At this point though, I had nothing to lose. Either the plan worked, and I got to find out what it felt like to risk my life, or we all went for a pleasant drive and came home.

There was something surreal about the fact that putting my life in danger equaled success.

Carlos performed a reconnaissance mission that afternoon and announced that he'd found the perfect place. "One entrance," he'd announced. "There is a back door, but it goes to the river. Whoever is tracking you can't escape that way. We control the access, we can cut them off, and keep any danger away from innocent bystanders."

"Too bad we won't be bystanders."

I opened my mouth to agree with Edward's *sotto voce* comment, only to discover that I didn't. I wanted to get to the bottom of this. To do that, I needed our mystery adversary to show.

I didn't have good party clothes with me, nor any makeup beyond the gloss that happened to be in my coat pocket when we left, but I couldn't stand not primping at all. I washed my short blonde locks in the sink—dear Lord, what I wouldn't give for an actual hot shower with soap that didn't come in a bar—and sat with my hair over the heater vent in the van as we all headed out to a pub on the river. Just four friends, tourists going out for a drink, wanting nothing more than to sip a pint of Guinness while gazing at the River Liffey. Make that a glass of whiskey. After all the ale that we'd had in the storage unit, I was Guinnessed out.

Jane drove us all downtown. She dropped Carlos off at the pub first, then parked illegally on the curb. "If they tow it, they'll be doing us a favor. That'll get rid of transport that might be recognized. We're walking distance from our base."

"What if we get into trouble?" Edward looked around as though expecting armed paratroopers. "How would we make a quick escape without a car?"

"If we need a getaway car, I'm taking the closest vehicle to hand."

Add hot-wiring cars to the list of Super Jane's skills.

Five minutes later Carlos called. "Found the perfect pub. Come join me. Quaint old place."

Code for *all clear*. That constituted the one tricky part of the plan, making sure the opposing team couldn't beat us there. The previous day Carlos had checked out at least a dozen different pubs, so hopefully any potential onlookers couldn't immediately narrow down our destination and fortify the place ahead of time. Evidently his ploy worked, because he'd used the word "quaint" on the phone, which told us the plan was a go. "Cozy" would have meant he spotted unfriendly types, and he'd get out as quickly as possible.

195

We walked into the pub and sadness descended on me like a rolling fog. The rich wood paneling and stained glass windows, shiny mahogany bar with brass trim, sturdy tables and chairs bearing faint marks from thousands, maybe millions of sweating drinks over the years. This could have, should have been my experience—a normal vacation. A jaunt over to Ireland for a few days? Just the kind of thing Marnie would have suggested. *You don't really have to go back today, do you, Emmy? Let's spend a few days in Ireland. I know a pub where a storyteller sits at the bar and shares tales handed down since one of her ancestors heard about a man named Patrick getting rid of some snakes...*

I shook my head. I wasn't here to soak up friendly ambiance. I was here to find out who wanted to kill me and put a stop to it.

"What'll you have, love?"

I looked at the bartender, a small balding man with one wrinkled hand on an empty pint glass.

If I was going to risk my life, I saw no reason not to have a drink first. A good one. "Glass of Jameson 21, thanks." *Cosmo* said it was better than the eighteen. Right now, whether it constituted enough of an improvement to justify the price difference didn't trouble me.

Edward signaled he'd have the same.

I looked at Jane, expecting her to tell me to stick to business. Instead, she smiled at the barman. "Shot of Sheridan's." She put a hand on the bar, looking for an instant like she might reach out and caress the guy's hand.

Really, Jane? You suddenly learn how to flirt and it has to be with a guy old enough to remember Vikings raiding monasteries? You can't save it for the thirty-something hottie by your side twenty-four/seven?

As always, however, Jane thought a step ahead of me. She leaned on the bar, as though getting closer to the guy now busy getting our drinks, then looked at the mirror on the wall like she'd just discovered something. "Is that another room? My friend is meeting us here, but I don't see him. Maybe he's back there."

The bartender glanced at the narrow doorway. "Tall fellow, Antonio Banderas type?" Seeing Jane nod, he inclined his head in that direction. "He's back there. Wanted to look at some of the old photos on the walls." He smiled. "Be sure he treats you right, love. If he gets to roving too much there's plenty of good Irish lads happy to pick up where he left off and make sure you've nothing to miss."

Jane laughed, a hint of pink touching her cheeks. "I'll keep that in mind." If she was acting, she was good.

I hoped the comment reached Carlos' ears, and then gave myself a mental slap. More pressing issues, Spencer.

The match-making barkeep assured us he'd bring our drinks back as soon as he got them ready. We thanked him and headed to the adjoining room.

Carlos sat in the corner, an untouched whiskey in front of him. He stood up as we entered the room. "You found it. Good. Great place, isn't it?"

Jane took his hand and leaned in to kiss him on the cheek. "Fabulous."

"Absolutely." I looked at every picture for one half a second. "Really Olde Worlde Irish." I landed the "E" on the end of each word as if it were worth an extra point.

"Definitely." Edward nodded so much, I feared he might break a vertebra. "Feels like a leprechaun should pop up in the corner."

Carlos took a sip of his whiskey and muttered, "Tone it down."

"I thought the point was for the bad guys to find us." I kept my mouth as still as possible while whispering my response and felt like a bad ventriloquist.

"Anyone playing 'Spot the Americans' is going to be irritated with you for making the game so easy."

Jane smiled and leaned toward me, as though sharing a joke. Under her breath, she said, "If we're too obvious, they'll know something is up."

At that moment, the proprietor came back in the room with our drinks so I could salve my ego with liquor. He placed the libations in front of us, taking great pride in bestowing such treasure. "Careful with those. I'm fair certain they're stronger than the stuff you get in the States."

"Good thing," Edward mumbled, taking a healthy swig of his. "I can't take much more of this sober."

Mercifully, the bartender was on his way out of the room right then and likely didn't hear Edward's footnote.

We toasted each other, clinking glasses hard enough to spill precious drops of my twenty-one-year-old whiskey onto the scarred oak table. I took two sips—smooth, winding its way through fruit, pepper and a mite of what tasted like fudge, finishing up back at the barley —before venturing under my breath, "Now what?"

"Now, we order another drink so everyone knows we're here for the duration." Jane downed her Sheridan's, drinking like the experienced college partier I knew she'd never been.

It continued like that for the next half hour, all drinks and false frivolity. I took Jane's advice and tried the Sheridan's next. Nice—chocolate, dark and light. If I lived through this, I'd have to remember that stuff. Just to soak up the alcohol and because it smelled damn good when it was delivered to the two men at the next table over, we ordered a couple of bowls of Irish stew, which arrived with a large chunk of Irish soda bread slathered in butter. If we died today, we'd go out well-fed.

By the time Jane and I excused ourselves to go to the loo, we had ordered a third round of drinks and settled into something that almost passed for authentic tourist chit-chat. It didn't look like our assailants would show, but at least we got in some good practice for our next sting operation.

Jane and I walked down the small hallway just to the right of the bar to the restroom. Jane used the facilities first and afterwards gave me the all-clear. "I'll wait out here for you."

I shook my head. "There's barely two feet of this hallway out of sight of the table. It'll look suspicious, won't it?"

Reluctantly, she conceded the point and returned to Carlos and Edward.

I took my turn in the minuscule lavatory. On my way out, three men walked by the opening to the hallway. Two of them had drinks in their hands and continued on to the back room. The third, a blond man with a ponytail, detoured into the hall.

I moved to one side to edge past him, but he stopped me with a hand. "I need a word with you, beauty."

The words and the smell of alcohol put me on guard, but a voice in my head said he could have mistaken me for someone else. It sounded like something Mom would say. Reasonable. Practical.

Of course, Mom hadn't been shot at lately.

"What word might that be?"

"Not so much a word as an action, really. I've got something I think you'll like." He reached down into his waistband. "It's quite a weapon."

"WEAPON!" I screamed, lurching forward to Carlos and Jane. Their tourist act fell to the ground with a thud as they leapt at him. Carlos wrenched the man across the small room and over a table as Jane frisked him.

"Nothing on him." She took over Carlos' grip on the guy now kissing the hardwood table top. "Where is it? Start talking."

"Where's what?" He spat, trying to talk around the cocktail napkin that constituted the only cushion to his fall.

"The weapon." Jane turned him over and leaned in toward him. "You and your friends have made our lives really unpleasant. You've got one minute to tell me where you stashed it before I let my colleague shoot you in the leg."

"What's all this?" The bartender stood in the doorway. "Come on, let him up for air. I run a respectable pub, and my wife will have my eyes if she hears I've let the place turn into a brothel." He stared at Jane's quarry and shook his head. "Will you never learn, Sean Rafferty? Showing off 'the weapon' again, are we? Wasn't last time disaster enough for you?"

Good grief. The only weapon this guy planned to flash was under his zipper. Of course every guy who tried an obscene pickup line in a bar probably deserved to be table-slammed by the CIA, but I felt reasonably certain this guy bore responsibility for the demise of nothing more than good taste. Well, that and the Irish stew, which now lay all over the floor.

After apologizing to the proprietor and leaving an exorbitant gratuity, we walked quickly out of the establishment. Outside, the whole idea of luring out our adversaries appeared ludicrous. Yes, I, in all my civilian, untrained glory, would assist in the takedown of a criminal, possibly a member of FTP wanted in several kidnappings. Right. Because wrangling evil-doers required much less fortitude than telling your boyfriend you didn't want to buy a house with him.

"Where to now?" Edward asked.

"Home base." I walked ahead of him. "I'm tired."

Jane has much longer legs than I do and had no problem keeping pace with me. "You okay?"

"Fine." I looked around and didn't see anybody else within earshot. "Just realizing I'm not secret agent material."

"You'd hate being an agent, Emmy. The hours stink and you have to do a lot of running."

A laugh nearly escaped my lips. Only the memory of my humiliation quelled it in time. "I expect you also have to know a terrorist threat from a pickup line."

"Hey, we all jumped to that same wrong conclusion. Side effect of an extended wait. You start seeing plots everywhere, whether they exist or not."

I squeezed her hand. "If you ever decide to give up the covert life, you can always be a diplomat. You'd do Marnie proud."

We reached the van in a few more steps. Still playing it safe, Jane started the engine remotely. No bombs under the car. I just wished I'd thought to pick up an entire bottle of Jameson 21 to bring back with me, overpriced or not.

The sliding door opened automatically at Jane's click. I climbed inside just as I heard Jane yell, "Don't, I haven't checked the car yet."

She hadn't finished the sentence when a smooth Scottish voice said, "Don't move."

CHAPTER TWENTY

That voice. That was it, the one that told soothing lies before chloroforming me. I whirled around to see a man whose chin and hairline both seemed to be creeping away from his vein-ridden nose sitting in the back seat, holding a handgun. He was smaller than I expected, but the gun was bigger, so I guess it all evened out.

"Careful now." He waved his firearm at Jane and Carlos, still outside the van, both reaching for their own guns. "Take out your weapons and put them under the car ahead of us or I shoot Emmaline here in the head." He pointed the muzzle from Edward to me. "Get in, make yourselves comfortable. We've a bit of a journey ahead."

Jane took out her gun and leaned over to put it away. Carlos put his gun on the ground and kicked it away with great ceremony. "We're following instructions," she said. "Now let's talk."

"You did, Carlos. Your partner, Jane, however, faked that throw, and intends to shoot me through the window." He used their names as easily as if he'd known them for years, despite no one introducing him. "Call her off or I put a hole in the little one here."

"Hey, I'm probably as tall as you are." I turned back toward him until my cheek hit steel. After that I faced front again, in time to see Jane tossing her gun under the Ford Focus parked ahead of us.

"Now the backup weapons. Both of you."

They both pulled smaller guns out and tossed them under the Focus' back end. I hoped the little car's owner could pull straight out of the parking spot. Running over guns cannot do good things for your alignment.

"Tell us what you want." Carlos got into the front passenger seat, his voice filled with calm and reason. He put his seat back a smidgen closer to my knees while Jane adjusted the driver's seat. Both of them looked like they were up to nothing more serious than a Sunday outing. "We can help you."

"Oh, you surely can." His Scottish accent made the words sound silky. Under any other circumstances, I would have melted. Interesting fact though, while the presence of a gun in the car raises the core body temperature, it renders melting impossible. "Right now, you can help me by driving the car."

Jane's measured tone matched her partner's. "Maybe you could give us your name, since you know all of ours."

"You can call me Ceann." He pronounced it "Kyown," so that it rhymed with *clown*. "It means boss, since I'm sure none of you speak Gaelic."

"Ceann." Jane's eyes flickered, but she managed not to gag, which impressed me. Calling this guy Boss in any language would've bought my last three meals a return trip through my esophagus. "We have connections. We can help you, if you help us."

He laughed. "Right now, what helps me helps you, because it stops you getting killed. That's help enough, I'd say. Now drive."

She drove.

***

We left downtown Dublin, passing an enormous park —bigger than Golden Gate Park and Hyde Park put together—with what looked like a copy of the White House on the grounds. Beyond that, sheep farms and small green hills dotted the landscape. I looked at the many colors the farmers had dyed their sheep and felt tears stinging my eyes. The fluffy creatures looked so incongruously adorable, like they'd started a hoofed punk group. I thought of the pictures I would have texted back to my family, and the names Pippa would have thought up for them. Mutton Rainbow. The Psychedelic Woolies. Ovine Distortion.

Now all I could think of was that the sheep had gotten hijacked, too. They hadn't asked for their technicolor hairdos any more than I had requested a gun in the back of my head.

No one said a word for an hour, maybe two. We passed more farms, more sheep, a lake, and finally more buildings. I wondered what city surrounded us until we passed a large park and I spotted the duplicate White House again.

"Where are we going?" I asked.

"Never you mind," came the velvet voice. "You'll find out soon enough."

"I don't know much about Irish geography, but we went by this park already. We're going in a big circle. Why?"

"Clever you. Figure it out yourself, if you're so keen to know."

"Are you going to kill us?" Practical Edward wasted no time on frivolous topics like location.

"That depends on you."

"Of course he's going to kill us." Jane's voice was measured, even, as though telling us the time. "We've seen his face. We can identify him. We have to go."

She had a point. The guy was so white he probably glowed in the dark. Who wouldn't recognize the pattern of broken capillaries on his nose? It looked like a map of the London Underground.

"So black and white." Our hijacker spoke with a lilt, almost a chuckle. "How very like an American. You all do like having the whole plot mapped out for you ahead of time. No sense of nuance."

"Not when it comes to death scenes, no." Carlos turned his head a fraction, as though using all his energy to keep from turning around.

"Behave yourself, pretty boy, and we'll see how it goes."

"You probably will kill us." I hated the thought, but it rang true. "You're driving us through the city again, but you're not telling Jane to stop. You want to take us somewhere with fewer people, maybe. Unless eventually you're heading for another city?" *Keep him talking,* said the voice in my head. Marnie, from Vietnam in 1975, while she waited for the chopper to rescue her from the city. She kept her head together in a crisis and she lived. She whispered that I could, too.

"There really aren't any other major cities in Ireland, not like this one," Edward said. "A quarter of the entire Irish population lives in Dublin. Even if you include Northern Ireland, Belfast is a fraction of the size."

"That's a fair bit of knowledge about a place outside of Britain, for an English toff." Our kidnapper didn't sound impressed, despite his words. "Good to know your fancy education included some geography lessons."

205

Edward didn't answer. We kept driving, mostly following the river. For once my gift of the gab came in handy. "Seems kind of risky, taking us prisoner all by yourself." Was it weird that I was genuinely curious about the workings of this disturbed man's mind? Probably, but what the hell—whatever worked. "What if Jane had gotten around the car quickly and shot you in the head?"

"Not my first outing. Shooting accurately through the outside of a car window is more difficult than you might think."

"I guess." I didn't want to agree with him, but even my imagination couldn't come up with a scenario where Jane could have pulled her gun and shot a guy already crouched down in the third seat of the van before he got the chance to kill one or all of us. I guessed the guy stood about 5'5" and weighed 120 pounds soaking wet, Carlos could almost definitely take him down in a fair fight, but something about the way this man talked told me he seldom allowed a fight to be fair.

"Don't worry." Jane didn't turn her head. From my position on the left-hand side of the backseat I could see her profile in the driver's seat. No tension in her face at all. She wouldn't give "Ceann" the satisfaction of open curiosity. "He'll have backup at our destination. He'll have it all planned."

He laughed. "Perhaps. You keep your wits about you, don't you, love?"

Everyone in the British Isles calls people "love" and normally I don't even notice it, but it sure got a lot creepier coming from this guy.

"You've thought it all out, haven't you?" I did my best to think like a soulless killer. "You'll take us somewhere that no one will see you kill us. Or hear you. The hearing is

206

important. That'll require space. You'll want to limit the forensic evidence you leave behind, and you'll need to dispose of our bodies." Bile rose in my throat as I forced myself to continue. "Four of us. That requires a lot of real estate. And time. Can't have your special spot disturbed while you're committing FTP's murders, can you?"

"Executions." Ceann corrected me, a professor instructing a dense pupil.

Edward gave a laugh divorced from all humor. "What difference does it make what you call it? We still end up dead."

"It makes all the difference." Psycho's tone lost a touch of control for the first time since we opened the van door. "People murder for selfish reasons. Your deaths are justified. Necessary for the greater good."

"How do you figure? We've done nothing wrong."

"Nothing wrong?" Ceann nearly shouted now. In the window, I could see the reflection of the gun vibrate. Great. Gesturing with firearms—that always ends well. "You've lived off the sweat of others your whole life, you useless shite. They didn't teach you anything productive at toff schools, did they? Did you learn to build houses or farm crops or nurse the sick? No. You learned bloody finance, how to take the money you inherited from dad and mum and use it to make more money for yourself, and help your blood-sucking friends to make more money, too. Drain the rest of the world dry, so you can float on your own personal sea." Bits of kidnapper spit hit the back of my neck. I narrowly resisted the urge to wipe it off or vomit or both. "Waste of space, the lot of you. Your death is no crime. It's a public service."

I whirled around. "I'm not aristocracy. I'm not even English." I gestured at Jane and Carlos. "Neither are they. What justification do you have for killing us?"

He nudged me with the edge of the gun to turn back around. I didn't want to. I wanted to look him in the face as he drummed up an excuse to dump our bodies in the river, when the real reason was as simple as "So you won't run to the police." However, the barrel of a gun does make an extraordinarily compelling argument.

"We did some checking on you, too. You're the niece of Marnie Quinn. She's spent her life making sure the corrupt regimes of the world stayed in business, hasn't she?"

"And making sure they stayed at peace with their neighbors, as best she could."

"Peace? At what cost? An ignoble peace is no cause for rejoicing. Better open rebellion where those that do all the work enjoy some possibility of gain."

My eyes rolled. "Who enjoys the gain after all those who've rebelled are dead?"

"Who are you to discuss the fate of the masses?" He'd moved from slight irritability to open froth. "You spend your time at cocktail parties thrown by the establishment, wearing clothes that cost as much as good men make in a month. And to what end? So you can whore yourself out to lads like our Edward here, hoping to become Lady Muck so you can watch your blood turn blue?"

"I don't whore myself out to anyone, thanks very much." For one glorious instant there had been a possibility of sex, but at no point in the exercise had anyone discussed an exchange of funds. Not in pounds, euros, or dollars. "We talked at that party. That was it."

"Of course." More spitting from the backseat. "Because you always leave a party to go to a secluded, dark corner of the garden and talk."

"She doesn't owe explanations to the likes of you." Edward's voice tightened to a brittle reed.

"Quick turn-round on your little Ashley, wasn't it?" This thread of the conversation seemed to have hit the re-set button on our terrorist's smug satisfaction. It was back now in abundance. "But then again, we all knew she was the re-bound girl after your hot little Saudi left. And she was so common, just a little teller at the bank. Better to go on to the ambassador's daughter."

"I'm not the ambassador's daughter."

Damn. Should have kept my mouth shut about that one. If he mistook Marnie for the ambassador, it might have given me some bargaining power.

"I know. Figure of bleeding speech."

Edward turned back to the kidnapper. "You'd best not have hurt Ashley, you bastard."

"Turn round." Our backseat guest nudged Edward with the gun this time, and then continued speaking, sounding as though chewing on something bitter. "No one hurt Ashley. There'd be no profit in that."

The man who'd assassinate all of us and take pride in it drew the line at hurting Edward's former not-quite-girl-friend? I couldn't buy that, which was funny because the deranged man actually sounded sincere.

"Take the next exit."

So, we were finally getting off the merry-go-round. Good thing. Jane had glanced at the fuel gauge five times in the last ten minutes. I doubted I'd like Ceann's destination, but I didn't fancy our chances if we ran out of gas in the middle of traffic, either, especially as the sun was very nearly down.

Carlos took in our surroundings. "Lovely. I've always enjoyed the beach at sunset."

"Yes, we've heard all about it. Your fantasy about shagging Tiffany while lying on the beach of a deserted is-

209

land gave us all a giggle, I have to say. Loved the part where you licked your way up her thighs, but I don't see how you could do it without ending up with a mouth full of sand."

Carlos' head whipped around to face the backseat. Ceann laughed, but I noticed he did stop talking. He gestured for Carlos to turn back around.

Carlos took a breath and said, "So that's how you knew where we were. You had Tiffany's phone bugged."

"Oh, no." Ceann sounded amused. "She did it for us."

"What did you do to her?"

Ceann had nerves of steel, I had to give him that. Carlos' calm tone scared the crap out of me and I wasn't his target. Yelling would have had much less effect than his deliberate moderation.

"We didn't do anything. The bank where she works has a manager that helps us clean funds, for a fee. One of my associates had a chat with her while taking care of our other business. They got rather friendly. After you started sniffing round, he talked her into having phone sex with you so we could see what you might let slip. Dead simple to monitor you after that."

Carlos snorted. "You're lying. Tiffany's no terrorist."

Ceann made a "tsk" sound. "Doesn't the Company teach you to be more discreet on a stakeout? Tiffany plays for all sorts of teams, mate. Of course, after the dream she told you last week about the threesome, I expect you know that." He caught Jane's eyes in the rearview mirror. "Your next left there, love."

"That was a secure cell phone," Carlos insisted. "You didn't track us from that line."

"No. You're right about that. But I believe she sent you a shiny new cell phone cover a while back. They make GPS trackers in the tiniest forms these days. Tiffany fit it right into the leather." He tapped my shoulder with the gun. "You did catch us with our pants down a bit when you snuck out of the safe house. My spy had fallen asleep. Had to wait until you were on your way back to catch you two without the escorts."

That explained the sloppiness of that attack, then. This one they'd planned better. It took all my effort not to shake.

Carlos, on the other hand, assumed a mental Secret Agent mask, just like they probably taught him in spy school. As we made the turn, I could see his reflection in the window for just a second. He looked as if he'd just watched a slightly disappointing movie of the week.

Jane flicked a glance at Carlos. Her own mask held steady, though I thought I saw a new vein throbbing in her temple.

Ceann directed Jane to a narrow road heading down toward the beach. Not a lot of street lights out here to break up the fog. The sun had disappeared over the horizon, but in the last rays following it down I could make out a stretch of large rocks in a row, rising up to form a natural barrier between the road and the sand. "Stop the car next to the boulders. This is where you all get out."

Jane threw the van into park, as Carlos reached for the door handle. "Stay close by, and behave yourselves when you get out," Ceann said. "I've a friend out there in the dark."

Something about the set of Jane's jaw told me she had no intention of doing that. Our tormentor must have agreed, because he added, "If you don't, your friend here will regret it."

Steel pressed against my neck. I guessed the soft click I heard was the sound of the safety going off. Jane and Carlos got out of the van.

Okay, Marnie…how do I get out of this one?

Create a window.

If I lived through this, Marnie and I needed to have a talk. Life and death crises, and that was the best her voice in my head could do? The van didn't have any windows this far back. I didn't have the tools to make one. Edward left the door open as he exited. Did that count?

Not that kind of window.

A new facet of myself I'd discovered—when guns are involved, I get very literal.

Window of opportunity…give Jane a clear line of sight. Sitting in the back of the car was a gamble for him. At some point, he had to get out, and this van didn't permit graceful upright exits. He needed to take his concentration off me for at least a second or two. Sure, Jane and Carlos didn't have their guns, but I was betting they could inflict lethal wounds with whatever was at hand. After the last conversation, Carlos could probably kill this guy with a clot of seaweed.

"You had quite a plan there, didn't you?" I leaned back in my seat, making no move to get out of the van. "I'm just curious. Which of us made the more lucrative kidnapping victim? Edward and I argued about this, down in that basement. Great place, by the way. Lovely decor. But back to the point. Who brings more prestige? The minor aristocrat, or the diplomat's niece?"

He pressed the gun into the back of my hair. "This isn't the time to chat. Get out of the van. Now."

"You don't want to shoot me here, with the van's upholstery soaking up all my blood. Too much evidence to clean up. So, I figure I should stay put."

The next second, he smacked the back of my head with the butt of the gun. My vision went blurry and I fell forward, clutching my head. As I blinked back tears and tried to make the ghosting images disappear, he said in my ear, "I don't have to shoot you to make you hurt, do I, love?"

I got out of the van.

CHAPTER TWENTY-ONE

Ceann kept the gun trained on me as long as he could, but did have to drop his gaze for just a second before getting out of the vehicle. I got as far ahead of him as I could. Jane looked from me to him and every muscle in her body tensed up.

"Careful there." Another voice. Irish accent this time, belonging to a skinny woman who moved from the left into the beam of the van's headlights. She took me by surprise, but then, with my second kidnapping this month to preoccupy me, that wasn't difficult. The wind blew her curly dark brown hair into a Medusa halo, but didn't seem to affect the steadiness with which she held the gun, specifically pointed at Jane.

"Ah, Lacey." Ceann nodded to her. "Everything ready?"

"They're ready to sail, as soon as you get out there."

I looked out at the distance. The wild grass at our feet mixed with a hundred feet or so of gravelly sand. Beyond that, the surf lapped up around an antiquated dock with three rowboats tied up to it. Squinting as hard as possible out at the ocean, I could just make out a ship floating in the distance. That explained the circling around the park. He not only had a destination in mind, he had a time. He didn't want us out of the car long enough to give him trouble, so we had to get here after our connecting transportation arrived. It wasn't a cruise ship, but it wasn't a small pleasure craft, either. Big enough to stay at sea for a couple of days. I had an uneasy feeling Ceann didn't intend to host us on it for long.

"Grand." Ceann turned to the four of us. "You're all going to die shortly, but rest easy. It's for the good of the cause."

"For FTP, you mean?" I asked, shouting over the wind. "Somehow killing all of us is going to unite Ireland?"

"FTP doesn't stop at Ireland, you slag." Lacey jabbed the gun toward me, and the wind died down as suddenly as it had stirred up. "Ceann has created a worldwide movement. We're going to cleanse every land that ever endured British rape."

"Really?" Jane said. "You're branching out now?" She asked casually, as though someone had just pointed out a new Starbucks in the neighborhood.

Our kidnapper's eyes shone. He didn't say, "Right you are, miss," but I felt certain he wanted to.

"Is she right?" Carlos asked. "I wouldn't especially care, but my partner and I have a bet going. She said you were on a crusade, and you couldn't stop at Ireland. I said you were an ordinary bastard, and you'd stop when you got yourself killed. Of course, it could be we're both right."

Our captor smiled so wide I could see silver fillings in the back of his mouth. "We're going to change the world with or without your good opinion." He eyed the dark waters. "Well, without you, period. That's rather a given." He inclined his head toward his partner. "Lacey, give me the cuffs."

215

Lacey produced a couple of pieces of plastic that looked like heavy duty trash bag ties from her pockets. The kind where you could slip one end through the other, but you couldn't get it back out again. Ceann handed his gun to Lacey as he grabbed the plastic strips. Faster than I would have thought possible, he slipped one around each of my wrists and bound them in front of me.

Lacey stood guard, a gun in each hand and a smirk on her face, looking like the protagonist of a particularly deranged video game. Ceann cuffed the rest of the group with a precision I imagine came from experience. After he took his gun back, he grabbed the plastic binding around my hands with his left hand and pulled me over the boulders toward the beach.

I followed, since I had no choice, but between my tied hands, the darkness, and someone else setting the pace, I kept stumbling. "Why didn't you kill us back in London, when you had us down in the basement?" I asked after a rock sliced into my knee on the third fall. "If it was so important, why did you wait this long?"

"Didn't need to." He waved the gun behind him, helping Lacey corral the others over the rocks. "You weren't a threat."

And we were somehow a threat now, while running away? It didn't make sense, but before I could ask anything else, a fierce gust picked up when we reached the beach, the kind of gale force wind that could knock you over if you weren't paying attention. My captor stopped, holding up an arm to protect his face from the sudden atmospheric attack. I dug my heels into the sandy earth. For that second, I could almost believe I'd developed telekinesis and controlled the very air. If I could, we had a hurricane coming any second. Really, though, if anyone could control the air, it would be

216

Jane. That would come right after yoga and martial arts training—honing her mind to bend the elements to her will.

The funniest things go through your mind when you're facing death.

The wind slapped me in the face, stinging my eyes. Tears welled up, my frustration and anger taking the climatic assault as a sign that self-control no longer mattered. "You kidnapped us!" I yelled. "You found a way to get us out of a heavily guarded house!"

"Shared back garden." He fought the wind, walking me over to a dilapidated dock with a couple of small rowboats tied off to it. "One of the ambassador's neighbors goes to the south of France every year around this time. We had a connection at the security company. Easy as pie."

I wanted to knife him right in that smug smile. "Then, after going to all that work to get us out, you let us go, only to track us down and kill us! What sense does that make? Why didn't you just kill us in the first place? Why all this drama?" The wind died down right before my last statement, so I didn't have to yell it, but I did anyway.

"Couldn't very well do that, now could I, lass? How would it look, killing the gimp?" Ceann shook his head. "Would have lost us the sympathy vote from all those lovely donors. Big thanks to your countrymen, by the way. More folks of Irish descent in America these days than there are in Ireland. Some of them dying to help take the Emerald Isle away from the Brits once and for all."

"So you couldn't kill us then, because of Edward's leg, but now it doesn't matter?"

"You told them about my tattoo." He tapped me on the nose. "And my accent. Oh, yes, we know all about what you told the police. They didn't believe you, and I had to stop you before you found someone who did."

217

The plastic dug into my wrists, as my hands begged to claw at his face. "What the hell do your accent and tattoo matter? You're hardly the only Scot on the planet. It's not like I could give them a voiceprint. And half the world has a tattoo, although most of them are nicer than that ugly plant on your hand."

He smacked me in the head. "A thistle, you twit. It's a Scottish thistle." Fortunately, this time he just used his hand, instead of the gun, but it still hurt like the devil.

"Then it's a lousy tattoo. It looks more like an alien."

Ceann continued, barely registering my reaction. "You heard your friends here. All the government agencies in the world think FTP stops recruiting at the Irish border. They have no idea how wide our network stretches, and you won't tell them, since you all will be dead."

"Doesn't killing three of their compatriots look sort of bad to your sympathetic American ATM?"

He twisted his mouth in confusion, and I wondered what exactly the Scottish called cash-dispensing machines, but I didn't get the chance to ask before he continued talking. "You won't be dead to them. Just missing. A few clues that you ran off together should fix that. After you spun them the tale about getting kidnapped, the police already think you're off your head. No one will find your bodies to make them think anything else."

"What about Jane and Carlos?"

"The American secret agents? Only your aunt knows that they even exist. Any newspaper starts bringing up theories about missing spies, and they'll sound completely barmy."

"He's wrong, you know," Jane said. I turned as far as I could and saw her talking to Lacey, who was guiding the other three along behind us at gunpoint. "Assuming he succeeds in killing all of us, dead bodies get found, eventually. You help him with this and you'll be on the hook, too. Are you ready to go to prison for this?"

Lacey's chin went up as she stared at Jane. "You don't scare me. Ceann is a brilliant leader. If he says you won't be found, you won't be. But even if I end up rotting in prison, it's worth it if it helps the Irish."

"I'm one quarter Irish!" The wind picked up again, and I screamed to be heard over it. "My mother's a Quinn, for pity's sake!"

Ceann shook his head. "A good Irish girl, willing to whore herself out to a Brit. Bit of self-loathing there, just like her aunt, serving the English."

"My aunt works for the American embassy, not the English one. Anyway, the CIA is on to you, and they notice when their agents go missing." At least, I hoped they did. "Give up now and see if they'll cut you a deal."

"She's right, you know." Carlos stared at Ceann. "End this. Give me the gun. Have you ever actually shot anyone? It's not as easy as you think, taking someone's life. Rips out a piece of your soul. You don't want to do that."

"I'd worry about your own soul, pretty boy. You're the one on your way to meet your maker."

"I don't think so." Carlos took a small step toward him. "You're standing here monologuing. You're stalling. If you wanted to shoot us, you'd just do it."

Ceann put a finger to his lips as though deep in thought. He said, "You know, I think you're right," and shot Carlos in the stomach.

＊

Carlos' six-foot-plus frame hit the ground before my brain could register what had happened. Jane screamed and ran to him, trying to check for a pulse.

Ceann pulled her up by her bound hands. "You want to ride out to the ship with the corpse here? Very romantic, if you fancy a bit of necrophilia."

"You bastard." Jane rounded on him, sweeping his leg in a very unstable move that sent them both to the ground. Lacey grabbed at her, pulling her away from Ceann before clicking the safety off her gun. Just as she was pulling the trigger, Jane bit her arm. The bullet sailed by Jane and hit Edward in the leg.

A sharp cracking sound rang in the air, over even the sound of the wind. Edward fell on his knees. I wondered how he could keep from screaming until I realized which leg Lacey had shot.

The shot diverted Jane enough for Ceann and Lacey to get her back under control, however. Ceann stood up and grabbed his gun. Then he looked at Edward and howled with laughter. "And the gimp's out of commission. Lovely. I couldn't have planned it better." He leaned over to Lacey. "I'm going to take the ladies with me on the first trip. Stand guard over the two bodies, and I'll come back for you and them."

I couldn't see her expression well, but Lacey seemed confused, staring at Edward. "This one's not dead."

Ceann laughed. "No, but he's not walking anywhere, either."

Now I did spit at him. "You worthless piece of shit! You'll rot in hell for this."

The maniac and his accomplice laughed.

Damn it. *Damn it.* I swiped an errant tear on my cheek against my shoulder and exhaled through my nose, trying to squash down panic. Do not let them get away with this. Summon every voice that has ever rented space in your head and find a way out. These two will live out the rest of their lives in a 6' x 8' cell.

Lacey forced me and Jane onto the dock. Ceann pulled Edward over toward the dock, Edward hopping along with him on his good leg. Tugging Edward's hands over a post on the railing, Ceann said, "Stay there like a good boy." He kicked Edward hard in the knee that was still attached to a live foot. "Not that you have any choice."

As Edward swore, Lacey helped Ceann get Jane and me into the boat, facing us back toward the shore so we could have a good view of Carlos' lifeless body. I stared at him, trying to see if maybe, against all odds, he might still be breathing.

Ceann pulled another zip tie out of Lacey's pocket. "Only one left?"

Lacey started to apologize, but he stopped her. "This will do." He bound my feet together. "She's little. It'll be easier to carry her onboard." He looked at Jane. "You behave yourself, now. Try any more clever business with those pretty legs of yours and she goes into the drink."

A cold wave of fear went through me. Water...me with my hands and legs zip-tied. Good Lord. I could wish he'd go ahead and shoot me.

He didn't oblige. "I'll be back." Ceann, the captain of this hell ship, waved to Lacey like we were going punting on the Thames. He turned around to start the engine on the skiff. I had fantasies about bringing my hands down in a firm chop on the back of his head and knocking him into the motor, but fear of accidentally flinging myself into the sea at the same time overruled the idea.

The motor wouldn't start, no matter how hard Ceann tried. He looked around, but neither of the other boats even had engines. For a fleeting moment I hoped he'd take it as a bad omen and abandon the plan. Instead, he yelled to Lacey to bring him oars from one of the other boats. Once she did, he stowed the gun at the small of his back and started rowing us out to his friends on the barge, steering the boat around so that now we had a perfect view of the ship waiting for us.

I wanted to feel relief that he'd put the gun aside, but with the two of us in handcuffs and surrounded by water, I doubted even Jane's ninja skills could get us out of trouble. After two minutes, I wondered if we all might freeze to death before we made it to the ship. With the crazy wind occasionally buffeting us about and the final disappearance of the sun, it dipped into the twenties, by my guess. Ceann clearly never made the varsity rowing team. He rowed straight toward the ship, which was a feat of its own in this weather, but about every other stroke, he splashed enough water into the boat that I feared we might sink. The sweaters we'd worn to the pub barely made a dent in the chill. Even disciplined Jane couldn't stop her teeth from chattering.

"Do you have to do that?" I spluttered after a particularly bad soaking. "My hair will be ruined."

"It's okay." Jane brushed water out of her eyes with her bound hands. "We'll still be in this boat twelve hours from now when the sun comes up. It'll dry us off."

He dowsed us again, on purpose this time. "Shut it, the pair of you, or I'll toss you over."

I shivered. Okay, I hadn't stopped shivering since we got on the boat, but now I shivered mentally, too. I looked to the ship and back to the shore. We approached the halfway mark between a ship of foes and the shore of inanimate friends.

222

Glancing back at the beach, I saw Lacey standing close to Edward. My stomach clenched as she raised the gun and I figured out she was going to shoot him. Edward had his hands off the post, resting at his stomach as though satisfied with his fate as he leaned against the railing.

The next movement happened so fast, I thought I'd imagined it. Edward waited until she was right next to him, and then jammed both hands into her stomach, almost falling toward her, making certain that his entire weight was behind it. Lacey went down.

I never thought I'd be glad to see a man hit a woman, but I almost cried out for joy, until Jane stepped on my foot. I glanced at her. She nodded toward Ceann. He hadn't noticed any of this. Putting all his effort into rowing and glancing over his shoulder to make sure he stayed on course, he had no energy left to monitor what he'd arranged as a static situation back on land. I bit my lip. Even if Edward had knocked Lacey out, there was still the whole tied-hands-and-leg-out-of-commission thing to deal with.

Only once he lifted his arms and brought them down hard over the railing, his hands weren't bound anymore. Hopping down the dock on his good leg, he made his way into the skiff that still had oars, untied it from its mooring and started rowing toward us.

Ceann concentrated on keeping his strokes even. The wind had died down from its earlier fury, but the low gusts stayed constant, creating a good chop in the water. I could make fun of his technique, but the fact that we still made headway toward the ship meant he knew something about rowing.

Apparently Edward did, as well. He rowed steadily toward us, his back to us, checking constantly over his shoulder to stay on course.

223

Was I dreaming, or was he gaining ground?

Ceann finally looked up and saw Edward. "Shite." He mumbled the word to his shoes, no breath to spare. He began to row faster. Even with his shoddy technique, we increased our speed.

Edward's constant rate beat him, though. Those beautiful biceps and triceps and pectorals and every other muscle that Edward worked so hard to perfect served him well. He glided toward us over the waves. I looked from him to the ship. Closer, closer, stroke by stroke. Ceann didn't have the build for this or the endurance. Even as he rowed faster, his strokes accomplished less.

The distance between our boats grew narrower with each stroke, until I could see the muscles in Edward's neck straining as he rowed. He was going to make it here before Ceann reached the ship. He pulled up to our boat, murder in his eyes. We were safe.

Or so I thought, right up until Ceann knocked me into the sea.

CHAPTER TWENTY-TWO

One flick of the oar, and I went into the water. The impact of the salty cold wet stung my skin like a burn. I pulled my hands apart as desperately as I could, but they stayed firmly together. My feet remained solidly joined, not an inch of slack available for a scissor kick.

Butterfly kick. Keep your feet together. Pippa's voice, from summers thirty years back. *Like a mermaid. You can be the princess of the sea.*

I flailed my legs around like a mermaid with a sprained tail. The surface shimmered above me. Flattening my hands, I ran them down my torso, doing as good an imitation of finning as I could with my hands bound together.

My head broke through the surface for a second, and I grabbed half a breath before sinking back down. I spent half my childhood in my parents' pool. Muscle memory kicked in, but muscle strength started to give out. I broke through once more for an even shorter breath.

My water-logged sweater felt lined with lead, and my running shoes kept pulling my feet down. I couldn't stop kicking or get my feet far enough apart to work them off. I felt myself going down again.

Maybe it was time to let go.

"Hold on, Emmaline!"

I blinked against water, willing strength into my feet. Damn, these voices in my head were getting eerily realistic.

"Emmaline!"

Edward. I heard his voice. It sounded a million miles away, but I didn't imagine it. He was up there.

I kicked my feet with all my strength, more than I thought I had left. I lifted my arms up, reaching for the air. Fingers closed over my arm and pulled up hard.

An instant later, Edward grabbed me around the waist. Jane clamped her tied hands on my arm and together, they managed to tug me into the boat.

Edward pulled me to him. "Emmaline! Talk to me. Say something."

I coughed, spat out some water, and coughed some more. "I'm good." Three more sharp coughs. "Okay, not good, but alive. Get these damn handcuffs off me."

Edward put his hands on my cheeks, pulling my mouth to his as though afraid of missing my face by accident. Nearly as soon as his lips landed on mine, he removed them again, grabbing the oars.

"Carlos," Jane said, grabbing my hands. "We have to get back to Carlos."

Edward rowed us back to shore in five minutes. My butt sat on the bench, but my mind kept going back to the water. I gasped four times, unable to convince myself that I no longer had to fight for air. My teeth chattered so badly my jaw hurt by the time we reached the shore.

Circumstances didn't allow full shock just now, however. Where had Ceann gone? I didn't see him. A few feet down the shore from the dock, I could just make out a groggy Lacey wading in the shallows a few feet away with her hands at her hips, probably trying to find her gun. Edward tied off

226

the boat onto the pier and boosted Jane up onto the dock. Sitting on the wooden landing and locking her legs around a post, she grabbed for my hands, and the two of them managed to shift me up onto the pier.

"The phone." Jane used the post to pull herself to a standing position. "Get a phone."

Edward nodded. "I'll head up to the road and try to find help."

Jane shook her head. "Cell phones in the car. Carlos and I dropped them when we first got taken, so they couldn't be confiscated."

I ran back over the scene in the car. Jane and Carlos both adjusted their seats when we first got in...dropping phones. Sneaky devils.

Lacey yelled to us to stay put as she fished through the waves.

As Edward made his careful way to the car, using an oar for a crutch, Jane held her arms as far apart as she could and then, like Edward had, smacked them down on the splintering wood railing. The cuffs snapped apart. She massaged her bruised wrists. "Cheap plastic."

I stared at her. "Thank God they didn't use the good stuff." I thought about trying to follow her lead. My muscles, still shaking from the mad swimming lesson and flash-frozen by the wind, said no. I sank down on to the dock, wondering if I'd ever have the strength to get back up again.

Edward turned on the headlights in the car and waved a phone at us. Before I could shout encouragement, Lacey located her water-logged gun and scrambled onto the dock, trying to threaten us with it and dry it on her jacket at the same time. Jane reached back for an oar and smacked Lacey in the head with it, as though she were an annoying fly. Edward rejoined us on the dock as Lacey sank down into un-

227

consciousness, the gun dropping from her flailing hand back into the Irish sea.

"Stay down," Jane told her, and ran to Carlos.

***

The next five minutes felt like someone had put the movie on pause. Jane knelt by Carlos. Either he still had a pulse or Jane couldn't accept that he was gone, because she pulled off her sweater and tried to staunch the bleeding in his side with it. Edward held the oar over Lacey, looking like all humanity had checked out of his soul and the calculating shell left behind had orders to strike at the first detected movement. My job was to shiver.

Once the backup arrived, someone upstairs pushed play.

Two cars and an ambulance sailed down a service road in the distance and headed on to the beach. In the beam from our van's headlights I could make out the word "GAR-DA" on both car hoods. Officers with drawn weapons emerged from them to surround Lacey. A short redheaded woman cut the plastic off my wrists and ankles. She nodded toward the captive. "Where's the other one?"

Edward pointed out to sea. In the dark I thought I could see the ship heading out. With Edward and Jane trying to get to me, had he managed to reach it?

The police officer—sorry, garda—yelled for her associate to call the Coast Guard, but Edward shook his head. "You won't find him on that ship. He's probably dead."

The redhead drew her mouth to one side. "And just how did he probably die?"

"I hit him rather hard in the head with an oar and he fell in the water. He was bleeding when he fell, and I didn't see him come back up. As soon as he fell in, the ship started preparations to leave. No one came for him."

The officer stared at him, and then looked at me. "Did you see this?"

I shook my head. Pieces of my wet hair slapped me in the face. "I was busy."

"Doing what, exactly?"

"Drowning."

"She's freezing, and we've had a full day," Edward said. He inclined his head to the car. "Can we continue this somewhere warmer? Somewhere that we can call our families and let them know we're all right?"

Yes. Oh, yes. I needed to call Marnie, and my mother. I really wanted to hear my mom's voice, and my dad's, and Sneakers'.

"Neil." I breathed the word out without thinking. God, I needed to talk to Neil and tell him we were as over as the eighth grade. I did not butterfly kick my way out of death in the deep blue sea just to waste my life in a house I didn't want with a man who didn't understand me. And who, to be honest with myself, I didn't really get either. "I have to call Neil. Please."

The garda looked from me to Edward and back to me. Then she yelled to a tall officer nearest the car. "O'Reilly! Get these people to the station. Make sure there's a change of clothes."

I exhaled a breath I hadn't realized I was holding. Edward turned and walked to the waiting car. I glanced at Jane before following him. She hovered over the stretcher on which the officers loaded Carlos. They put a blanket over his body, but not his head. Thank God. There was hope. Maybe not much, but some. "I'm going with him." She shook off the emergency tech trying to take her pulse. "I'm fine. I'm going

229

with him." She didn't look a lot better than Carlos did, but no one tried to stop her.

The redheaded officer put a hand on my back. "Where are we going?" I asked her. "Are we going to dinner?"

She pushed me forward. "We're going to the station."

"Is there food there?" Well, at least that's what I tried to say, but my tongue twitched. Maybe I bit it while I was drowning? I stepped forward and tripped over something, but I didn't see anything there. I lifted my foot up to keep walking and tipped to the side. "Wers sa ressina?"

The officer steadied me and put a hand on my forehead. "We need an EMT over here."

Nice people with blankets took me away for a little lie-down after that.

CHAPTER TWENTY-THREE

Prying my eyelids apart seemed like a bad idea, so I didn't.

I lay there, hearing voices that sounded familiar. I thought maybe I might be awake. It didn't exactly feel like a dream anymore. It didn't feel like reality either, until something cold assaulted my chest.

Blinking a couple of times, I tried to muster the energy to slap someone for molesting me in my sleep until I realized my assailant had on scrubs and wanted to check my heart with a stethoscope. It was just as well. Not even indignation at the invasion of my personal space could give me the energy to lift my arm.

"Welcome back." The Irish-accented doctor took her instrument of cold metal torture and thrust a light into my eye instead.

If you want to welcome someone back into the land of the living, you greet them with a vanilla latte or a blueberry scone, or maybe both. You do not assault all of their senses in turn with medical equipment.

"Trying to say something there, darlin'?" the doctor asked.

"She's asking for a scone." Marnie. She lived, and she still spoke my language. Thank God. She sat forward, leaning toward me from a banana yellow vinyl chair. It clashed with the pastel pink wallpaper.

"Perhaps a spot of chicken broth for now," the doctor said. "You've been asleep for two days, love. Mild hypothermia. We'll wait till tomorrow for pastries."

What did I bother waking up for? I thought, before promptly falling back to sleep.

***

That afternoon I finally came out of the stupor, staying awake long enough to have chicken broth and watch television. They only had four stations. A third of the shows were presented in Gaelic and my knowledge of the language stops at *Erin Go Bragh*, so my understanding was limited, but with accents so musical, I didn't really mind.

Marnie sat with me, assuring me she'd called California to let the family know I was all right. Only Neil required a separate call. My entire family, even Harry, kept vigil for me over at Mom and Dad's house.

"Harry was particularly curious to know all the details about what happened. Never heard him so talkative."

Well, at least my imminent demise brought the family together.

"Edward has been here keeping me company. I sent him to the hotel to get some sleep." Marnie smiled and shook her head. "Chivalrous to a fault, that one. Kept saying he owed it to your boyfriend to send you home healthy."

I missed the next part of her monologue. Edward wanted to send me home to Neil? I didn't want to go home to Neil. I wanted to stay here, with Edward. Just thinking about

232

the kiss in the safe house made my temperature go up several degrees. And then he rescued me from drowning. It had to mean something, didn't it?

Just as I was clearing my head to stop thinking about seducing Edward and tune back in to Marnie, Jane slipped in the door. Her long hair hung limp around her face, looking mousier than ever, as though it hadn't seen shampoo in days. The hue of her skin made me think she hadn't slept in just as long. If her face were on TV, I'd have said someone needed to check the contrast because the yellow was up too high.

She hugged me gently. After letting me go, she gave Marnie's hand a quick squeeze. "How are you feeling, Emmy?"

"Better. Even though they won't let me have scones, or a latte." I held out my hand and she took it. "As soon as I get real food, I'll be fine."

"Thank God." She hugged me again.

"How's Carlos?"

The color control on Jane's face went even further out of whack. Now the blue exceeded limits too. She looked sick. "He's alive. The bullet was small caliber, non-expanding, and it hit his stomach, not his heart or liver. The doctors worried most about infection, but by some miracle, they've kept him free of it so far. He's not out of the woods yet, but there's a good chance he'll make it." She let go of my hand and folded her arms over her stomach.

I didn't have the brain power to interpret *small caliber* or *non-expanding*, so I concentrated on the *he'll make it* part. "That's good news, isn't it?"

"Yes. Yes, it is."

She tried to smile, pressing her lips together too hard. Whatever it was, she didn't want to spill it in front of Marnie.

As ever, my aunt could read the room. She stood up. "I'm going to get some coffee. Can I get you anything, Jane?"

Jane shook her head.

"You can get me a latte," I told her.

"Tomorrow, if you're good." She blew me a kiss on her way out. Marnie, ever the diplomat. Don't say no, just not now.

I looked at Jane. "Marnie won't make herself scarce forever. Spill it. What's going on with you and Carlos?"

Jane sighed, rolling her eyes, blinking a lot and curling her lip at the same time. It was like the expression Olympics. Nine point five, with a half-point deduction for the raspberry noise that robbed it of decorum. "There has never been anything between me and Carlos."

"Except for the fact that you adore him, you mean."

She stood so still I thought she might have stopped breathing. "Yes. I do."

"Which means you have excellent taste, because, let's face it, the man is yummy, but that was true a week ago. From the look on your face, something changed. What is it?"

"I adore him." She sat on the edge of the bed and rocked herself forward and back. "I thought he was gone, Emmy. When I saw him get shot, I really thought I had lost him."

I sat up a little more and put a hand on her shoulder. "But you didn't."

"But for an hour there, I thought I did. God, Emmy, I've never felt that desolate in my life. Until now."

"Why now?" I resisted beating her with the pillow, but only just. "You said he's going to be okay." Probably.

234

"Probably." Of course, Jane had to say it out loud. "And they expect me to keep working with him, just like before."

"Honey, I've just woken up from a forty-eight-hour nap and I'm not conscious enough to be subtle. Spell it out for me."

She breathed in and exhaled hard. "I knew there'd never be anything romantic between us, but I told myself that I had an important place in his life. If it ever came to that, I had his back. I'm good at my job, Emmy. I have the highest accuracy rate in our unit at the shooting range. I can run a five-minute mile without breathing hard. Drop me in the Amazon rainforest with nothing but a fruit roll-up and I'll find my way back to D.C. in three days. But when it came right down to it, none of that mattered. I couldn't protect him."

If I used that litmus test, I'd never date again. I can't run for five minutes at any speed without feeling like I damaged something irreparably. "He stepped in Ceann's way, honey. He was trying to stop the guy. You couldn't have done anything."

"I know. He was trying to protect you and Edward—"

"And you."

"And me. I'm his partner. We're trained to protect each other."

"So now he knows he can't protect you all the time, either. You fought like a lioness protecting her pride, Jane. I know I'll think twice before picking on your choice of outfit again."

This got me a weak smile. "No, you won't."

"Okay, no, I won't. But only because I know you love me too much to judo-chop me."

"Yes, I do." She patted my arm and then went limp again. "I fought as hard as I could. I was as smart as I knew how to be. He got shot anyway."

"So, since you can't protect him all the time, now you think you don't have any place in his life?"

"I don't." She looked at me, the sincerity in her hazel eyes almost more than I could bear. "I failed at playing guardian angel. I don't know how to be around him and be nothing to him."

I wanted to refute that, or maybe box her about the ears, but unfortunately, she believed it. "Have you ever told Carlos how you feel?"

She sighed, the exhalation of the ages. "He's had three years to send me a signal, Emmy. He's never given me one sign that he looks at me as anything but good backup. Now I don't even have that appeal."

"Maybe that's a good thing."

Her eyebrows narrowed. "I think your hypothermia is making a comeback."

"Now he knows you're not perfect. Maybe you shined a little too brightly in the secret agent firmament. Might have put him off his game."

Her eyes went dark. "So I'm supposed to screw up to make him feel superior?"

"No. You're supposed to admit that you're a human being and you have limits. Think of all those talents you just listed. You're kind of intimidating, sweetie."

She laughed. A genuine laugh this time. "What's so funny?" I asked.

She slipped off her shoes and put her feet on the bed. It reminded me of our late-night gab sessions in college. "Life. You think that I'm intimidating and I've spent our entire friendship feeling intimidated by you."

"By me? Why?"

"You could always get any guy you wanted. Maybe not forever, but at least for a while." She smiled. "I guess that's good, right? Made us both rise to the competition?"

I clapped my hands together. "Competition! That's what you need for Carlos!"

The smile disappeared. "Honey, I've competed with the entire Eastern Seaboard. I lost."

"Not for you. For him. Has there ever been anyone in the picture?"

She looked away, and then shook her head.

"Then find someone. After he's recovered, let him know he's not the only bull in the pen."

"How? I'd have to evolve into someone else."

"Remember what you told me about clinging to the nearest guy around?"

She held up a hand. "Forget it, Emmy. I was being stupid."

"I don't want to forget it. At least, not all of it. I want to evolve." I took her hand. "If you want to grow too, then I won't have to do it alone. Not really."

She bit her lip, then nodded. "I'll try."

"Promise?"

"Promise." She clasped my hand. "Good Lord. Enough about me. You're barely recovered from your stint as an oceanic popsicle. How are you? Really?"

I laughed. "I'm fine. Or at least, I will be soon. Just tired."

"Me, too. Do you suppose they've got a room for me here?"

"I'm sure they've got rooms for all of us, with nice padded walls."

237

Marnie stuck her head around the door. "I've got tea. Brought some for you as well, Miss Jane."

Jane and I relieved Marnie of her load. As I took a sip of my tea—surprisingly good for a hospital beverage—Marnie opened the door wider. "Someone else here to see you, too."

Edward looked in, as if checking for bugs. He stood on two legs, so I guessed Marnie had managed to find him another prosthesis. It had never occurred to me to ask if he owned a spare, but that would only make sense. I beckoned him over, but he stopped at the foot of the bed. "Just wanted to see that you were all right."

In addition to her crazy ninja skills, Jane was also scarcely less the diplomat than my aunt. She stood up and walked to the door. "I've got to check on Carlos."

I put my tea on the side table and sat up straighter. "Remember, confidence. You're evolving."

She smiled. It looked like someone had painted the wrong smile on the sad clown. "Right."

"Go give him a thrill."

She glanced at Marnie and Edward, blushing furiously, and said, "Baby steps. Evolution takes time," before disappearing into the hallway.

Edward cleared his throat. I patted the space beside me that Jane had vacated, but he stayed put. "Has the doctor given you a clean bill of health then?"

"They're keeping me till tomorrow, but after that, I should be a free woman."

"I suppose you'll be heading home."

"Oh, not quite yet." I glanced over at Marnie. "I'd like to spend a few days in London to get used to solid food again before flying to California and adding jet lag to the mix."

"Your boyfriend is no doubt on his way here, then."

"No, I don't think so." I looked to Marnie for confirmation that I didn't need. She took a second away from checking something on her phone to shake her head. I stared at the iPhone in her hand. "I really need to call him."

Edward looked at me. I met his gaze and thought I might drown in that sea of blue. He took a breath like he had something big to say and then turned and left. It was a good thing he chose to go because if he'd looked at me like that for one more instant, like he could see my whole soul at once, I'd have ripped his clothes off and taken him right there on the hospital bed, even with my aunt in the room.

Marnie wouldn't have appreciated that.

As soon as the door shut behind Edward, I leaned over to her. "Can I borrow your phone?"

CHAPTER TWENTY-FOUR

The conversation with Neil lasted seventeen minutes, and that included several lengthy silences. I don't know what I expected, but it was more than what I got. I'd never broken up with anyone before. Jane nailed it during her speech in that warehouse. I had a great knack for leaving the door open and waiting for the other party to walk through it. I told myself that I didn't want to hurt them, that it would be healthier for them to come to the decision on their own. I'd even allowed myself a measure of self-pity when the guys finally walked through that wide-open door.

Neil demonstrated no heartbreak.

He said the right things. "We shouldn't decide this over the phone, Emmaline. Come home. Let's—"

"I've already decided, Neil. I'm sorry." My eyes ached. I waited for tears, but my body didn't have the energy. "It just isn't the right place for me. It hasn't been for a while."

"Well."

Long, awkward silence.

I opened my mouth to say something three times, but nothing felt right.

At last, he cleared his throat. "If that's the way you feel, then I guess that's it."

And that was it. No tears, no *I'll die if you leave me,* no *How could you do this to me?* Neil didn't sound like a man hiding his pain. He sounded like someone trying to mask his relief.

Somewhere in the recesses of my brain a voice told me that this was what I'd dreaded all along—not hearing that someone couldn't live without me, but finding out how easily he could.

At least I didn't have to wonder whose voice spoke in my head. This time, it was my own.

***

The next morning, Marnie greeted me with a latte, covered in enough caramel syrup to make my teeth rot from twenty paces out, along with a batch of scones fresh from the bakery across the street. I had asked for them on instinct. I realized now I hadn't experienced enough of Ireland to know whether they even made them here. I fell on them like a wanderer in the Sahara on a stray bottle of Evian.

Caffeine, quality baked goods, and no one wanting me dead. For the moment, this was enough.

Between that and the new outfit Marnie supplied me —jeans and a cashmere sweater complete with Stella Mc-Cartney lingerie—I felt almost human. My good mood lasted right up until we stopped by Carlos' hospital room on the way out. It took my breath away to see the handsome, vibrant man lying motionless and be-tubed on a narrow bed. He shifted his head toward me. I didn't know whether he remembered my name, but at least he was conscious. "Believe it or not, he looks tons better today," Jane said. She looked better than yesterday, too, so I believed her. "I'm sorry to hold you up, but would you stay with him for a minute? I see Carlos' surgeon passing by and I want to get an update from him."

I turned around and saw an Asian man nearly as tall as Jane who managed to make scrubs into a good look, trying to jot something on a clipboard while holding a paper coffee cup. I looked to Marnie, who nodded. "We've got time before our flight leaves."

Jane walked to the hospital bed. "Emmaline is here, Carlos. She wanted to say good-bye."

I watched Jane disappear to the relative freedom of the hallway and then forced my eyes back to Carlos. He made an effort to sit up, before I stopped him. "Hope you're...okay." His voice came out raspy and weak.

"I'm fine. Thanks to you and Jane and Edward. I owe all of you." I swallowed. "How are you?"

His hand came up no more than a fraction of an inch, but I still caught the dismissive gesture. "Flesh wound."

"How long are they going to keep you here?"

"Don't know." He took two steadying breaths. "Week...maybe two."

Maybe more.

"Got to get...back to work."

I gave the closest thing to a smile I could muster. "FTP lost its leader. I think your work here is done."

We continued our awkward conversation, pausing a second after each comment as he caught his breath, until I saw Jane walk through the door holding a cup of coffee. I gave his hand a quick squeeze and backed away. His face gained some color as he talked, but his breathing grew more labored with each word he spoke. "I'll let you be. Take care, and thanks again. From the bottom of my heart."

242

"My pleasure," he managed.

I turned to go, but before I got to the end of the bed, he choked out, "Watch yourself. Something…not done."

Jane pointed her finger at him. "Quiet now, or I'll sic the nurse on you. The mean one with the rectal thermometer." While Carlos gave a pathetic attempt at a laugh, Jane walked me to the door. "He's still a little incoherent. Don't worry about it."

Something bothered her, but I didn't know if it stemmed from Carlos' words or the surgeon's. "What did his doctor say?"

She took a sip of the coffee. "Everything looks the same. He really just stopped by to bring me a coffee, since I couldn't get away."

"He looks good in scrubs and he brings you coffee? Why couldn't I have gotten that doctor?"

She gave me a scolding cluck of her tongue. "I'm sure your doctor was just as good as Ben."

I stared at her, and lowered my voice to a whisper. "Ben, is it? You and Carlos' surgeon are on a first name basis?"

"Things were touch and go with Carlos for the first thirty-six hours. Ben came by a lot to check in. He saw me drinking a coffee from the cafeteria and said they had better stuff in the staff lounge, so he brought me a cup. Now he brings me some whenever he's on this floor."

I tried to keep a straight face and failed. "Be sure you let Carlos know about your new coffee delivery boy."

She rolled her eyes. "Please, Emmy. Carlos won't care if I go out with someone else. You saw how he reacted when I said Kevin asked me out. He just laughed."

I took her arm and pulled her into the hallway, around the door jamb. "You said men are my forte, so let me

243

straighten this out for you. The bureaucrat who plays with his ferret? He's not competition for a guy like Carlos." I pointed down the hall, where Gentle Ben stood talking with a patient. "Now, the thirty-something trauma surgeon who looks like Chow Yun-Fat's sexier younger brother? He's competition."

Jane turned a shade of red I didn't know her skin could get. "Ben is a nice man with good taste in coffee." She took a sip of the beverage and then, in a voice so low I could barely hear it, added, "The fact that he's sexy is just a bonus."

"Does Carlos know that *Crouching Tiger, Hidden Dragon* is your favorite movie ever? Because if not, I'm so going to tell him."

She gave me a tight hug. "Get out of here before I have to hurt you and you get readmitted."

I hugged her back. I desperately wanted to get out of the hospital, but abandoning Jane felt wrong. "When you're back in the States, call me. We need some best friend time."

"I promise." She gave me one last squeeze. "Now go."

"In a second." I gestured to her to stay put and walked back over to the patient. "Carlos, do you feel up to talking to your surgeon?"

He yawned. "No...kind of sleepy."

"Okay." I patted the edge of his bed. "I'll tell Jane to go ahead. I'll stay with you till she gets back."

"She's talking to him?"

"They're going to get some coffee in the doctors' lounge. She'll be back in fifteen or twenty minutes."

He looked at me and then used all his energy to lift his head a smidgen off his pillow. "Cali..."

He didn't yell, he didn't have the strength for that, but he said it louder than he'd said anything else this morning. Jane came running back to his side. "What? What is it?"

I pulled Marnie out of the room while they were talking.

"What was that all about?" Marnie asked.

I smiled back at the hospital room as I jabbed the elevator button. "Just giving Jane's evolution a little push."

***

On the way to the airport, after I filled Marnie in on our impolite departure, I puzzled over Carlos' earlier comment. He was weak, and his breathing sounded like an eighty-year-old emphysema victim, but he didn't strike me as incoherent. What wasn't finished?

When the taxi dropped us off, I still had no answer. Forget it, I told myself. He's on a lot of painkillers.

We met up with Edward at the terminal. He surveyed me critically. "You seem ready to take on the world again."

"I'm perfectly happy to let the world fend for itself, thanks." I put my hand through the crook of Marnie's arm. "I plan to spend the next few days doing some extremely low-key sight-seeing and letting Marnie wait on me hand and foot."

She made a face, but squeezed my hand as though afraid of losing track of it. "Which, for once, you just might get, dear girl. As long as you promise to never, ever scare me like that again."

"My days of having my life threatened are over, Marnie. Never again. I promise."

I should have listened to that voice in my head saying *Never say never.*

***

The Aer Lingus jet touched down peacefully in London after barely an hour in the air. I compared the journey in my head to the midnight escape that had taken us out of Britain. Daylight and windows add a lot to a journey. Sure, Marnie had to pull off a diplomatic miracle to get the customs agents to let us into Britain when our passports showed no stamp out, but even so, it beat the CIA red-eye service.

Once on the ground, Marnie stuck me with her bag and headed to the ladies' room, leaving me alone with Edward at last.

"You must be glad to be home." Well, that took the prize for the stupidest opening line I have ever resorted to in all of my thirty-nine years. Why had my brain suddenly ceased to function?

"Indeed." He knew Marnie's bag constituted our one and only carry-on, but he looked at it as though searching for the rest of the luggage. I couldn't remember ever flying before and taking nothing with me. Marnie brought Edward's and my passports with her to Ireland and restored them to us. Other than that, we had no possessions. I supposed at some point my suitcase back in the first safe house might be restored to me, but somehow finding out didn't rank high on my priority list just now. "You must be thrilled to be out of Ireland."

I thought about that for a second. "Oddly enough, no. I mean, I'm glad to be away from Ceann and Lacey and anyone else who wanted to kill us, but..." My voice trailed off as I thought about all the non-lethal experiences I'd had there. Kissing Edward. Toasting life with Paddy and Fi. Walking through some of the most beautiful greenery on the planet. Drinking Sheridan's. Kissing Edward.

246

He smiled. "I know how you feel."

I knew it. I knew he—

"Considering how awful the English have treated the Irish over the years, the surprising thing isn't how many people there want to kill us. It's that most people there don't. Most of the Irish people we encountered just saw me as a tourist, not the emissary of a culture that caused them pain."

Okay, yes, that was a miracle and a testament to the Irish spirit, but I hadn't been thinking that at all. I waited for him to say more, something slightly more personal, but he didn't. I cleared my throat. "You might want to know—I broke up with Neil."

His eyes met mine for a heated instant and then scanned Marnie's luggage with the same intensity. "That's a big step. How do you feel about that?"

I put one foot behind the other and rubbed my ankle as if the top of my left sneaker needed polishing. "It went better than I expected, really. He wasn't upset. Sounded kind of grateful, almost."

"I didn't ask what he thought." Edward snapped the words like dry sticks. "You're the one who made the decision."

I blinked a couple of times, staring out the window that substituted for a wall in this corridor. Pale London sunshine battled with clouds and seemed likely to lose. "We both made the decision. I was just the first to say it out loud."

"Funny thing—I called Ashley last night and asked if she might try going out with me again."

The world tilted in front of me as if his words had pushed me back into the Irish Sea. I felt for the handle on Marnie's roller bag, trying to find my balance. "You...you're sure that's what you want?"

"I think so."

Marnie exited the bathroom and headed our way. Before I could signal her to give us a minute, Edward saw her, too. "I realize you didn't ask for my advice, Emmaline, but if you had, I'd say you should give yourself some time. I'd say that if you dated anyone right now, you'd just do it because you thought you couldn't survive on your own, when in fact you're much stronger than you think. Not that you asked." He waved at my aunt and then walked away without looking back.

Marnie arrived at my side and caught me a split second before I would have fallen to the ground.

***

I was alone.

Okay, not literally. Marnie drove me home, and my mother and father called on the way, and everyone but the dog had to take a turn talking to me. They put the phone up to Sneakers' head, but he didn't have anything to say.

Pippa took the phone after the Sneakers snub. "I ran into Neil today at the Java Stop. He said you guys broke up."

My eyes flew open. "He told you that?"

"Yeah, after I almost tackled him. I thought he was being rude, ducking out without saying anything to me. Once he told me, I couldn't blame him for trying to give me the slip. Why didn't you tell me you were thinking of breaking up? Is there someone else?"

"No." Not for lack of trying, but... "I've been through a lot. It made me think about what I want."

"And you want to be alone?" She couldn't have sounded more shocked if I'd said I wanted to take up random acts of cannibalism.

248

"No." I rubbed my temples with the thumb and index finger of my free hand. "I really don't, but I don't want to mark time in a dead relationship, either."

"Maybe you just need to try harder. Neil looked lost without you, Emmy. I bet you could patch things up. Just tell him you've gone through a traumatic time and you weren't thinking straight when you broke up with him."

A huge sigh escaped my lips. "I'd have to lie to do it, Pippa. If anything, the trauma helped me to think more clearly, at least about this."

Silence reigned for five seconds. Five blessed, wonderful seconds.

"You'd really rather be alone than with Neil?"

I thought about that. I still wanted to believe something could happen with Edward, but if it didn't? If Neil and alone really comprised my only choices, I'd choose singlehood?

"Yes."

That stunned us both into silence.

At last she took a breath. "Wow. Well...good for you, Emmy."

"Thanks."

"Now, grab a pen. Mom just gave me a list of souvenirs she wants you to bring home."

Harry took the phone from Pippa after I got the list. I heard voices passing, letting me know he was walking somewhere, and then suddenly all I heard was silence. Unless I missed my guess, he'd just found a place in the house where no one could hear him. "Emmy, when you get back we need to talk."

Harry and I talked easily enough the two or three times a year we were actually in the same room, but I couldn't recall a time when we ever *needed* to before. "Okay…what's up?"

"Jane called me and told me about your examination of the files on Edward's family. She thought I might want to offer you a job."

"A job?" My stomach clenched. "You work for the CIA too?"

"No."

I exhaled all the breath in my body. I couldn't handle any more surprises just now.

"I work for the FBI."

Well, it couldn't be worse than working for the CIA. The FBI might let me look out the window.

***

When we got to Marnie's townhouse, she poured me a large glass of wine and put me to bed. With a little help from the alcohol, my brain switched to the off position for the next couple of hours. Strange dreams swam through my sleep though. The house in Ireland. Jane shoving me and Edward into the closet "because you deserve it." Other times, a ghost chasing after us, yelling, "Not till you say you're sorry," in an accent that alternated between English, Scottish and Irish.

Did ghosts yell? I always thought they just moaned or whispered. Perhaps it depended on how mad they were.

Not till you say you're sorry.

When I woke up from these dreams, I flashed back to Carlos in the hospital room. *Something not done.*

I ran all this by Marnie over breakfast. "It's nuts, right? Carlos' drug-induced paranoia. Evidently it's catching."

The perfectly made-up cupid's bow lips didn't part for some time.

I leaned toward her. "They confessed. The megalomaniac told me all about the kidnapping, right before sending me to what was supposed to be a watery grave. That didn't leave any loose ends. Right?"

She took a deep breath and held it. I was ready to drop the whole thing and get another cup of tea when she finally said, "He told you someone convinced him to kidnap Edward. Did he ever say who?"

A picture formed in my head, like a kaleidoscope that had finally shifted random pieces into a recognizable shape. "Oh, hell, Marnie...I think I know."

CHAPTER TWENTY-FIVE

"Ashley?" Marnie said the name for the fourth time as she shifted onto the M20. She hated the suggestion that we drive down to the Alderwood ancestral home and explain my suspicions to Edward, but she couldn't find a hole in my theory. Within ten minutes we were on the road.

"It all adds up."

"What adds up? Everything you've said is circumstantial. You have no proof."

I ticked the points off on my fingers. "Edward said the man convicted of killing his father and mother never confessed. He said John and Mary fought to put the man in prison. The man had a baby daughter when the trial happened. A daughter who grew up without her dad."

"Just because Ashley is about the right age doesn't make her the one."

"She's the right age. She's a redhead, just like her father was."

"Which could be a dye job for all you know."

"She works at the bank that has Edward's money. She handles his accounts. That's how they met." I shook my head. "Marnie, she had to know that last deposit came from a different account. She knew, and she didn't tell him."

Marnie's eyes cut from the road to me and back, and then she stepped on the gas.

***

He had to be there. He had to.

Marnie drove faster than any sane person should and it still didn't satisfy me. Even if I'd ever known Edward's number, his phone had disappeared in the kidnapping from the embassy party, just like mine had. Jane had replaced her phone and Carlos' when we'd set up our pub sting, but no one had seen any point in getting one for Edward or me. Marnie had a number for the main house, the one she'd found to get Edward's passport for him, but no mobile number for anyone. Dialing the landline got me a recording. I left a message, trying my best to sound urgent but not insane. "Edward, it's Emmaline. I think you might be in trouble. Don't trust Ashley, okay? Please call me the second you get this."

It sounded insane anyway. Oh, well. Right now, I had more important things to worry about than how I might be perceived on voicemail. I put the phone back in Marnie's purse. "How much farther do we have to go?"

Marnie stared at the road in steely concentration. "Another fifteen minutes. If I drive any faster we're going to get pulled over." She gave a mirthless laugh. "Maybe that's a good thing. We probably should call the police anyhow."

"I thought of that, but what would I tell them? You still have your doubts and you know all the details. As far as I know, the CIA and British Intelligence kept the local police out of the loop. There was something in the tabloids about the Irish police intercepting the head of FTP, but the CIA pulled some strings and kept all of our names out of it."

Marnie pushed the little Austin Mini faster down the highway.

We made a journey that should have taken us ninety minutes in sixty-eight. For better or worse, no police interfered. The house stood at the end of a quarter-mile hedge-lined drive, shuttered and silent, with two cars parked in front. I couldn't tell whether either belonged to Edward, or his adoptive mother Mary, or Ashley, for that matter.

The bone-white house, imposing in its Georgian grandeur, didn't reveal anything except the architect's obsession with symmetry. Nothing moved inside its two rows of double-hung sash windows and no one leapt from behind the columns flanking the front entrance. We walked out into the grounds. At last, my straining ears detected noise. I might have imagined it. Heck, I'd never been here before, the repetitive scraping sound could occur every morning during elevensies for all I knew. I couldn't see anything unusual, but I moved toward the sound anyhow.

Marnie followed me. "What are you —"

I turned to her and put my finger to my lips. No sense giving advance warning if someone was up to no good.

Or maybe Paddy was right, I had gone right round the bend, and the sound meant only that the Alderwood estate had extraordinarily organized squirrels. At the moment I could imagine nothing more wonderful than finding out I'd overreacted. The fact that I might enjoy being incorrect cemented the knowledge in my soul that something was very wrong indeed.

For about ten minutes, we walked quietly into the forest adjacent to Edward's family home. I listened intently. An occasional breeze brushing the leaves together. A bird or two. Scratching noises that sounded random enough to come from unchoreographed rodents.

And then finally, voices. I couldn't make out any words, but I knew that one of them belonged to Edward.

Another two steps and I saw figures. Forcing myself to go slower, I used the trees as cover. Marnie stuck close by me, each of us trying desperately to blend in with the foliage.

Ashley stood over a hole in the ground, holding a gun aimed at Edward and looking considerably less elegant than when I'd seen her at Marnie's party. Edward stood at the bottom of an oblong hole, alternately shoveling dirt into a bucket and then tossing the bucket's contents out on to the ground above to make space.

I couldn't believe we'd made it here before she shot him, until I got a better look. Ashley leaned against a tree. Edward stood chest-deep in the hole. It had probably taken him hours to get this far.

I motioned to Marnie for her to go back to the house. She shook her head and pointed at the ground. She was staying put. Damn it. She pulled out her phone and pressed the "9" button three times. The U.K. emergency number. Waiting till Edward started to shovel again, she pressed *send* and put the phone in her pocket.

"9-9-9, what is your emergency?"

On a London street, no one would even have registered the words, but in this quiet forest, it came through like a bullhorn. Marnie tried to end the call, dropping her cell in the attempt, and Ashley's head snapped toward us.

First, she shot the phone.

Damn. Evidently the woman had some marksmanship skills. I stepped forward and pushed Marnie behind me, willing my eyes away from the fractured gadget. "Hi, Ashley."

She backed up, sweeping the gun back and forth from Edward to me and Marnie. At least that meant she couldn't concentrate on any one of us for long. That was progress, right?

I tried to smile at her, but the corners of my mouth wouldn't go up. "I don't think we've met. I'm Emmaline —"

"I know who you are." She waved the gun at me. "You're the new chippy. Edward hasn't been able to take his eyes off you since you walked into that absurd party." Her upper lip curled into a farcical smile, her lower lip looking as though it had been dragged along in the expression against its will. "As you can see, Edward's busy just now. You two have just made him busier."

I took a deep breath. "Ashley, you don't want to do this."

She laughed. Not a forced, *your words don't affect me* chuckle, but an actual guffaw. "Oh, how absurd, Emmaline. There is nothing in life I want to do more than this. Surely you understand that."

"No, I don't." Crap. I had just finished stalling for time with the Free the People lunatics, and now it was time to start with Ashley. I'd have to wrestle with my feelings of frustration later, though. Just now I needed to focus. "Explain it to me."

"Please," Marnie said. "Maybe it'll help to tell us."

"You're an optimist, aren't you?" Ashley's smile made the chilly forest seem positively glacial. "Thinking you'll be around long enough to hear."

Marnie didn't flinch. "I'm a realist. You plan to bury us out here, and it'll take Edward time to dig two more graves."

"I could have you two dig your own graves."

"Then you'd have to wait several days. Look at his arm muscles and look at mine. I'll drop dead of a heart attack and then you'll have to finish digging the hole yourself."

256

Ashley looked like she wanted to argue, but Marnie's logic was tight. My new adversary focused on me instead. "You couldn't understand if I did tell you. You grew up with your whole family. What could you possibly know about loss?"

I swallowed hard. I'd nursed a grudge for a lost dream for fifteen years. What if that dream had been for a father of my own? "I can't imagine how hard it must have been to grow up without your father, Ashley."

"That was only part of it." Her mouth puckered, like the memory tasted sour. "I had no father and I grew up as the daughter of a murderer. Clever trick, to deprive a person of a parent and still saddle her with his reputation. Do you know how hard my mum struggled to keep a roof over our heads?"

"I'm sure it was awful." I tried not to look at the gun she kept moving between us and Edward. "Your father always maintained his innocence, didn't he?"

"Right up till the day he died." She vented several shallow breaths, maybe to stop herself from hyperventilating. "He didn't do anything, but someone had to go to prison. An earl died. The world needed a scapegoat." She flicked the hand with the gun in the air. I really wished she'd stop gesturing with that hand.

"But why go after Edward?" I folded my arms. Weak sunlight broke through the clouds elsewhere on the estate, but it was dark and cold under these trees, and I hadn't thought to bring a heavy coat on this rescue mission. "Surely he of all people suffered as much as you did. He lost both parents, gained a guardian with a dicey reputation, and forfeited a limb. Wasn't that enough?"

For the first time since Marnie and I arrived, a shadow of uncertainty passed over Ashley's face. "I never wanted to hurt Edward, really." She looked at him with something

257

approaching tenderness. "You actually handled things rather well, breaking up with me because you knew you weren't over your former wife."

I gritted my teeth. "Then why are you out here, ready to kill him?"

"It has to be done. It's justice. His adoptive mother, Mary, pushed for my father to go to prison. She'll tell you she was doing it for Edward, but that wasn't all she got. Taking care of him gave her and her husband control over lots of money. They moved into the main house. Edward never treated them like servants. They lost nothing, and they gained everything. Now, when I kill Edward, she'll lose him, and she'll get kicked out of that fancy house. She's not blood family. The National Heritage Trust won't let her continue to live there after he dies. Maybe she'll finally understand what it's like to have someone take away what you love."

Staring at Ashley, I felt an unwanted stab of pity. She had completely devoted herself to this idea of retribution by the death of another person—someone she didn't even particularly dislike.

I looked back at my aunt. The stolid diplomatic mask remained in place. There's a reason I never play poker with Marnie.

A glint off Marnie's late iPhone caught my eye. Did she succeed in ending the call before she dropped the phone, or did the emergency operator hear the shot? Was help on the way? For now, I could only stall and pray.

God, please don't tell me you sent me back to London to die.

"I'm curious, Ashley. How long have you been involved with FTP?"

A corner of her mouth turned up, a wry smile that battled with the rest of her determined face. "The accountant is playing detective. How cute. Stick with numbers, slag."

"You know, people don't understand accounting. It isn't really about numbers. It's about details. You categorize things so you can see what matches and what doesn't."

Ashley yawned.

"FTP goes after people to get money. Yet, deposits from one of the accounts affiliated with FTP put money *into* Edward's account." I studied her face. "It was you, right? You found a way to move funds around at the bank. You put that money into Edward's account to make him an attractive target."

"FTP loved that I worked in a bank." She pursed her lips, as though trying not to smile. "I could help them find ways to launder the funds they raised, and I bloody rescued them when one of their less intelligent members tried to bring a bag full of cash donations from sympathetic Americans. The cretin didn't realize that bringing that much money on a plane would raise eyebrows. A couple of calls and some back-dated paperwork, I was able to convince them the man owed Edward a debt and agreed to pay in cash to avoid tax issues on both sides of the Atlantic."

"Given Edward's finances, you must have had to work some magic to make him look good enough to kidnap."

"God, yes. His accounts were pathetic. When his father-in-law's money stopped coming in I worried they'd find him not worth the trouble." She gave a short sigh. "I didn't know you'd be there with him, so they'd have to lift you, too."

"Of course, you knew the money wasn't really an issue. You never intended for him to live long enough to ransom."

The setting on her features switched over to grim. "I had it all worked out with MacCallum—you know him as Ceann, probably. I was going to take over guard duty on the second day and, while I stood watch, there would have been an incident where I had no choice but to shoot him. MacCallum would've disposed of the body and FTP would get the blame for the disappearance. No one would connect it to me."

"Only you forgot to tell him that I was a poor little cripple." Edward spoke for the first time since I'd arrived. His voice sounded raw. No water breaks for the grave-digger, I gathered.

"Who'd have thought MacCallum was so worried about his image?" Ashley shook her head. "Thought it'd look bad to shake down a toff just because he had a fake leg. MacCallum's grandfather wouldn't have worried about it, I can tell you that." She bared her teeth at Edward—you could call it a smile, but I wouldn't. "His grandfather was involved with an Irish separatist group—the people actually responsible for your parents' death. Did you know?"

Edward's skin, even in this shaded grove, went pale. "How do you know that?"

"He told me when I brought you up as a potential target. Seems your father fleeced the entire village where his company was located in Ireland, and the locals tired of it. One of the more radical groups decided to make an example out of him. Something the police might have found out if your family hadn't already thrown all their weight into putting my father away."

We all fell silent after that.

***

Ashley enlisted Marnie and me to scoop dirt out of the hole with the bucket after Edward shoveled earth into it. As the minutes crept silently by one question got cleared up; no one was coming to help. Whether they thought the call a hoax or just lost any signal to trace when Ashley shot the phone, I didn't know, but it amounted to the same result.

Edward had nearly finished the second hole—I refused to call it a grave, even in my own head—when I stood up to ease my back. Pitching dirt involved a lot of crouching. "I'm curious, Ashley. Your buddy MacCallum told us he had connections with the police and that's how he found out the details I gave them. Who was the mole in the precinct?" I tried to keep my voice even. "You're going to kill us, so there's no harm in telling. We won't be able to pass the information on."

Edward dropped the shovel, and Marnie had a coughing fit.

Ashley shrugged. "There is no mole." She looked at Edward, who picked the shovel up and tossed a last clot of dirt out into the trees. "You called Mary and she was good enough to call me. I guess you don't keep her up to date on your love life, dearest, because she thought I'd be worried. She told me the whole story."

"Thoughtful of her." Marnie rubbed each of her arms with the other hand. Clearly I wasn't the only one with aching muscles. "And you promptly relayed all this information to MacCallum?"

Ashley giggled. "I might have sent a text. He was cross with me for not telling him about Edward's lack of limb, but he still trusted me enough to listen when I said you knew too much." She took a deep breath and exhaled slowly. "We met at the funeral of a man who'd shared a cell with both of our fathers at different times. We bonded over our shared experience of jailbird parents. You don't know what it's like unless you've lived it."

Edward leaned on the shovel. "Ashley, I'm sorry. You had a hard life and you didn't deserve that." He took a deep breath. "You can still walk away from this. Put the gun down. You haven't actually hurt anyone yet. You can have a good life from here."

"I have nothing!" Ashley screamed, gesticulating with the gun. Dear God, please let her stop doing that. "My parents are both dead. I have no friends. By now, FTP knows that I used their money in your accounts, so they're probably going to kill me. Don't you see? There's no going back now."

I risked looking away from her long enough to glance at Marnie, but her expression confirmed that she agreed with my assessment. Ashley was done telling stories.

Our captor shoved the gun toward Edward. "Get out. This hole is deep enough. Start on the last one."

I thought about pointing out that the hole measured maybe four feet deep, instead of the six that television told me were industry standard, but Ashley didn't seem worried. It gave her less dirt to shovel back on afterwards, so maybe she liked it that way. It'd still give her a good head start before any animals dug up the corpse.

Edward put the shovel on the ground outside the hole. He reached up to Ashley. "I need a bit of leverage to get out. Lend a hand?"

He probably could have hoisted himself out, but after—at a guess—six hours of digging, maybe not. Ashley scowled. "Not bloody likely. Get your chippy here to do it."

I lay flat on the ground and extended a hand. Marnie sat on my legs, to give maximum leverage. Between all of us, he managed to clamber up to ground level again. Reaching the top, he fell down on his knees and stretched his arms out

262

in front of him. Yoga—child's pose. At this moment, I don't think even Jane's hand on his fanny could have gotten him as far as downward-facing dog.

Ashley jabbed him with the butt of the gun. "Get up. You've one more to go. Likely no one is close enough to hear the shots, but I'd rather shoot you all together so no one has time to investigate before I finish the job."

Edward groaned. "Ashley, give me a minute. I've been digging for hours."

She grabbed the barrel of the gun and hit Edward in the head with the butt of it. "Move!"

In the second it took her to readjust the gun, I grabbed the shovel and swung at her. She saw it coming and moved, but the steel end made solid contact with her upper arm.

She screamed and fell, tumbling over Edward's still outstretched body. The gun flew out of her hand and landed in the dirt. I dropped the shovel and dove for it at the same time as she scrambled over. I moved fast, but she didn't have as far to go. Her fingers clawed toward it, her nails brushing against the metal.

Something moved to my left. I heard a loud crunch and Ashley's fingers retreated.

I grabbed the gun and wrapped my fingers around it as though I intended it to become part of my flesh. "Get in the hole, lunatic!"

Marnie prodded her with the shovel. Ashley glared at me, drenched in loathing. She held her right hand, the wrist dangling at an unnatural angle. Pissed off Marnie and a shovel are not good for bone health.

Ashley swung her legs over the edge, but not before shooting me one more glare. "Die, you bloody whore."

263

I kicked her into the hole and backed away, aiming the gun at her and clicking the safety lever. "Nobody dies today, damn it. Now shut the hell up."

Edward crawled on his hands and knees toward a nearby tree and found Ashley's purse. He dug out her phone and dialed 999. This time, Emergency Services got the whole story. We heard sirens before Edward got off the phone.

Marnie eased up next to me and put a hand over the one I used to hold the gun. She pressed her face next to mine. I took a deep breath and thought how soft my aunt's cheek felt when she said in my ear, "You know you just turned the safety on instead of off, right?"

"Of course. Would you take this?" I handed her the gun and, for the first time in my life, fainted dead away.

Good thing my ancestors were already dead, because the shame would have killed them.

CHAPTER TWENTY-SIX

By the time I came to, the police had Ashley out of the pit and in handcuffs—the genuine metal article. She spat invectives at us every step of the way as they led her to the police car.

Edward shook his head. "I've got to call my lawyer."

My thoughts still had fuzzy edges, and I thought I'd heard him wrong. "What do you need a lawyer for?"

"Not for me. For Ashley."

I stared at him. "You're kidding. After everything she did today, you still want her?"

He narrowed his eyes at me. "Good Lord, no. I'm not that much a glutton for punishment." His face grew grim. "Trouble is, she's not completely wrong. Mary, John and my uncle all used every ounce of influence my family name had to put her father away. I was only eleven when the trial took place, but even I remember that much. To be fair, I think they truly believed him guilty, but I doubt very much that the investigation of the crash was as thorough as it should have been." He scraped his prosthetic foot through the brush. "My family caused Ashley a lot of pain. My father took the bread out of thousands of people's mouths. I have a lot of karma to make up for, and getting Ashley some help seems like the place to start."

My rampant skepticism must have colored my face because he smiled. "By 'help,' I'm thinking a good psychiatric facility somewhere."

I glanced at the police car. "For a start."

The police drove back to the main house, flattening a bed of poppies along the way. All this vehicular traffic played havoc with the landscaping, but Edward didn't seem to mind. I guess two brushes with death inside of a week had focused his priorities.

Two officers dispatched Ashley to the local jail, while the remaining four stayed to question the rest of us in the estate's kitchen. They found Mary tied to the pipes under the sink. Aside from the awkward position, she was unharmed, but that didn't stop her from bursting into tears as soon as she saw Edward. Once the police freed her, Edward put his arms around her and led her to the table. A gray-haired officer named Sanderson talked to her in low tones but got nothing besides sobs for a good ten minutes.

I wondered whether Ashley might try to spin the blame our way. When the police arrived, she had stood in a shallow grave and Marnie had a gun on her. I might have tried, if I'd been her. From what I heard the officers saying, however, Ashley spent all her vocal power bemoaning her lack of success.

Given his cash constraints, I wondered if Edward had enough money to take care of Ashley's psychiatric care. She was going to need a lot of it.

The police questioned us for several hours, before deciding they had enough information. After they left and Mary force-fed us dinner, the clock said 8:00pm, and my eyelids said *bedtime*. Edward and Mary insisted that we stay the night. They only had one guest room made up, but it would not take long to make up another. I didn't let Marnie get all the way through her token protest before saying, "We'd be so grateful, thank you." I told them one bed would be fine. At the moment, isolating myself from the herd had zero appeal.

I remember climbing into a queen size bed, telling Marnie I loved her as she got into the other side, and thinking what a fun habit Edward and I had developed of pressing hospitality on one another after police questioning. Then I think both Marnie and I fell asleep before we finished lying down. Good thing gravity took care of the rest.

***

When I woke up, the digital clock on the end table said one in the morning.

Apparently, I had developed a pattern. Face death, sleep for a few hours, wake up to relive the horror. You know you've had too much trauma in your life when you've formed a routine around it.

Wide awake, I got out of bed gently so as not to wake Marnie. She, at least, appeared to be sleeping peacefully. I crept downstairs and headed toward the kitchen. No one could begrudge me a cup of tea and a scone, given the circumstances.

The door separating the kitchen from the main hallway was closed when I got to my destination, but light already shone through the crack in the doorframe. I froze and listened. Paranoid? Yep. With my recent past, I figured I was entitled.

I heard liquid pouring, the refrigerator door opening, and a second later the sound of a spoon making a quiet clatter in a cup. Probably someone breaking into the house to complete Ashley's mission wouldn't sit down and make a cup of tea first.

I pushed the door open and saw Edward sitting at a table on the left side of the pristine dark wood kitchen, a cup in his hand as he stared out the window to the back garden. "Hey."

I spoke as softly as I could, so as not to spook him, but he still jostled the cup and spilled a few drops as he turned to me. "Hello." He dabbed ineffectually at the liquid on the table with his finger. "You couldn't sleep, either?"

"Not for long. Too much adrenaline still in my system, I guess."

He put the cup down and stood up. Since he still had the prosthetic leg attached, I suspected he hadn't gone to bed at all. Having enough experience of Edward's sleeping habits, I knew he took it off whenever he wanted serious shut-eye. He gestured toward the cup. "Care for some?"

"Yes, please." I sat at the table and watched as he prepared it. "Your brain still racing too?"

He smiled, the weariness of the day stopping his mouth from spreading too wide. "Can't stop hearing threats in every innocent creak. I suppose that'll take a few days to work out of my system."

"Too bad I'm not Jane. I'm sure she could show you some handy yoga poses to soothe your mind...or at least massage your backside for you."

He turned to me, eyebrows an inch higher than usual. "How did you—"

"You had the door open a little too wide, and I woke up from my nap a bit too early." I looked out the window, straining to see something besides my own reflection. "I don't blame you, you know. Jane's very pretty."

"She is, but if I'm going to have someone caressing my backside, I'd rather it were you. Of course, I suspect you already knew that."

I looked up and found him staring at me. All thoughts of tea left my head. "You were the one who wanted to go off with Ashley. You said I was just using you so I wouldn't be lonely."

"Maybe I don't mind so much just now." He walked over and took my hand, gently pulling me up out of the chair.

A cavalcade of voices ran through my head, telling me all the reasons why this was a bad idea. Too soon, too much trauma, heightened emotions…I gave them all the boot and reached for him. "Your room," I whispered. "Mine's occupied."

By some miracle, we made it up to his room without waking anyone. Kicking the door closed, he pulled me to him and kissed me, licking into my mouth like I held undiscovered treasures. After a few seconds, he switched to nuzzling my ear. "Where did we leave off, when we got interrupted?"

I guided his hand up under my shirt. "I think it was just about here."

This time, we finished what we started.

***

Sun streaked through a gap in the curtains in laser fashion, landing right on my eye. Good Lord. Some adjustments to the drapes would have to happen before I spent any more nights here.

I sat bolt upright. Spend more nights here? Did Edward want that? Did *I* want that? Was I ready to forgive London, to move into what was basically a suburb—no farther than Santa Rosa was from San Francisco?

269

Get a grip, Spencer, I told myself. Barely two days after you broke up with Neil and here you are ready to annex yourself to the next available male. You had one night together. That doesn't usually lead to happily ever after.

Edward slept soundly. Small wonder, after a day of digging graves and a night of enthusiastic and—damn it—extraordinarily satisfying sex. His ex must have had psychological issues. No sane woman could prefer money over what that man could do with his tongue. Prosthetic leg? I barely even noticed.

I sighed and leaned my head back against the headboard, which creaked like it might split in two. Edward stirred beside me and cast a lazy eye in my direction. "Good morning."

"Hi." I chewed on my pinky finger.

He propped himself up on an elbow. "Something wrong?"

He looked perfectly calm. Where were his roiling emotions? How could he just lay there, looking like his big decision was what to have for breakfast?

I clutched the sheet to my naked torso. "Nothing. No problem. I'll just get my things."

He sat up, grogginess fading. "In a rush, are you?"

I felt down to the floor for my clothes, trying to expose as little flesh as possible while putting them on. "No, I just don't want to be in the way."

"You're not."

"Edward, I'm a grown woman. I know what this was, okay?"

"Really? Care to enlighten me?"

"It was a...singular event." Somehow, the phrase *one-night stand* caught in my throat like a mouthful of cotton. "Look, you don't need to let me down easy. I know you're

270

still getting over your ex, and I just broke up with Neil. I'm not ready to give up my whole life in California to move here. Not that I'm assuming you want that, I just—"

"And I'm not ready to chuck everything and move to San Francisco." He put out his hand and clasped mine, stopping me from doing up any more buttons. "But I could think about making a visit, sometime soon. You see..." he kissed each of my fingers, "I just met this incredible woman who saved my life, and she lives around there."

The temptation to take the shirt off and let him continue kissing things ran through me for a second, but another thought chilled it. "Long distance? Right after a huge trauma? You know that's generally a terrible idea, right?"

"Generally, yes." He stopped kissing my fingers but didn't let them go. "Yesterday morning I thought going back to Ashley meant safety. It turned out to be the most dangerous choice I've ever made. Now, risky doesn't look so bad."

I sighed. "Jane had it right, you know. I don't do well being alone, and long distance is kind of like being alone, but worse."

Edward let go of my hand. "It is a gamble."

I forced myself to look him straight in the eyes. "Do you want to gamble on someone when you don't even know her middle name?"

The beginnings of a smile lit his face. "Why? Is it hideous?"

I swatted his arm. "It's Anne. With an E. All of us girls have the middle name Anne, because my mother was obsessed with *Anne of Green Gables* back then."

He frowned. "You're right. That does rather put a damper on things."

I searched his face for clues, but didn't find any. "Why?"

271

"My mother loved those books too, and she made me read them when I was small. Terribly sappy."

I swatted his arm. "You take that back. I love those books."

He grinned. "You don't expect me to change my middle name to Gilbert, do you?"

"No, I expect you to kiss me rather thoroughly before we have to go downstairs and get grilled by your mother and my aunt."

"Yes, ma'am." He put an arm around me and guided me back down to the bed. "Anything for my kindred spirit."

***

The flight to San Francisco ran three hours late and hit a minefield of turbulence on the way. Somehow, though, as Edward, Marnie and I made our way through customs, I still found myself smiling.

"Cordelia, Philippa and Harrison, right?" Edward ticked off my siblings' names on his fingers.

"Very good. Get through meeting them without dashing back on the plane and I'll buy you a drink."

Marnie clapped her hands together. "We passed a cute little place in the Mission District on the way home. Let's all get a drink."

"The Mission District." Edward stared out the window, as though he could see the city instead of just endless acres of tarmac. "I was there once. It'll be interesting to see how the place has changed."

"You visited San Francisco?" I couldn't remember him ever mentioning it. "When was this?"

"Fifteen years ago. Came to see a cousin who worked at a magazine around here. She tried to set me up with one of her Anglophile friends."

I ran my fingers along his arm. "Let's steer clear of the Mission District. I met your last old flame. It didn't go well."

He laughed. "The lady declined the invitation. As I recall, she threw some drink in Shelley's lap. Made me almost sorry I didn't get to meet her. She certainly had spirit."

Magazine...Shelley...throwing a drink...I stopped walking.

It couldn't be. The Shelley I worked with? All those years ago, she tried to set me up with Edward?

For a second, I could swear I heard God laughing.

"Emmaline?" Edward stood twenty feet ahead. "Something wrong?"

Fifteen years, I wasted. My bad relationships...the heartbreak Edward's ex put him through...could we have skipped all of that, if I'd just trusted that destiny thing long enough to go out with an English guy after I got back from London?

Doubtful. The laughing deity up there probably always knew we'd both have to take the scenic route to get where we needed to go.

Or perhaps there were lots of Shelleys in San Francisco, and they all got drinks thrown in their laps.

"No." I beamed at Edward. "Everything's fine."

He extended a hand to me, and I ran to catch up with my destiny.

ABOUT THE AUTHOR

Kimberly Emerson lives in Los Angeles. She divides her time between writing stories and working off her indentured servitude to a cat. The day job in accounting is just a cover. This is her first book (that she's been willing to show people, anyway).

gbd

49599405R00168

Made in the USA
San Bernardino, CA
24 August 2019